When God Came Running to Light The Darkness

Women's Inspirational Fiction by Nancy Williams

Bookman LLC
Publishing & Marketing
Providing Quality, Professional Author Services
www.bookmanmarketing.com

This book is a work of fiction. Any resemblances to any persons, living or dead, is completely coincidental.

ISBN: 1-59453-624-4

ONE

Narrowly escaping death has a way of changing its near-victim forever, and I was no exception. Consequently, the way I look at life has changed, and I no longer take anything for granted.

A clunking sound filled the air. "What was that?" I asked no one in particular. The dogs looked at me as if I had lost my mind, and lately I've wondered that myself.

I had never been fearful before, but now, the smallest foreign sound startled me, and certain fragrances set off anxious alarms in my head. As a Christian, I keep thinking I should be on top of this, and I know it could be worse. I could be a total basket case. I mean, I'm not exactly curled up in fetal position in the corner, but neither has it been the lead pipe cinch I would've liked.

In fact the whole past month has been difficult. I was chased and barely escaped death the week of my wedding. And not two weeks later, I landed in a Boston hospital, right in the middle of our honeymoon, with encephalitis. Poor Drew.

After all that happened, I had hoped to come home and melt into a peaceful, mundane, even mind-numbing routine. It would be a nice change.

I had hoped to put the past behind me, but just when I was so ready for a normal life, with no excitement and no mystery, I could see it starting all over again.

The first part of this week, Drew had to go back to work at the Kansas City office of the FBI, and I began to get in touch with old friends. That's when the trouble began.

My second day home, I tried phoning my girlfriend, Neely Watson, but got no answer.

I had already checked in with my quilting group, the seniors at Shady Acres Nursing Home and Mom's Peachtree Street neighbors. Then I had called my friend, Suse Reilly and chatted for two hours. Suse is seven months pregnant at age fifty-two, having her own grandchildren, as she put it, since none of her three children are cooperating in that area.

Everyone but Neely was accounted for, and I really missed her. She has a weight complex, but then, who doesn't have one in this day and age? Including me. Neely, always upbeat, with her wry wit and great ideas, was nowhere to be found.

By Friday morning, my curiosity had gotten the best of me, and I drove to her work. Neely has been a school librarian for over twenty years, so she's one of the few people whose whereabouts was predictable. Or at least that's what I thought when I strode through the library door.

Mrs. Hakes, the Media Liaison, was sitting at the massive oak desk, wearing a small gold pin announcing her title. I was barely acquainted with Mrs. Hakes, who seemed somewhat reserved. And from what I could tell, no one else really knew her either. Maybe that's why no one ever called her by her first name, whatever that is. But everybody knows me, including Mrs. Hakes. My life in this town has been an open book, at least in the past seven months, since it was turned upside down.

Mrs. Hakes looked up from stamping books with the school name, and her attitude was cool as she bobbed her head slightly. "Makkie."

Talk about stereotypes. The woman epitomized the word *librarian*. Thin, with slightly stooped shoulders, she has dark, hooded eyes, and wears rimless gold-framed glasses. Her short, graying brown hair seemed to have a mind of its own, and stuck out, as if she'd barely escaped a tsunami. I wondered if her lips had ever cracked a smile or laughed at a joke. Chances were good they had not.

I smiled at her cryptic greeting. "Hi, Mrs. Hakes. I need to see Neely Watson. I've tried to get a hold of her for the past several days, but haven't been able to reach her."

I waited, watching her, and wondered if it was my imagination, or if her eyes seemed sly as she answered. "I don't know exactly where she is," she said in a tone that was terse, almost oppositional.

"Well, listen, do you know—is she in the building?"

She looked past me, with eyebrows lifted. "You'd have to check with the office about that."

I'd expected her to say, 'Oh, she's just down the hall at the copy machine, running off some library materials.' But she didn't.

That was my first inkling that something was really off. I knew that if something was wrong, the whole place had to be buzzing with gossip, with me being the only one out of the loop. I made my way to the office in a mental fog, trying to sort it all out.

In the office, a student aid was the only one on duty, so I said, "Hi, Jill. Could I please speak to the principal?"

I recognized the girl, a shy blonde, as the granddaughter of one of the women in my quilting group, and I smiled, though I didn't know her well.

She looked up at me from a geometry book. "He's not in just now. Could I take your name and number, and have him get back to you?"

I said hopefully, "Well, maybe you can help me. I'm looking for my friend, Neely Watson, the librarian? Do you have any idea where she might be?"

She stammered, obviously uncomfortable at being put on the spot. "Well, um…I'm not allowed to give out that information."

I sighed as I turned to leave. This wasn't the first time I had run into brick walls in this town.

Azalea Missouri is a town of nine hundred something, about thirty-five miles southeast of Kansas City. It's one of those bucolic places that could be pictured on the page of a calendar, with straight, level streets, and huge mature oaks and sycamores overhanging each one. Each street is named for a flower of some kind, and there are no homes for sale. The housing is tight and desirable, close enough to commute to Kansas City, but not close enough to feel urbanized.

Maybe this would be a good time to introduce myself. My name is Makkie Yeats Livingston. I'm fifty-two years old and a retired RN. I've lived here since I was small, so I know the town inside out and upside down. Most of the people are my friends, more or less, and I have always felt safe here. That is, until seven months ago, when a crime wave hit our town. To say that it rocked my emotional boat is an understatement of legendary proportions.

First there was the murder of my friend, Ferdy Wallace, which hit us all pretty hard. We had never, in recorded history, had a murder in Azalea. When it happened, we made the Kansas City Star Newspaper, front page, bold-print in the Sunday edition. *What a way to gain a reputation.*

Then the residents next door, at Fair Oaks Bed and Board began to die under suspicious circumstances, with my eighty-year old mother parked smack in the middle of the action. Not only that, but we discovered, quite by accident, that the authorities were not keen on investigating anything, but had their hands in the till, and were into other illegal activities up to their eyeballs. It made me wonder what the world was coming to.

Right now, I needed to get back to the issue of Neely. I grabbed my cell phone, and dialed Milt's number. Milt is Neely's Dad.

I have all the numbers of the important people in my life memorized, but I can't accumulate many more friends, or I'll have to start writing them down.

Milt's answering machine groaned, "Ya know the drill…at the tone, leave a message, and maybe I'll get back to ya."

I frowned. Just how long had that terse message been playing? I've known Milt forever. He has an annoying habit of defaulting to military mode at the slightest provocation, though I don't believe he's ever actually served in the armed forces. I can't help but wonder if that behavior has made Neely's life somewhat difficult.

He does odd jobs, repairing leaky roofs, mending porch steps and keeping very busy. Heaven only knew where he was right now.

I was worried enough about Neely that I had already called some of our mutual friends, who all said they hadn't seen her in a while. It was only after pressing the point that I learned that my friend and beautician, Nadine Rutlege, was the last to have heard from Neely, five days ago.

At home again, I made myself a cup of hot, spiced cider and took my handful of vitamins and herbs, hoping to improve my resistance, and restore my body to at least its status quo of energy and stamina.

Glancing in the bottom of my mug, I noticed that the cinnamon stick I re-use was now totally soggy, a nearly unrecognizable lump of brown bark. I scooped it out, leaving tiny grains behind, and dumped it in the trash. I tend to pride myself on recycling, not so much of cans, bottles, and paper, but tea bags, cinnamon sticks, tin foil and zippered storage bags.

I made a piece of toast and checked my e-mail.

I keep trying to get back into writing mode, to work on the sequel to my first book, but it's a hard sell, when distractions come at me from all directions. I am presently putting together a cookbook, called *Recipes for Hot People*, which I hope will be of interest to a publisher, to accompany my two book inspirational fiction series.

I e-mailed my sister Zoe, to let her know we were back in town. She's not much for returning phone calls or even staying home for that matter, so who knew when we'd actually speak to one another.

Although I tried, I didn't get much done in the way of housework or writing, since my thoughts continually strayed back to my missing friend.

Neely hates to travel. She has rarely left the boundaries of our fair city, except when compelled to, for further education classes at the university. She's a homebody of the first order, which makes this whole disappearing act all the more bizarre.

I was still sorting clean laundry that I had been working on since we arrived home from our honeymoon three days ago. I was pacing myself, still tiring easily after being ill.

Living for six months with my older sister Zoe, was basic training of sorts for marriage. She whipped me into shape, in spite of myself, where laundry and housekeeping were concerned. She was given, I found later, to taking up to ten showers a day when she was overheated, which left me with mountains of laundry to do.

At first, I thought it was because of my lack of organizational skills that I couldn't keep up with the laundry, but since I've been more or less organized most of my adult life, I decided to check it out. Zoe.

Of course. I should've known. The source of much of the misery in my life.

She is a professor of Psychology at the University and a widow of some ten years. She is fifty-four, slender, classy and intelligent, with great taste, and the money to support it. Unfortunately, she also gives me *attitude*.

I am two years younger and five feet three, to her five feet eight inch frame. Where she is thin, I am slightly rounded. She has great cheekbones, whereas mine are practically nonexistent.

We've never had anything except genes in common, or for that matter, liked each other very much, Christianity notwithstanding. Because she's domineering, I have made it my life's goal to simply stay out of her way.

It was neither her fault nor mine, when we accidentally moved back in together. In fact, it was Mom's.

Mom, widowed ten years earlier, had let me know in mid-April that she wanted to give up her home and move into the mansion next door, recently turned Senior Bed and Board, called Fair Oaks. Because she didn't want the house sitting empty, she asked me to move back home.

Regrettably, she didn't tell me she had also invited Zoe to move back in. Unwary, we both ended up on Peachtree Street, moving vans parked nose to nose, ready to unload, when we learned we were moving back in together. Zoe had sold her home, and I had already given up my apartment, one of a rare few in Azalea, so neither of us could simply return home.

You can't imagine the strain. Zoe had been ordering me around since my earliest recollection, and I wasn't thrilled at the prospect of repeating history. But there wasn't another housing unit available within thirty miles, and my life was here, so I prayed a lot and dug in for the long haul.

I found out that I really *can* do all things through Christ who strengthens me. Literally. It had to be Him, or she'd be dead by now.

When questioned, Mom admitted that before she dies, she wants to see her girls become friends and had done what she could to make that happen. Now, she is nearly eighty-one years old, but her health is good overall, and she'll probably outlive us both, making her last wish a moot point.

Our summer together tested the limits of my sanity. Zoe is a gardener, canner and cook extraordinaire and made sure I had picking, weeding, watering, slicing and dicing to keep me off the streets and out of trouble. But only until I mustered the courage to forego my passive behavior and *just say no.*

She also made all the rules at Mom's and enforced them to the letter, my least favorite being: *no air conditioning until June first.* Unfortunately for me, the month of May made the record books for heat and humidity, and there I was without my air. It wouldn't have been a problem, had I not still been in the throes of menopause, dripping and overheated day and night. But I suppose you had to be there to appreciate the whole thing.

TWO

I finished the last load of laundry and tucked folded items into drawers for my new husband and me and stepped on the scale for the first time in months. We middle-aged, slightly rounded, menopausal females don't generally stand on scales, for very good reasons, but I had been ill long enough to make me curious about my weight.

The scale reported that I had dropped twelve pounds, most probably from being intravenously fed, for the better part of a week. You'd think that no food for that long would benefit a gal by at least a twenty-pound loss, but *no*.

After cleaning out the litter box, I dusted a half-inch of silt off the furniture, and started to fill the sink to do dishes, then scrubbed out the pet dishes and refilled them. After such a whirlwind of activity, I felt like I could sleep for a week. But I could see the dogs, Duke and Fred, looking in my direction, in silent anticipation of a customary romp in the meadow next door. I had been tired and distracted since coming home, and knew they were feeling neglected, so I said, "Okay, guys, go get your sticks." I didn't have to ask twice.

I followed them out to the meadow, where I dragged a lawn chair, so I could sit while throwing the sticks.

Fred was in good form, leaping high into the air to catch his stick in mid-flight. Duke, too, excitedly bounded along the ground, retrieving his with zest. I could only dream about that kind of energy. So far, it was all I could do to stand at the kitchen sink for the ten minutes it took to do dishes.

My mind once again zeroed in on my missing friend. *Where are you, Neely? This isn't like you at all.*

Once back inside the cottage, I tried Milt's place and again got his machine, only this time I decided to leave my number. Maybe he was one of those who actually called in for messages.

After fixing myself a tuna on whole wheat, I sank down on the sofa, pulled a quilt over me and dropped off to sleep. When I woke about two hours later, I felt somewhat rested and remembered I had planned nothing for supper.

I needed to do marketing and fast. Drew had stopped for a few things the night we got home, but there would be little creative cooking after tonight. The thought of peanut butter soup did little to tempt my appetite.

I grabbed my handbag and grocery list, and fished the coupon file from a drawer; then with the engine already running and my seatbelt fastened, I had to go back for my checkbook. I sighed. It's getting so it takes me two or three trips to gather my own wits these days.

At the Piggly Wiggly, I found my mind wandering, steering my warp-wheeled shopping cart down the aisle. Why is it you don't realize the problem until you've traversed at least one entire aisle? I hurriedly pulled things off the shelves, tossed them into the cart and crossed them off the list, as grocery shopping is one of my least favorite occupations.

I could hear, before I could see, Absey Applebee, a large elderly woman, with a shrill, yet masculine voice.

"Dave, don't you carry that wonderful nine-grain bread, you know the one, Hearth Grains, or Earth—something. Are you hearing what I'm saying to you?"

There was no doubt in my mind, that the entire Piggly Wiggly and perhaps the entire block had heard every word.

Looking chagrined, poor Dave steered her toward the office, where they could visit in private. Absey's visits around town are greeted with great ambivalence; she has plenty of money to spend, but you have to put up with a lot to get it. I wondered if it was worth the effort.

Already worn out from simply pushing my basket around, I was relieved to see my groceries being bagged and loaded into a cart. The young man hadn't even bothered to ask, 'Paper or plastic, Ma'am?' for which I was eternally grateful. No woman alone, unless she's into weight lifting ever answers *paper*.

I took the long way home, past Neely's charming gray bungalow, unable to help myself. After parking my car in her driveway, I went to look through her back French doors.

I peered in and knocked, only to be met by silence. I tried the door, snoop that I am, and was surprised to find it unlocked. Neely, a single woman, never *ever* leaves her doors unlocked. I was wary, walking into her pristine white kitchen with its blue and yellow French country accents, but nothing was out of place.

I tiptoed through the house as though someone were sleeping. Her living room, filled with stunning heirloom antiques, was tidy, but it felt close, as if no one had been there for some time.

The guest bedroom looked as it always did, but in her room I did a double take. In the corner of her large feminine room, her computer was on. The screen saver displayed a panorama of hard-to-ignore shooting stars. I sat down in her chair and pushed the space bar to bring up the screen.

Outlook Express was open to a letter from someone calling himself *Your everlovin' guy*, but using no other name, dated October thirtieth. *Who on earth is this person?* Neely and I have been like sisters, and I thought she felt comfortable enough to tell me almost anything, but obviously I was wrong.

I made a copy of the current e-mail, then scanned through old ones, and it looked, by the dates, as if they had kept in touch for several weeks. I felt like an interloper, reading her mail, but the content wasn't as important as the leads I might find.

She was the one friend for whom this was totally out of character, and I couldn't help but worry. This girl was as predictable as a sunrise; being unpredictable was a dead giveaway that something was wrong.

Next to her heart-of-pine pencil post bed, I was surprised to see her medications, including hormones, allergy and blood pressure pills still in the drawer of her bedside table.

In the bathroom, I looked around, alert now, and noted that her toothbrush was in its holder above the sink, and her contact lens case was perched on the vanity ledge. I opened the case; her lavender-tinted contacts were plainly visible. Neely didn't wear glasses that I knew of, and I couldn't imagine her leaving without her contact lenses. I refused to let my mind run wild.

I hesitantly approached the coat closet, where she kept her purse, and opened the door. My heart skipped a beat. Her light *tan* purse was in its place, which was odd, for two reasons. For one thing, no woman ever goes very far without her handbag, and for the second, Neely is obsessive about seasonally appropriate handbags and shoes.

The white things are stowed before September first, and the tans she packs away by November first, in favor of deep browns and blacks. I've known her for so long that I've memorized her rituals.

She had attended my wedding on October thirteenth, and at that point I'd noticed nothing unusual. Today is November fourth, and I couldn't squelch the feeling—something was definitely wrong.

I steered my reeling mind toward her refrigerator and opened it. Everything she owns is labeled, one way or another, so I wasn't surprised to see labels on the containers inside. The problem was the date. The latest date I could see was October thirtieth.

Oh, God, please help Neely, wherever she is, I prayed. Neely leaves food in her fridge exactly three days, never longer. She obviously hadn't been here to remove the food by November second. Where was she?

I snooped a little longer in her bedroom. I couldn't remember if she kept a diary, but it sure would've helped if it had popped up right then, and said, *here I am.*

I found no diary, but a Daytimer lay open on her bureau, dust thick around it. Neely doesn't do dust, because of her allergies.

My heart thumped loudly in my ears as I studied the page for the thirtieth of October, and saw the notation, 'D here at 4' followed by one question mark and one exclamation point.

In the address section, I skimmed through to see whose name might start with a D. There was only one entry, her nearest neighbor, Darlene Dittmer.

I stuck the Daytimer in my purse and looked toward Darlene's, where I saw no activity and no lights on, even on such a dreary gray day. I rang her bell a minute later. As she opened the door, I could see her thin, wiry, sixty-year old frame, with steel-gray curly hair. I suppose she's nice enough, if you like thin-lipped, crabby women, which I generally do not.

I wasn't surprised that she said nothing, waiting for me to speak first. Not exactly the outgoing type.

I said, "Darlene, I've been trying to get in touch with Neely."

When she still said nothing, I said, "You know Neely…your neighbor. Have you seen her?"

She looked at me through black, horn-rimmed glasses, a throwback from the sixties if I didn't miss my guess.

"The last time I saw her was a week ago, when she was watering her lawn. Haven't seen her since, actually. And it occurred to me, I might even have to call and remind her to mow that mangy-looking lawn of hers." Because of the long Indian summer, the grass had yet to stop growing.

What a joy, this woman. "Well, thanks, Darlene. You've been helpful."

She shut the door in my face without another word, and left me staring at it. She had last seen Neely a week ago, two days before she disappeared. I pulled out my pen and jotted it down on my palm, in lieu of paper—before I forgot.

I returned to Neely's place just long enough to lock up, taking a spare key from her key caddy in the kitchen. Before leaving, I walked around the outside of the house, surveying the scene. I've learned, the hard way, that it pays dividends to pay attention to details.

The first odd thing I noticed was the flowerbed under Neely's bedroom window, where her spent annuals were badly trampled. Pushing them aside, I could see faint footprints, but nothing identifiable. I frowned.

THREE

This was getting weird. I didn't know if I should wait until I could contact Milt or go ahead and call the police or Drew, my favorite FBI agent. I knew he would rather I exhaust the local channels, so I did none of the above, at least for the moment, since, so far, I had nothing but hunches. Having gone this route before, I already knew how the authorities feel about hunches. Particularly those belonging to me.

Mom and Snooky were sitting on the porch, in their easy chairs, feet up, on this unseasonably warm November day, when I stepped out of my car and waved.

Smiling, Mom waved back. "Well, hello, dear. Beautiful day, isn't it? How are you feeling by now?"

As I walked toward her, I said nothing, since there was no need. I could see her evaluating my appearance for herself.

"Your color still isn't the best, you know," she said, hugging me a moment later.

"I know. Am I interrupting anything?"

Snooky smiled. "You could never interrupt. You're family."

"That's sweet of you, Snooky. Listen, I need to talk to you."

They both nodded, and I plunged in.

"Mom, I've been trying to contact Neely ever since I got home, and I think something's wrong."

"What do you mean, 'something's wrong'?"

"Well, I called and left several messages, but she never returned my call. And when I stopped at the school, they wouldn't tell me anything. I saw Mrs. Hakes in the library, where Neely usually does her work, and she seems to have moved right into Neely's position as head librarian. Then I stopped at Neely's house a few minutes ago, and the back door was unlocked. She *never* leaves her doors unlocked."

After a short beat, I added, "There was nothing out of place, and I mean nothing. It's as if she left to do marketing or something, and will be right back. Her toothbrush and meds are in their places, as are her purse and contact lenses.

"Mom, you know how obsessive she is about putting away summer purses and shoes by a certain time? Well, her tan handbag is still there, in her coat closet. She never changed over to her winter things."

I shook my head, fretting. "Her computer was on, and this is the message that was on her e-mail screen." I handed Mom the printout and continued. "I can't think of anyone she might know whose name begins with a D, but his initial was in her Daytimer, with the message that read, *D coming @ 4.* Her address book has no D's except her neighbor, Darlene Dittmer, and she was no help. Only mad because Neely's yard is overgrown. She said she hasn't seen her for a week."

Mom nodded in encouragement.

"I thought about whether she could've taken a trip, but you know how Neely hates to travel. Her home is her whole life. Oh, and there are trampled flowers in the flowerbed under her window."

"Oh, my," said Mom, looking concerned.

I asked, "You haven't seen her lately, have you? I mean, while we were gone?"

She sighed, squinted her eyes, gently tapping her cheek with her index finger, which is how she does some of her best thinking.

"The last time I saw her was at the wedding. Have you checked with your mutual friends yet?"

"I have, and the last person to see her was Nadine, who said Neely called just as she was leaving for a meeting, and that was five days ago. Sounds like they didn't have time to visit."

"What about Milt—have you talked to him?"

"I tried to call and finally left a message on his machine. Mom, I'm worried. This is so unlike Neely."

"I was just thinking the same thing. Well," she said, looking at Snooky and me, "what do you think we should do next?"

Snooky said, "I think it might be good to try Milt one more time."

A minute later, Mom dialed Milt's number, and I was relieved to hear her say, "Oh, Milt, we're so glad to finally reach you."

She listened a minute and then said, "Well, Makkie's been trying like the dickens to contact Neely, and no one seems to know where she is. What?"

After a pause, she continued, "Milt, I think maybe we should come there and talk. Is that all right with you?"

We arrived within five minutes to find Milt standing on the porch, waiting.

Milt is your average, aging seventy-two year old male, medium height, with gray hair and brown eyes. He's one of those slightly hyperactive men, who can't seem to sit still without at least wiggling a pinky finger, as if his energy demands an outlet.

I hugged him. He held the door, and Mom and Snooky followed me inside the tidy, two-bedroom bungalow. Milt motioned us to sit, then sat down across from us.

With furrowed brows, he began, "I don't know what to tell y'all. Neely came by one day about a week ago, while I was at work and said she needed to talk."

I asked, "What day was that? Can you remember?"

He wrinkled his nose in deep thought. "It was a Friday if my recollection is any good."

"What else did she say?"

"Well, you know, she caught me right in the middle of jackhammerin' Poochie Lynche's driveway. You know Poochie, over in Primrose? Anyway I couldn't hear too good after listenin' to all that racket, so if she said somethin', I don't remember. Does that make sense?"

Snooky looked doubtfully at me, and I said, "Unfortunately, it makes perfect sense. So you haven't seen or heard anything from her since?"

"I was thinkin' about that the other night, wonderin' why I hadn't heard from her, but I've been so busy the past few months that there are sometimes whole entire weeks when we don't see each other, so it didn't seem that unusual."

"Has she mentioned anyone lately, some new friend, a guy, with a name that starts with a D?" I asked.

He frowned. "Not that I recollect." After a few more minutes of small talk, we left, telling Milt we would keep him informed.

In the car, I said, "Mom, I need to get home to Drew in a few minutes, but how about going with me to Neely's tomorrow and digging through her old e-mails, to see what we can find?"

"You know how I love a good challenge," she said with a mischievous smile. "What time?"

"I'll pick you up at nine, okay?"

I headed to the cottage that Drew and I now call home, left to me by my elderly friend and mentor, Ernie Kellogg, who had died several months earlier.

I was exiting my station wagon, when Drew pulled up in his Bronco. "Hi, Sweet Cakes," he said with a wide smile, "how's my best girl?"

My heart beat faster just seeing him. Tall and slender, he has broad shoulders, salt and pepper hair and the most beautiful blue eyes I'd ever seen. He still reminds me of a slightly older George Clooney, clear down to the widow's peak at his hairline and the cleft in his chin.

"Okay, I guess. How did your day go?"

"Oh, nothing very exciting. Mostly paperwork." He glanced at my face, and frowned, adding, "Something's up. What is it?"

"I was going to tell you. I just thought I'd let you have a few minutes before saying anything. The thing is…"

"Oh-oh, I don't know if I want to hear this," he said in a slightly singsong tone of voice. He held the door for me then followed me into the house.

I tilted my head. "You brought it up. Now, hear me out, will you? You know I've been trying to call Neely for the last two days and gotten nowhere? Well, today, I went to the school and then to her house. Mom and Snooky and I went to see Milt, and he said he hasn't heard from her since a week ago Friday."

"Well, maybe she decided to travel or visit a friend."

I sighed and sank onto the sofa, tucking my feet under me.

"Drew, I know Neely as well as I know myself. She hates traveling, only leaves home when she absolutely has to. She even went to those compulsory continuing education classes in the city, practically kicking and screaming." I paused, sighing.

"Drew, Neely is not here. It's like she's vanished into thin air. Her things are all there. You know—toothbrush, medications, her purse and even her contact lenses, without which she can't see a lick." After a beat, I added, "I have never known her to do anything remotely like this, and I'm worried."

I saw him about to protest and held up my hand. "Don't worry, I'm not asking you to do anything—just to understand. Mom and I are going over to Neely's tomorrow and sift through her e-mail messages to see if we can learn the identity of the guy she's been talking to."

He frowned, the lines in his face deepening in concern. "Listen, honey, I don't want you two getting into any trouble. If you have something that needs investigating, you need to call the police." He paused, lifted my chin so our eyes met, and kissed the tip of my nose. "Do you need me to repeat that, my love?"

I frowned at him. "You want to rain on my parade, is that it?"

"Not at all, Makkie, but some of what you've gotten yourself into has been dangerous. I know that somewhere deep inside you, you have some kind of weird *need to know*, but I don't want to spend the rest of my life worrying about you, so please, pray for discernment, and then listen when you hear that still small voice say, *stop now*. Agreed?"

I sighed. "Agreed."

He drew me into his arms, bent down and rested his cheek on the top of my head. "I don't know what I'd do if anything happened to you. I've already experienced being within a hair's breadth of losing you, and I can tell you, it's like part of me is dying."

He caressed my hair and whispered, "What can I say? I'm trusting the Lord for many great years together, so please—just use your head, will you?"

He smiled, then sighed and shook his head. "I know I can't stop you from checking this out any more than I can ask you to stop breathing, but please, you and your mother, look before you leap. And I'll try to remember that Jehovah Nissi is your Protector and pray that He surrounds you with His angels, because knowing you two, you'll probably need it."

FOUR

Mom and I were at Neely's door by five minutes after nine, and I let us in with my key.

As I led her through the kitchen, I said, "Mom, you know, Neely always throws out all the food in her fridge on the third day. Well, everything in there," I said, pointing to the fridge, "is labeled the thirtieth, so it's been way over three days. What would you say to helping me toss the outdated stuff, so I can set it out for the trash man?"

Mom agreed, and we dug out a trash bag, tossing things right and left. I found a box of Arm and Hammer Baking Soda, opened it, and set it in the refrigerator after wiping it out, not that it needed it. Her place always looked as if the cleaning lady had just left.

I dragged the trashcan out to the curb and felt frustrated by my lack of stamina, already worn out by the time I joined Mom in the bedroom. She had pulled up Outlook Express and was scrolling through the list of e-mail messages. She stopped and opened a note, also signed, *Your everlovin' guy*.

Mom said, "Here's another one. 'Hey, Neely, how's it goin'? Haven't heard from you in awhile, so thought I'd drop a line to let you know I been missin' you. I want us to get together soon, maybe do that white water rafting thing I mentioned. I know you'll just love it. Can't wait to finally meet you in person and get to know you better. I was thinking I'd book us a raft for the weekend of the first, so let me know, okay'"?

Mom couldn't hide her shock when she looked at me. "It's not like Neely to associate with total strangers, is it?"

"Not that I know of." I paused. "Mom, scroll down and see if there are any more messages from that guy."

I frowned, shaking my head. "Who would want to go white water rafting in the month of November anyway? The water and wind would be freezing."

She scrolled through several messages and found another, dated October twenty-sixth. *Hey, Neely, I went ahead and booked that raft like I promised and plan to pick you up on the thirtieth. We'll do some sightseeing and then get to our launching sight on the first. Be ready. Your everlovin' guy.*

I looked at Mom. "None of this makes any sense. Why would Neely leave behind everything she would need if she planned to travel? I don't get it."

"Didn't she hate to travel?" We both knew the answer to that.

After a long beat, I shook my head. "Mom, I can't imagine her making plans to meet anyone she met on the Internet. She teaches classes on *Stranger Danger* to first graders in Library Science. She would never willingly go anywhere with a stranger."

"Then where is she?" Mom puzzled aloud, resting her chin on her palm.

"Keep scrolling down, Mom."

She flipped through more odds and ends of e-mail and found one with a picture attachment, which we opened. It was the face of a man, with the signature, *Your everlovin' guy.*

Mom said, "Well, look at that. At least now we know what he looks like. Let's print this out and hang onto it."

The man looked to be in his mid to late thirties and was thin, with dark, straggly-looking brown hair and angular features. It was just a first impression, but the look in his eyes bothered me. They were vague looking, as if he had trouble concentrating. Like I had seen in schizophrenics in the psych ward in nursing school. I felt my anxiety level rise, just looking at those eyes. I've been known to be wrong in the past, and for Neely's sake, I was hoping against hope that I was wrong now.

We finished up on the computer, seeing no further communications from *guy,* and took one last stroll through the house, trying to observe anything amiss. Once more in her room, I was horrified, when the wind blew against the window and I noticed the screen, not a foot from her computer desk, almost invisibly slit at the very bottom edge and then up the sides. Why hadn't I noticed it before? I mentally kicked myself. It was evidence that this wasn't a pleasure trip for Neely.

My emotions flew into roller coaster mode, and I felt frantic.

"Oh, Mom, I feel so bad that I didn't go to the police yesterday. Maybe they'd already have found her if I had."

"Now don't be so hard on yourself, dear," she said, trying to comfort me, "you've been trying to find her for several days, and even Milt wasn't the least bit suspicious."

She hugged me. "Well, why don't we ask the Lord to protect Neely and show us what to do next." We bowed our heads, and she prayed.

A minute later, I scoured the room with my gaze, trying to cover all our bases.

As we were leaving, I thought about Neely's purse in the coat closet. "Wait, Mom. I need to check something."

I opened the tan saddlebag style purse and dug through it. Neely carries huge purses, always ready for any contingency, and the pile on her kitchen table grew bigger as I dumped out its contents. There was an address book, a makeup organizer, full of her cosmetics, a tiny first aid kit, two pens, a manicure set, a hairbrush, wallet, and checkbook, but something was missing. I had to think a minute, before I realized what it was.

"Mom, Neely's cell phone isn't here, and it's not on the charger in the kitchen. Maybe she has it with her." Until now, it had never occurred to me to call her cell phone.

Mom frowned. "If Neely has her phone, why hasn't she called us?"

"Maybe she hasn't had the opportunity. Just to be on the safe side, maybe we should let her call us, huh?"

We sat down at her kitchen table, a small white drop leaf on which she had decopaged a blue, white and yellow French country design.

I stood up, then, suddenly remembering we hadn't checked her answering machine for old messages. I hit rewind, and we started listening, to various ordinary messages from various ordinary voices, some familiar, some not. Including my own.

Then came a message that said, "Neely, why haven't you responded to my e-mails? I'm going to be there by four on the thirtieth and you'd better be ready."

His voice didn't sound everlovin', or even the least bit cordial, to me. The message tape droned that the message had been received at noon, on the twenty-seventh. I wondered if Neely had tried to back out of the relationship. If she had, we could find no evidence that she had made a note of it or tried to ask for help.

I glanced around one more time, and there, under the kitchen table, I saw something I hadn't noticed before. A small, yellow Post-It note lay so the writing was against the floor. I picked it up and handed it to Mom. My nerves were shot.

"Mom, what is this? You look. I just can't."

She read it silently. "I think Neely was trying to leave a trail for us to follow. It says, David Bremer, 415 Del Monte Street, St Louis, MO. 413-555-6832."

"Mom, we need to get the police on this ASAP."

"Let's go." She drove, while I rested my head against the seat and closed my eyes, suddenly exhausted.

The youthful, blond officer at the desk was someone neither of us recognized. He looked up as Mom cleared her throat. "We need to speak to the chief."

The young man, whose nametag read S. Parks, obviously didn't recognize Mother the Mayor. He said with attitude, "And what do you need with the chief, may I ask?"

I frowned. Since when did the chief need someone to screen his calls?

Mom sighed then looked at him with slits for eyes and pursed lips. "Forget it, Junior, I can find my own way. I don't need you or anyone else to announce me to the chief. I'm the one who put him in office." She strode past him, turned around and glared at him. "And your name, if I'm not mistaken—is Parks. Is that correct?"

Now wide-eyed with regret, S. Parks flew from his chair, knocking it over, and banged his hip on the desk, sending it screeching an inch or two. He headed toward Mom. "Please, ma'am, let me apologize. I'll take you to him right now."

She gave him a withering glare, one eyebrow upraised. "Too late. You had your chance."

He stood in front of her, barring her way. Her eyes flamed, and he instantly moved as if scalded.

After knocking, she burst through Ace Grimm's office door. "Ace, if you don't mind, we need a moment of your time."

S. Parks stood in the doorway, biting his lip, as if waiting for the ax to fall. Ace strode purposefully to the door. "What do you want? Get back to the desk," he demanded and slammed the door in Parks' face.

Ace turned, smiled at Mom, and motioned us to chairs. I felt like I could sleep standing up by now.

"And what may I do for her honor, the mayor?" Ace's gray hair had been trimmed to look more professional, and his wide smile highlighted the deep wrinkles that creased his face.

Mom handed him the sticky note, a copy of the e-mail message, and the picture, which he studied in puzzlement. When he looked up, she said, "Listen, Ace. We have a situation here that needs your immediate attention."

She filled him in on the details of Neely's disappearance and our findings. He took notes and held up his hand. "If you'll excuse me, I'll get Steve Parks on this right away."

Mom held up her index finger and raised her left eyebrow, catching Ace's attention. "Are you referring to the S. Parks that mans the front desk for you?"

"Yes. He's my nephew, and he needed a job, so I hired him."

With a frown, Mom said sarcastically, "I can't imagine why."

"Excuse me?" His eyes widened in question.

"For one thing, Ace, nepotism is always highly suspect, and for another, he's an insolent so and so. Rude. And not the kind of person I want representing the police department in Azalea. He's out."

"Okay, boss—whatever you say," Ace agreed, waving his hands in deference. Ace had only had the job a few short weeks, and it looked like he wanted to keep it.

Squaring her shoulders, Mom said, "All right now, Ace. Get me a mature officer looking to do some serious investigating, and do it now, please."

He pressed the intercom button. "Brenda, I need Dale Cuthbert. Call him in for me, will you?"

"Now you're talkin'," said Mom, with a knowing grin. The choice of police officers was limited to two, Mike Margolis and Dale Cuthbert, and of the two, Dale was the elder.

Dale is an honest man, a man of integrity, whose sixteen year-old son cuts Mom's grass each summer and whose wife, Amelia is in my quilting group.

The chief got a call back over the intercom, and Brenda announced that Dale was on a call, but would be in as soon as he finished.

Mom shook her head. "Don't bring him in on our account. I just need you guys to look into Neely's disappearance. Right now, I need to get Makkie home. She's been feeling a little under the weather lately."

I looked at her askance and frowned, gritting my teeth. It's not like we needed to broadcast to the world my current wretched state of health.

Ace looked in my direction, appraising me. "I heard something about that. Well," he said, patting my shoulder, "I hope you get to feeling better soon."

As we turned to leave, he added, "We'll get on this first thing, okay? See ya, boss."

Mom yelled back, "Don't call me boss."

FIVE

I pulled into the drive just as Drew slid from his car.

"Hi, beautiful," he smiled, slamming the car door. "How did your investigation go?"

"Okay. Listen, hon, I need to lie down. Could we talk about this later?"

He took my arm and helped me to bed, where he pulled off my shoes and tucked a quilt up to my waist.

"You really need to go easy, babe. You look all in."

"Thanks, honey."

"I just came home for lunch. Want me to make you something to eat?"

I sighed. "Not right now, but thanks for the offer."

I thought I could feel Drew kissing my cheek as my eyes closed.

I heard nothing more, until I woke at 3:30.

I woke to Duke, nuzzling my hand and whining to go out.

After splashing water on my face on my way to the door, I sat on the patio for a few minutes, feeling the gentle southerly breeze against my face. The day was sunny and warm for November, in the high fifties.

I grabbed the phone on the third ring to hear Mom's voice. She said Dale Cuthbert had called. He said he would contact the St. Louis authorities, write up Neely as a missing person, and add her name to the missing person's data bank.

My heart sank. I knew she was missing, but hearing it like that triggered sudden shivers that involuntarily skipped up my spine.

Drew would be home in an hour, and I had to start supper. *Thank you, Lord, for mundane activities that keep us going when we're in crisis.* Once I heard someone say, "When things are out of your control, just put one foot in front of the other and do the next thing." It was a comforting thought.

I dug through the freezer, found a package of pre-tenderized patio steaks, and browned them in the electric skillet, adding seasoning, then scrubbed two potatoes, and stuck them in the oven to bake. A salad would complete the meal.

I turned the heat down in the electric skillet and headed for the shower. The phone rang while I still had shampoo in my hair, so I let the call go, knowing the machine would pick up. I hurriedly finished and grabbed a towel. Throwing it around me, I pushed the play button on the answering machine.

The voice was Neely's. It sounded shaky. I turned the volume up and heard her say, "Makkie, I'm in trouble. Please pick up if you're there. If not, call my cell phone ASAP, *please*."

I grabbed the phone and punched in her cell number. It rang once, and I heard someone grab it.

"Hello, Neely?" I said, frantic. "Neely, is that you?"

"Shhh," she whispered into the phone.

"Neely," I responded with a loud whisper, "is that you?"

Her voice shook as she whispered, "He's in the shower, but I don't want to take a chance he'll hear. I had to stick my cell under a pillow so he wouldn't hear it ring. Makkie, I'm being held against my will. It's a guy I met online, and I thought he was nice, but when I tried to break it off, he got pushy and forced me to come with him."

"Neely, where are you? I'll get you some help."

"We're in the Sundowner Motel on Kipling Street in St. Louis, room eighteen. He's been watching me so closely, I didn't dare use my cell until now." I grabbed a pen and jotted her words on my palm.

"Neely, I love you. We're all praying, and we'll get to you. You aren't hurt, are you?"

"Not really, but this guy is nuts. He's been talking about us going white water rafting, like its some kind of dream of his, but I'm not going. Can you imagine me trying to balance my heft in a raft, fighting to stay afloat? No way. Besides, it's too cold to be doing that this time of year."

"My thoughts exactly. Hang in there, sweetie," I said, "and don't go anywhere."

She muffled a laugh. I hung up the phone, threw on some shoes, and called Mom, then Ace. I picked up Mom and headed toward the chief's office within five minutes.

I showed him my hand.

He laughed. "What's this? No paper?"

Mom gave him a playful hit on the arm. "Get serious, Ace."

He punched a button on the intercom. "Dale, we know where Neely Watson is."

Dale came in with his pen poised to write, while Ace reached over and extended my hand. Dale, stretching his neck, looked toward my hand in puzzlement.

I frowned. "Well, better to have it on my hand than not at all, right?"

He shrugged then copied it down. "I'll get this to the St. Louis authorities. Thanks for the help," he added, smiling.

To my surprise, tears burned my eyes, and seeing them, Mom smiled and hugged me. "You're just feeling relief, dear."

Ace looked at me. "How did you come by this information?"

"Neely phoned and left a message, telling me to call her cell."

"Well, you two are in the thick of things, as usual, but I think we can take it from here. I'll let you know when I hear any news, Jane."

"Thanks Ace," Mom said as her shoulders sagged in relief. "We'll be waiting to hear."

Walking to the car, Mom said, "Honey, why don't you come home with me? That way Snooky and I can fuss over you. You know we how much we enjoy that." We dropped my car off at the cottage, since Drew would retrieve me later.

Mom drove us home, while I got a hold of Drew on my cell and gave him an update.

I lay down in Mom's guest room and slept. When Drew arrived an hour later, he woke me with a kiss. He seemed revved. He sank onto the bed, pulling me into his arms.

"Hi, babe. I punched Bremer's name into the data bank, and guess what? The guy's got quite a record. Sounds like a mental case. He's even been known to crawl over security fences in DC to talk to the President. It's too bad they can't keep nuts like that off the street permanently."

He held me for a long moment, nestling me into a warm embrace. His voice was just above a whisper. "Hmm, have I been missing this—You smell so good. So, are you feeling any better after your nap?"

He caressed my cheek with the back of his hand and worked his magic, his dazzling smile turning my insides to Jell-O.

I gave him a silly grin. "I'm happy to announce I'm beginning to feel like my old self again."

His eyes twinkled as he laughed. "Oh-oh, I don't know if that's a good thing or not. The old Makkie has a tendency to go over the top, remember?"

"Well, I don't feel good enough to be doing that yet. But I do *like* the idea."

"All right then. Are you ready to head home?"

"As ready as I'll ever be."

When we walked in our front door, Duke and Fred bounded up to greet us, letting me know they were starved. I started warming up our dinner and shortly poured food into the massive rubber dog dishes on the floor.

"How can you guys eat so much?" I asked. "All you do is sleep all day, and that shouldn't require much in the way of calories."

They eyed me, looking confused, and then ate like it was their last meal.

Drew came out of the bedroom, dressed in his favorite slouchy sweat shorts and tee shirt.

"Isn't it a little chilly for shorts?" I asked, stifling a chuckle.

"Any day in November that reaches fifty degrees is a day to celebrate with shorts," he announced cheerfully. "It's too cold to go without socks, though, even for me. My feet are freezing after about the middle of October for some reason."

"You know, don't you," I teased, "that that's a sure sign of aging?"

He laughed. "Well, that's a fact you certainly could've kept to yourself, my love," he said, as he grabbed me and kissed my neck.

"Ooh, stop. That tickles," I said, cringing.

A few minutes later, he brought his newspaper to the table with him as I set down our plates.

I thought hard about how to word my next comment.

"I hope you don't take this wrong, but I really don't like it when you read the paper at the table. It makes me feel ignored. Could we agree to read anywhere but at the table?"

Lowering his paper, he paused, in deep thought and then smiled, "You know, now that you mention it, I think that's a good idea. I may add it to my list. You know…of those things that will keep us happily married."

I smiled.

He laughed. "I'd promise you anything for one of your smiles. I feel like I could lose myself in your eyes, you know." I made a face and felt a flush crawl up my neck.

He stood, took me into his arms and gave me a serious kiss. "We need to snuggle in front of a fire tonight, and *talk*, don't you think?"

Over dinner, I asked about his upcoming work schedule.

"Well, we'll be transporting some documents next week, but it's only for a couple of days. Why do you ask?"

"Well, I just hate it when you're away. I mean, I don't want to seem like a complainer, but I still struggle when I'm alone at night."

His brows furrowed in concern. "Oh, honey, I know, and I'm sorry. I hate being away from you. In fact, that's the worst thing about this job. Really."

A short time later, the dogs snuggled on the hearthrug, and the cats curled up nearby.

As I slid our plates into a sink full of suds, I asked, "Don't you think we should have heard something about Neely's release by now?"

He picked up his newspaper and headed toward his recliner. "What time did Dale get the St. Louis authorities in on it?"

"Well, all I know is that I gave him the information about four, and he said he'd get right on it."

Just then, the phone rang, sending a jolt through my shaky frame. I picked up with a hammering heartbeat and heard Mom's voice, "Makkie, we have good news. You'll want to join us as soon as you can." She refused to say more.

I hurriedly finished the dishes and flipped away the dishtowel I had tucked in the neckline of my shirt.

"Honey, we need to get to Mom's. I'll bet they've found Neely. Let's get going."

At Mom's there were several law enforcement units and an unmarked white Chevy Caprice that had never fooled a single soul.

I jumped from the car and ran toward the house as the door opened, and Neely flew into my arms.

"Oh, Neely, I was frantic about you. Are you okay?"

"Thanks to you, I am. It wasn't twenty minutes after we spoke that the police broke into the room and arrested Bremer."

She hugged me tightly, and I scolded, "You need to get rid of that chat room capability on your computer."

"It's as good as done, boss," she said, saluting me.

Drew hugged her. "Glad that you're home safe and sound, kiddo."

Inside the house, everyone was talking at once. Mom held up her hand for silence. "I want to thank our police chief and his able officers for getting on this so fast. I can't help but think they saved the day."

Drew asked, "Did the arresting officer say what they were going to do with Bremer?"

"Well, for one thing," Dale said, "he's being charged with kidnapping, and that alone should keep him behind bars for a long time."

Mom handed around a plate of sandwiches, since the officers hadn't had any supper. Plates of her hot water fudge cake with fudge icing tempted me as they passed, and neither Drew nor I could resist.

A short time later, I beckoned Neely to follow me into the office, where I motioned her to sit down. I closed the door and tilted my head. "Neely, did he hurt you? How are you really doing?"

I guess I must've sounded motherly, because she stood, fell into my arms, and burst into tears. Her dark eyes were fearful, and her face flushed as she broke down.

"Makkie, I was so afraid he was going to hurt me. He was crazy, schizophrenic or something. Kept talking to invisible people, even arguing with them. I thought I'd never see you again. I can't tell you how glad I am this is over."

"Neely, do you want me to spend the night with you?" Without letting her speak, I added, "You shouldn't be alone your first night home."

After a beat, I frowned. "Hey, I noticed he slit the screen on your bedroom window. What exactly happened?"

"Well, he kept e-mailing me that he wanted to get together and go white water rafting. I told him repeatedly that I'm not athletic and didn't want to go, but he seemed obsessed with the idea. He told me to expect him on the thirtieth at four o'clock. I e-mailed him repeatedly, telling him I wasn't going, but somehow that only seemed to make him more determined."

She shook her head. "I knew things were getting out of hand, so I tried to contact Dad and found him on his break at work, but for some reason, it was like he was deaf when I finally told him the problem. When I tried again to phone, he never returned my calls. I was planning to go stay with Dad the night of the thirtieth, but couldn't get hold of him and had no key to his house. I didn't know what to do.

"Since you were out of town, I called Nadine, who said she had a meeting and wouldn't be home till late. I hesitated to impose, since I don't know her that well. Suse was away, and I didn't know anyone else to call.

"Anyway, when he arrived, I wouldn't answer the door, so he found a window that wouldn't lock properly, slit the screen, came in the bedroom window and forced me to leave immediately."

"Neely, you could've called Mom. She would've done everything in her power to help you."

"I know, but she's newly married, and I hated to bother her."

"Why didn't you at least call the police?"

"I did," she said with a grimace. "Unfortunately, I got some guy named Parks, who simply wouldn't take me seriously. What else was I supposed to do?"

I hugged her to me tightly. "Listen, if anything like this ever happens again, just get out of there--go anywhere, but don't be at home, like a sitting duck, okay?"

"Got it. And believe me, you don't have to tell me twice. I've never felt so stupid in my entire life. I mean I even teach a class to the little kids on Stranger Danger."

"I heard about that."

A minute later, I went out and pulled Ace aside. "Ace, I hope you've fired Steve Parks, because Neely spoke to him when this was all going down, trying to get help from the police, and he ignored her—wouldn't give her the time of day."

He looked at me, sighed, and grumbled, with gritted teeth, "I might have known that idiot would eventually endanger someone's life. He's gone. I fired him as soon as you guys left today. I'm really sorry, Makkie."

"Don't tell me. Tell Neely."

He looked apologetic when he turned to her. "I'm sorry if his actions jeopardized your safety in any way. I wouldn't have wanted that to happen for anything."

He held out his hand, and she took it. Then he took her hand in both of his and squeezed it, with tears in his eyes. To me, he said, "You know, Makkie, I used to throw Neely's ball back across the fence when she was pre-K. She was my bud," he added, blinking back tears.

Neely pulled him into a hug. "It's okay, Ace, the Lord was with me. But you need to get some better help."

"Your wish is my command." He smiled, swiping at his eyes with his shirttail.

I pulled Drew aside. "I hope you don't mind, but I need to stay with Neely tonight, and help her sort through what's happened. Will you be okay?"

"Sure, honey. Count on me. How about me dropping the two of you off?"

"That would be great."

I turned to Neely. "Drew is going to drop us at your place. I'm keeping you company tonight and tomorrow. Do you have a jacket?"

"Makkie, I'm not going to let you spend a night away from your new husband."

I frowned. "Neely, this is not up for discussion. Get your coat."

We drove to her place in the light of a full moon, and he dropped us off, saying he'd be back with my bag in a few minutes.

As we walked up the drive, Neely looked wistfully at her home.

"Listen, Neely, I hope you don't mind, but Mom and I were here yesterday and cleaned out your refrigerator. I know how you hate food moldering inside."

She laughed. "Only you would think to do something like that."

We sat curled up on the sofa in her cozy living room when I said, "Listen, Ace is going to have Ronny come out in the morning and install a new screen at his expense, since he feels responsible for the entire mess going as far as it has."

"Really? That's awfully nice of him."

She got up when she heard the microwave beep, left the room, and shortly handed me a cup of hot chocolate. I sipped its warm sweetness, enjoying the first stress-free moment I had known in several days. I had been on adrenaline overdrive for so long that it felt foreign coming down.

Drew stuck his head in the door and said, "Yoohoo ...Delivery man."

I met him in the entry as he set down my bag. He kissed me, hugged me tightly and said, "See you tomorrow, okay, babe? Love you." He waved at Neely. "See you, kiddo."

After he left, I joined Neely in the living room, where we were quiet for several minutes, and I could feel fatigue wash over me.

She said, "You know, Makkie, when I got on that chat line, I thought I still might meet Mr. Right. But after what happened, I can't help but think this was God, giving me a clear signal that He must be my Mr. Right."

"An astute observation, my dear Watson," I replied.

She laughed. "Listen, I'm pooped. Let's go to bed." She hugged me as we stood and turned toward the hallway.

"Neely, I can't tell you how glad I am you're okay. It feels like Christmas, and you are my gift."

I paused then continued, "You know that story in scripture where the shepherd had lost one little lamb, out of his flock of one hundred and left the entire flock to go search for the one? Well, I think I know how the shepherd felt. You were the only one missing, but the hole left by your absence was enormous. Do you know what I mean?"

"I think I do," she said. Then she added, "I don't know what I'd do without you."

I stopped walking and turned to look at her. "Neely, I know you may think things have changed now that I'm married to Drew, but they haven't. Drew and I agree that no matter what time it is, day or night, if you need us, we are there for you, and I know Mom and Snooky feel the same way. You aren't isolated and you're not intruding. You are family, and I want you to repeat to yourself one hundred times, *I am family, I can ask for help*. Got that? I mean it."

"Thanks…"

I went on, "I know, I know, you hate to interrupt the newlyweds, but listen. You and I go way back, he's the new kid on the block. Say," I said, suddenly changing the subject, "you wouldn't like a couple of cats, would you?"

She laughed. "What? Why? How many do you have?"

"Too many. Three to be exact."

"Are they fixed and declawed?" she asked.

"They sure are."

"So how many can you spare?"

"Are you serious?"

She nodded. "I've been thinking about getting a cat, just for the companionship."

"Really? With all these antiques?"

"Listen, what good are antiques when you're lonely? Not much, I can tell you. I'd love the company."

"Glad to hear it. I'll move them over tomorrow. You'll be crazy about them."

"But didn't you say you thought Hairy might crump at any minute?"

I laughed. "I did, but that was my mistake. He has a new lease on life, now that Patty Cake attached herself to him. Remember me saying we had seven kittens to give away? Well, guess who sired them?"

Her jaw dropped. "You're kidding? How old is he in people years anyway?"

"You're asking me?"

SIX

By eight the next morning, Ronnie Grimm was at the door, struggling with an armload of tools and a wide roll of screening material. His brown hair always looked like he'd taken an eggbeater to it, and today was no exception. Dark circles shadowed his brown eyes, as if he wasn't getting enough sleep.

He gave Neely an embarrassed smile and said he'd forgotten his ladder. She showed him where the ladder was, and he got busy, making lots of masculine racket outside the bedroom window. Neely mentioned how comforting it was to hear it. I thought so, too. Not long after, he volunteered to fix the broken window lock as well, and Neely quickly agreed.

By noon, she and I had collected two cats and all their junk and loaded them into my station wagon, for the trip to her place. Patty Cake, unfortunately, is not a good rider, and, within minutes, had upchucked on the backseat floor. It made me glad we weren't in Neely's pristine sports car.

After I set them down and opened the crate door, we watched as they crept stealthily out and scouted out their new home turf, sniffing, and looking into corners and cavities. The two shortly leapt from the floor to the counter to the top of the refrigerator and stood looking down on us. With a smile she couldn't quite squelch, Neely scolded them.

"Hey you two, get down from there." Frowning, she said, "I guess I'm going to have to move my pottery off the top of my refrigerator. Wouldn't want them knocking if off during the night, giving me a heart attack."

Just watching their antics seemed to tickle her. She said, "It's like they have some kind of silent sign language we humans don't get. I love it."

We unloaded their paraphernalia, and an empty paper bag fell unnoticed to the floor. Hearing the crackling of paper a minute later, we turned to see the cats curling up in the deep end of the bag, which then flipped upright, with cats howling and yowling to get out. Neely laughed until she cried.

"I think I'm really going to get a kick out of this."

She treated me to lunch at Verlene's and was greeted by people she barely knew, who said they were glad to see her safely home. The grapevine in our town works better than the newest state-of-the-art satellite communication system.

With a look of surprise, she shrugged. "I didn't know so many people would care one way or the other."

We spent the afternoon shopping for groceries and lolling in her living room. The afternoon sun perched low in the sky when I stowed my bag in the car. When I finally hugged her goodbye, I knew she would be okay.

I had just parked my car in front of Mom's, when Zoe ran down the porch steps, and got into a waiting black sedan.

"Hey, Makkie," she said cheerfully. I always tread lightly around her, since I never know what her mood will be.

Mom opened the door, and I gestured toward Zoe. "So what's she so cheerful about?"

She smiled. "Oh, she's really excited about the wedding. It's only a little over two weeks away, remember?"

"Hey, that's right."

"So how is Neely doing, dear?"

"I think she's going to be fine. She even made room at her place for Hairy and Patty Cake." I paused. "She said she had been thinking about getting a cat for a companion anyway."

"I'm sure they'll do wonders for her."

"Oh, I almost forgot. I need to go clean out my car. Patty offloaded her dinner in the back seat. Got any 409, Mom?"

She handed me a couple of rags and a spray bottle of some kind of cleaner. "Just throw the rags in the trash when you've finished, okay?"

I was on my way home a few minutes later, wondering what to fix for supper, when I took a notion to stop off at Peking Express. The parking lot was just starting to fill up with the usual pickup trucks, when I joined the string of cars in the drive-thru line.

I hurried home, captivated by the fragrances emitting from the Styrofoam cartons, trying to restrain myself from eating the entire bag of Crab Rangoon.

I unloaded the car, noting that Drew wasn't home yet. Tossing the bags onto the counter, I ran toward the ringing phone.

Suse said, "Oh, Makkie, I'm so glad to hear your voice. How's Neely doing?"

We talked for a few minutes, and I asked how she was feeling, at seven months pregnant. She said, as she always does, "Pretty good, for an old lady."

Shortly, Drew strode in. He looked really handsome in a long sleeved, blue shirt and a blue and green plaid sweater vest. It did great things for his blue eyes. He kissed me, enfolding me into a warm embrace.

"How's my best girl, today? Missed you last night." After a beat, he added, "How's Neely doing?"

"She met Bremer online, and my first words to her were, 'Get rid of that chat line.' She agreed, saying she thought he was mentally ill, always talking with invisible people. She was totally terrified, but she seems okay now. Thanks for understanding that I needed to be with her. I think she really needed me."

His eyes twinkled. "I know exactly how she feels."

He sniffed and smiled. "Mmm…what smells so good? Did you bring home Chinese?"

I grinned. "Um-yup."

"Great. I'm starving. I've cooked my own meals my entire adult life, but now that you've assumed the position, it's like I can't remember how to do the simplest things for myself." He added, "What do you suppose causes that?"

"Beats me. I just hope you haven't completely lost your touch in the kitchen, because that's one of the reasons I married you."

"Oh-oh, I think we're in trouble now," he said with a delighted chuckle.

Studying the oriental writing on the carton while we ate, I said, "I wonder why they never put any nutritional information on these containers."

He smiled. "If they did, they'd probably have to issue a warning: *These products may be hazardous to your health—not to be taken internally*."

I was surprised when Drew helped me clean up the supper mess a short time later. Most husbands go read their newspaper while the wife does all the work.

I smiled. "What—are you starting a tradition of helping in the kitchen?"

"I think that would be companionable, don't you?" He grinned. "That way I can keep my eye on you."

"It would be a novelty, that's for sure."

I pulled him down and kissed his cheek.

He gave me a wide, slow grin. "Hey, now. Sure you want to start something you might not be able to finish?"

"I'm sure."

He built a fire in the hearth, and we settled down to watch the flames, before he turned to me. "You know, sweetheart, it just occurred to me that you have an unusual gift."

I frowned in puzzlement. "What are you talking about?"

I snuggled deeper into his arms, as he tipped my chin up to look in his eyes. "I know you see yourself as ordinary, but you're not. You have a huge heart, with enough room for everyone. You love all the way—something I've rarely seen in my lifetime." As long as he thought so.

Sometime during the night, I began to see Day Barclay's face in my dreams and heard his threats echoing in my mind. I fought the bedcovers trying to get away, heard screams, and woke as Drew pulled me into his arms and swept the damp hair out of my face.

"Sweetheart, wake up. It's just a nightmare. You're safe now, okay? Just relax and take slow deep breaths." He paused. "Same nightmare?"

I nodded.

"Well, you probably need a dry nightgown. You're soaked."

I slid out of bed in a daze and pulled a dry nightshirt on, before crawling back under the covers.

"You going to be okay, hon?"

"I'm fine."

"Makkie, honey, I'm worried about you. Don't you think maybe you need to see someone about this?"

"Ask me in the morning, okay?" Maybe by then he would have forgotten about it. I wished I could.

I had struggled with the same recurring nightmare since Day Barclay, a suitor I had rejected, chased me, with murder on his mind. He was caught in a thick bramble patch after I fled, but continued making threats on my life even as the EMTs accompanied him to the hospital. In fact, he'd broken one EMT's jaw en route. He was now incarcerated, but his violent threats still haunted my dreams.

The next morning, I slept until seven, waking to a note from Drew that said he wanted to let me sleep in.

It ended with his love, and a heart, with an arrow through it, with a postscript suggesting that I find a therapist to consult.

I pulled out my Bible, and started reading in my favorite book, Psalms.

Psalm 138 echoed my own gratitude: *I will praise Thee with my whole heart; before the gods will I sing praise unto Thee. I will worship toward Thy holy temple, and praise Thy name for Thy lovingkindness and for Thy truth. For Thou has magnified Thy word above all Thy name.*

I felt unbelievably grateful for Neely's safe return.

I gathered up the soiled laundry, and started a load of whites, then sat down to call Mom. She said she and Snooky were getting ready to go house hunting with Zoe and Bryce. She invited me to go, and though it sounded like fun, I declined. I had plenty of things to catch up on at home.

The leaden skies held little promise of sunshine when I got out my basket and gardening shears, and the dogs and I went to pick the last of the wildflowers in the south meadow before the first hard freeze. While I was there, I trimmed the grass around the two small grave markers I had discovered only days before our wedding. The dogs romped around me, while I picked up the brass cache pots, dumped out the old flowers and brackish water, and filled them with the last of the season's wildflowers, then brushed away the dirt that had accumulated in the engraving.

The graves were those of the wife and daughter of my friend, Ernie. They had been killed in a car accident, in 1955. I had known none of this until just before the wedding, and I hadn't handled it well.

I felt totally confused when I found the graves. In a letter that arrived from his lawyer just before the wedding, Ernie explained the accident, for which he was responsible, while driving drunk. He admitted being in rebellion to the Lord.

He had made a pledge after their deaths, to put away anything that would distract him from God's will for his life, which meant not tending these two precious graves. But the most important thing he had said, was *Don't let anything paralyze you, or distract you from listening to the Lord, and being in the center of His will.*

I never wanted to forget those words.

The dogs followed me back to the cottage, as I thought, *Lord, what would you have me to do today?*

I flipped on my DVD of Nat King Cole's Christmas Hits, and listened, teary-eyed, to *O come let us adore Him, o come let us adore Him, o come let us adore Him, Christ, the Lord.* I shook my head, with no idea why I felt so weepy today.

The phone rang, interrupting my reverie, and I picked it up to hear the voice of my friend, Mouse, a dear elderly saint, who always seems to know exactly when I need an encouraging word.

"The Lord laid it on my heart to call, dear. Are you all right?"

When I didn't answer immediately, she began to pray. "Lord, you told us in Your Word that You are with us, ready to hear and answer our prayers. I bring my dear sister, Makkie to You, Lord, knowing there is heaviness in her heart, for reasons only You know. Be there for her, Lord, minister to her needs, surround with Your loving presence, and be the lifter of her head. Pick up the load she's carrying, and carry it for her, in Jesus name, Amen."

"Oh, Mouse, thanks. You always seem to be listening, hearing the Lord so clearly when He speaks to you. I want to be like that."

After a thoughtful beat, she said, "Well, honey, by the time you get to be my age, you have little else to do but listen, and I must say that I see you already listening, training your ear to hear His voice. And that's a good thing, isn't it?"

We chatted for a few minutes, and in the background, I heard a raucous voice say, "Awk—Who is it? Who is it?"

Mouse said, "Excuse me for a minute, dear." Her voice faded, as I knew she'd turned away from the phone. She said, "Clemmy, get a grip. It's only Makkie."

"Awk! Clemmy loves Makkie."

"Did you hear that?" Mouse asked with a chuckle.

"I heard. You give that crazy parrot my love."

She hung up a few minutes later, and I felt as though someone had lifted a huge weight off my heart. I turned up the music again, and this time I sang along as I unloaded the dishwasher and sorted laundry.

I'd decided I needed to give at least two hours a day to my writing, or I'd never finish anything, so within only minutes, I sat down at my pc and lost myself in the writing process, as my crazy characters immediately ran away with the story, in a direction I would never have dreamed.

Two hours later, I stood and stretched, feeling good to have accomplished my goal. One thing was crystal clear. I was a writing junky, who needed my fix to get through each day.

After feeding the dogs, I glanced outside. Today would be another excellent day for garage sales, according to the Azalea Sentinel. Clear, fifty-five degrees and mild. Our friend and newspaperman, Ken Greenlee, had recently begun to print a weather forecast for those of us die-hard garage sale nuts, calling his little column *The Junker's Forecast*. We garage sale enthusiasts are thrilled to be forewarned about the need for an umbrella or a hooded sweatshirt.

Garage sales used to be limited to the period from April fifteenth to October fifteenth, or maybe a little later, weather permitting. However, people had started using their garages, which all have side doors, at least in our area, and stationed auxiliary heating units nearby to warm their frozen clientele. Some even offer coffee or hot chocolate during more extreme weather.

I hit the road with my duffel bag of trusty garage sale supplies, including tape measure, pocketknife, scissors, pen and pad, magnet, flashlight and magnifying glass, rope and adjustable tie down straps. Grabbing it out of the closet, I can be ready to roll at a moment's notice.

The paper had said there were two sales just east of town, one of which was a moving sale, which could be an excellent source of bargains, and the other, not far away, that listed antiques among its offerings.

I located the moving sale and found a slight young woman, in her early twenties parting out a household. She had beautiful brown eyes and shiny light brown hair. She had the face of youth, carrying a heavy load, and her eyes looked puffy, as though she'd been crying.

When I stepped into the garage of her darling little bungalow, I smiled. "Hi, I love your place. So you're moving. Where are you moving to?"

She made a weak attempt to smile, but failed. "Back to Chicago, where my parents live, and I sure can't take all this with me."

"Wow, that's a shame. It looks like these things are practically new." I glanced up at her and saw tears shimmering in her eyes.

"They are. We've only been married a couple of months, but he's decided he doesn't want to be married anymore. Says he's got too much living to do to be tied down to me or any other woman right now."

"Oh, bless your heart," I said before I could stop myself. And at that, she turned away and broke into racking sobs, her shoulders heaving. I gently pulled her into my arms and let her cry. It was fortunate there were no other shoppers.

"What's your name, sweetie?" I asked, drying her eyes with the clean hanky I keep in my pocket for just such occasions.

"Jackie Parsons. Or at least it is until I take my maiden name back, if I decide to."

"Jackie, would you mind if I prayed for you?"

"Oh, would you? I could sure use it. I feel like I'm losing it."

I held her hands. "Lord, You love Jackie with a love that never ends, and I ask that You show Yourself to her, through Your Word and Your mighty presence. Wrap Your arms around her and comfort her. Bless her in Jesus' name, Amen."

"Thanks," she whispered, "you can't know what that means to me."

"You'll be in my thoughts and prayers, okay?"

She smiled.

As my glance swept the table, I said, "You're selling your things for so little."

"Well, I have to give him half of everything I get, and I'm so mad right now that if the court didn't demand I sell it, I'd probably give it away, just to teach him a lesson."

The tables were covered with gardening supplies, small kitchen appliances and utensils, rugs, curtains, expensive designer linens and towels, wall décor, tools and a few grooming aids.

I said, "Listen, don't you think you're going to need some of this stuff, no matter where you go?"

She frowned. "I guess I just want to get rid of everything and start fresh. Anything he's touched, I want out of here. I never want to see it again."

"Are you sure?"

"I am, so if there's anything you want, I'll make you a deal you can't refuse."

After a thoughtful pause, I ventured, "You know, when I was twenty-two, my husband left me after only two months of marriage."

"He did? So you know what I'm going through?"

"Yes. It really knocked me for a loop emotionally."

"How did you handle it?"

"One day at a time. I tried to focus on helping others, to get my focus off myself."

She frowned. "I can't see myself doing something like that. I've always been a little shy around other people. In fact, I'm surprised we're even having this conversation."

Unable to think of another thing to say, I scanned the table and picked up two beautiful sheet sets, and set them on the table. "Okay, I'm starting a pile."

She smiled. "I promise I won't let anyone run off with your stash."

I picked up a sleek white clock radio and turned it over, reading *do not reset; smart clock resets itself.* She had it marked three dollars.

I frowned. "What does it mean—*do not reset clock*? Do you know?"

"It's called a smart clock. You plug it in, and it knows what time it is and sets itself. I think it's computerized."

"Wow, I've never even heard of such a thing." I shook my head. "What will they think of next?"

"I know—mind blowing isn't it?"

I set it on my pile. It was exactly what I needed—something that could function completely independently of me, or my ability to figure it out.

I gathered up a few more things, including a couple of large candles in fancy metal and glass holders, several fluffy towel sets in my favorite colors, pale pink and sea foam green.

I paid her for my loot and helped her bag it. I glanced around, unable to believe that not one other person had darkened the door.

"Have you had much business?"

"Not much. I don't think people like leaving the city to garage sale, especially not this time of year. Holidays are coming," she said, bursting into sudden tears, "and I'm going to be alone." I knew that wasn't what she'd meant to say, but I understood.

"Do you have any friends? Anyone to help you get through this?"

She swiped at a tear running down her cheek. "We haven't been here long enough to meet many people. And who'd want to be my friend now?"

I handed her my card. "If you need to talk or need someone to help you pack, please call me."

"Really?" She looked surprised.

"Sure, we could even go out to lunch, if you're not too picky. There are two choices, Chinese or Verlene's."

She made a face. "I know. Pretty pathetic, huh?"

"Well, I guess that's one of the joys of living in a small town. You don't get your expectations up a whole lot."

"Ain't it the truth."

She looked at my card. "Makkie Yeats. Cool name."

"You think so?"

She lowered her chin. "That bad, huh?"

"Yup. Oh well. You can't have everything, I guess."

When I unloaded my treasures an hour later, I suddenly wished I had gotten Jackie Parsons' phone number. I wanted to check on her. She seemed rather fragile, and I couldn't help but wonder about her state of mind. *Take care of her, Lord.*

As soon as I got home, I hooked up the clock radio, and sure enough, the thing ran through a series of numbers, blinked, and then set itself to the exact time my watch revealed. I shook my head. It was humbling, actually. I hate it when my appliances are brighter than I.

Shortly after that, I had a call from Suse, asking me to meet her for lunch at Ying Lang's Peking Express. We met a few minutes later, and I still couldn't believe she was seven months pregnant. She looked stunning, in a navy, tan and white crepe pants outfit.

I smiled. "Wow, you look great when you're pregnant. What is that anyway?"

"Beats me. But I sure would hate to stay pregnant all the time just to accomplish the 'look'."

"Right. Forget I said anything."

Suse draped her coat over the chair back. "You know, I think I need this lunch just to cheer me up. I know winter does yucky things to my disposition, and much as I hate to admit it, I need my friends to keep me going."

I had to agree.

Ying Lang's is a buffet, so I had a little bit of several favorites. Unfortunately, some of General Tao's fiery peppers had found their way onto my plate, and my esophagus, with its reflux, was not one bit happy about the situation.

I choked, coughed and drank water, which only made it worse. Finally, when nothing else would help, I had to resort to vanilla ice cream to douse the flame. I dug around on my plate and unearthed another long red string, which I set aside.

When I had finally settled down, I asked Suse, "So do you and Elvee want to know the gender of the baby?"

"Well, he says no, but then he doesn't have to worry about dressing it in pink or blue, so I'm pressing to know. I'd like to get a head start on shopping. I got started this summer, during garage sale season, and you know, the Lord really did provide.

"I found a new white crib, or maybe I should say hardly used, for twenty dollars, with only one screw missing—that Elvee had to scrounge. But I have to ask myself, how does anyone end up with a practically new crib? My kids used to chew on the rails, beat on the trim, and scribble on the ends whenever they got hold of a stray crayon. So I have no concept whatsoever of a gently used crib. Anyway, I also ran across a Peter Rabbit layette that I couldn't resist."

I swiped at my lips with my napkin. "Oh, I've seen that one, and it's perfect for either a boy or a girl. The colors are so subtle."

"That's what I thought."

"Now, listen Suse, don't go buying everything for that baby, or there won't be anything left for the rest of us to do."

She paused, changing the subject. "So how does it feel to be a married woman again?"

I couldn't suppress a grin as I broke open a fortune cookie. It said, *Your sunny disposition lights up the world.* I rolled my eyes.

"I think I can live with it. Drew has waited so long for the right woman that he feels a sort of reverence about the whole thing. It's a very humbling experience."

Suse worked for a few minutes on her egg roll and Crab Rangoon, which she had saved for last, then said thoughtfully, "You know, I can make better egg rolls than these."

"I think you're right." I personally never eat the egg rolls at Chinese restaurants. They tend to overcook them and dry them out.

I said, "So how's Elvie doing with the pregnancy thing?"

"It's funny. I don't remember him being a hypochondriac the last time I was pregnant. He actually didn't take much interest, as I recall. But this time, he's got morning sickness, heartburn and even backaches." She laughed. "If I didn't know better, I'd think he was the one who was pregnant."

I swallowed a sip of water and set down my glass. "Is he excited?"

"Oh, sure. You'd think he was Eric the Red just home from pillaging the Huns or something."

I laughed. I had never heard her talk this way before. "Men are funny, aren't they?"

"Well, sure, but did you have anything specific in mind?"

"I just mean they do that macho male routine and then get mushy over pregnancy and babies. Go figure."

"Right," she agreed, "go figure."

I felt so much better after lunch that I hugged Suse. "You know, if you did this for my benefit, it worked."

She giggled. "Neely said she thought you might be needing a lift. Hafta do my part, you know."

As I drove away from the restaurant, I decided I'd spent too much time alone lately, and drove straight to Peachtree Street to see what was up. I parked in front of Mac and Blanche Finchley's house, where Blanche was just pulling into the drive.

Blanche and Mac are in their early seventies, avid golfers and congenial neighbors. Blanche is an active Mary Kay distributor and her own best advertising.

She slid from her pink Cadillac and hugged me.

"Makkie, dear, it's so good to see you. How are you feeling?"

When I looked at her in puzzlement, she said, "Your mother has been keeping us informed." *Of course, I should have known.*

"Oh, I think I'm finally beginning to bounce back." She beckoned me into the house, where she offered me a cup of cappuccino and a minute later, jumped to her feet after a glance out the window.

"Quick, close the door. I'll pull the shades. Noogy Gotsch is at it again."

Noogy is the elderly town eccentric, who insists on riding her red Schwinn up and down the streets every few weeks, buttonholing whoever she sees, trying to convince them to buy magazines for double what she just paid for them at the Piggly Wiggly. She doesn't need the money. Her parents were comfortably well off when they died, and she was their only heir.

Not only that, but she's pushy and embarrassing, dressing in the most outrageous combinations imaginable. Today, her attire was a little subdued; she wore no hat, just some cut off polyester shorts in chartreuse green, with pink knee high socks, a faded red and white checked shirt, and her usual, purple tennis shoes.

It's not that anyone hates her, but she has no desire for a relationship of any kind with anyone. Her only goal is to sell, sell, sell, so we all rush to shut curtains and doors, hoping she'll just disappear.

She finally did leave when no one answered her knock. It was then that Blanche visibly relaxed. "I know she isn't dangerous or anything, but it still sends my stress levels up, seeing her heading in my direction."

"I hear that," I agreed.

Sipping a cappuccino, I listened while Blanche told me she had a new Cadillac on the way, compliments of Mary Kay, due to her continuing sales success.

I could see it coming when she said, "Makkie, I know I've said it before, but you have the most beautiful complexion. Won't you reconsider becoming a Mary Kay Beauty Consultant?"

I gave her my most indulgent smile. "Thanks for the compliment, Blanche, but I can't see myself selling anything. In fact, I'd probably starve to death if I had to make a living in sales."

"Oh, well," she said with a sigh. "You know I had to ask, dear."

I figure it must her in her contract that she has to approach her friends at least once every six months with the same worn out sales pitch.

SEVEN

As I walked across the street to Mom's, I noticed she and Snooky sitting on the front porch, once again enjoying the mild weather.

I said, "Hey, guys."

Mom said, "I thought that was your car."

Snooky stood as I approached. "How about some hot cider, honey?"

I hugged him. "Oh, Snooky, that's sounds wonderful. Thanks."

He grinned, reminding me more than ever of Charlie Ruggles, the handsome elderly actor.

"There's nothin' too good for my girl."

He had been amazingly supportive in the last month, and I felt closer to him than ever.

He handed me a steaming mug of fragrant cider a minute later. "Sit down, Makkie and take a load off. I can imagine you're still building up your endurance. Is that a good guess?"

"It's a perfect guess, Snooky."

Changing the subject, Mom said, "Oh, Makkie, we found the perfect house for Bryce and Zoe, over in Primrose."

"Well, I'm happy for them. I really am."

I let her rattle on, telling me all about it, absorbing every word, and when she finished, she gave a contented sigh.

I hugged Mom and Snooky then took my leave. Once again, I had forgotten to take anything out of the freezer for supper, so I'd have to wing it.

I hugged the dogs when I got home and let them out to run. When I got back inside, I saw the message light blinking on the answering machine.

When I pushed play, Drew said, "Hon, you must not have had your cell phone on. I've been ordered to board a plane at four, so I won't be home tonight. I already stopped by and picked up my bag. Sorry I missed you. I'll call when I have time. Love you, babe."

So much for worrying about dinner. *Lord, please take care of Drew.*

Mom's neighbor and my friend, Libby Peters called just then, asking how I liked married life. We visited for a while before she finally said, "You know the pool the French sisters were going to install? Well, it was finished yesterday. They came over, to let me know I'm welcome to come for a swim anytime. How do you like that?"

"I thought they were on the list for next July."

"I guess their contractor had some cancellations. Besides, it's been an unusually warm fall." After a thoughtful pause, she added, "I don't suppose that means winter will be mild. That'd probably be too much to ask, don't you think?"

I sighed. "We can only hope."

I had scarcely hung up the phone before Freezia Harcourt called.

"Honey," she said, "I just wanted to let you know that I'm selling Tuppermaid now, and I need to recruit hostesses for my parties. Will you have one for me sometime in the next couple weeks?"

I made a face, wishing I never had to be put on the spot.

"Oh, Freezia, I hate to disappoint you, but I'm not a party person. I hate them—always have and always will, I'm afraid."

She cackled. "Oh, well that's normal. Everyone hates them, but that doesn't mean a body can't still have one to oblige an old friend, now does it, dearie?"

"Listen, Freezia, I hope you'll understand when I say I won't be able to do it. I just can't deal with the party scene."

"Well, at least you're honest with me about it, not like some who say they'll have a party just to get me off their backs, then back out at the last minute."

"So, Freezia, how are you doing otherwise?"

"Well, Mamie helped me get rid of those tenants I told you about. It turns out that the two men in the basement were actually wards of the state their caseworker had pawned off on me, with their mental illness."

"You didn't have any trouble getting them to leave?"

"Oh, well, I had to do some fast talking to that social worker. She started giving me this line about how I couldn't discriminate against the mentally ill, but I just told her, 'Listen here. You never informed me of this little mental health problem. If you had, I might have said yes. But since you didn't, they're out of here. So come and get them."

"And what did she say?"

"Oh, she was mad as a wet settin' hen. She said, 'They have a signed lease. You can't kick them out. I have nowhere else to put them.'

"And I said, 'Well, that's not my problem, now, is it? If you don't cooperate with me, you'll wish you had. Now come and get them. And she said, 'They're not dangerous when they're on their meds. So what's the problem?'

"And I said, 'Listen lady, I looked up Haldol in the Physician's Desk Reference at the library. It says Haldol is used for the treatment of hebephrenic schizophrenia. You didn't think I'd be up on this stuff, did you? Well, I am, and since you can't guarantee they're taking their meds unless you live with them, then you can't guarantee my personal safety either. Isn't that right?'

"She hemmed and hawed, but she knew right then and there that I had her over the proverbial barrel, and she agreed to come and get them within the hour."

"Oh, well, that's a relief."

"You're not just whistling Dixie."

In a financial bind due to her last harebrained scheme, Freezia had recently hatched a plan to rent rooms in her home. One gentleman had been a veritable virtuoso of violin and accordion, which he played all hours of the day and night.

One had been a sweet, visually impaired woman, whom Freezia had called a spook, simply because she was so quiet and would appear out of nowhere, scaring poor Freezia out of a year's growth. Now both she and I have known some wonderful visual impaired people, and are in no way prejudiced against them, but it was the spook part of the lady's demeanor that had presented the problem.

Almost immediately, she'd reported that the two men who occupied her basement had been on Haldol, which was our first clue something was very wrong. For some reason she has a habit of calling me for advice, after she's already in way over her head, expecting me to come up with solutions to magically dispense with the problem. It's happened repeatedly, to the point where I now dread taking her phone calls.

I had given her a couple of scripture passages to memorize that dealt with counting the cost before jumping in with both feet. I was hoping she had taken them to heart, but at least selling Tuppermaid seemed like a harmless occupation. *How much trouble can she get into, doing that?*

"So you finally talked to Mamie about it, huh?" Mamie is her ninety-two year old mother, who thinks her daughter is at least one sandwich short of a picnic and doesn't make any bones about saying so.

"Sure did. She wants me to keep in touch and run things by her before initiating any more of my nutty ideas. She seems to think she can keep me on the straight and narrow. What do you think, dear?"

I laughed. "Well, if Mamie can't do it, no one can."

We hung up a few minutes later, with me promising to check my supply of Tuppermaid and let her know if I needed anything. Fat chance of that, when it seems to multiply like rabbits when you're not looking, and can sometimes be bought at garage sales for pennies on the dollar.

I worked for several hours on my book, adding another two chapters to the total. I had one elderly female character, who bore a distinct likeness to our own Freezia Harcourt, and I wondered if that would present a problem.

The house grew cold as daylight faded, so I built a fire in the hearth and located the box of mysteries Mom had left me when she moved to Fair Oaks six months earlier. Even though I read like crazy, I hadn't made a dent in the box, so it would be perfect for a night like this. I dug until I found a book by one of my favorite authors, Sue Grafton.

I immersed myself in reading for several hours, and got up to let the dogs out about 8:30.

I went out in my bare feet and realized instantly that our Indian summer had disappeared, leaving a biting, cold chill in its wake. As if to convince me, the wind whipped into a sudden frenzy, and sent me, shivering, back inside for a jacket and shoes. By the time I returned to the door, the dogs were nowhere to be found. I called repeatedly, and I could hear them barking in the distance, but felt puzzled when they didn't respond to my call, since both are trained to come immediately.

Bundled in layers of fleece, I banked the fire and grabbed my keys, thinking that if I drove up the road and called, maybe I could coax them to come home.

The Taurus was freezing and hesitated when I turned the key in the ignition. After a few false starts, I revved it the moment it finally kicked in and shortly backed out the drive, with a flashlight in one hand and the other on the wheel.

Through the open window, I called, "Duke, Fred, where are you guys?"

I could hardly hear the barking now and became increasingly worried; this was so unlike them. Feeling anxious to find them and get home, I parked at the side of the road and started walking, but could neither see nor hear them anymore.

After walking for a few minutes, I was chilled to the bone in the icy wind and decided I shouldn't have left the car. Training my flashlight around the area, I headed back.

Once again in my warm car, I turned around in a wide spot in the road, thinking maybe the dogs had gone in the opposite direction. I opened the windows to listen, letting in the frigid night air as I called their names. I shook my head in bewilderment; they never did stuff like this. What on God's green earth was going on?

With my attention on the roadsides, I drove slowly, craning my neck, struggling to see through the inky darkness. As the wind died down, low-lying fog began accumulating due to moisture at ground level. At that moment, the car shuddered with a dull but riveting thud.

"Oh, God," I prayed out loud. "What did I hit?"

I put the car in reverse and stopped just a few feet away, getting out, with my flashlight poised, eyes straining, but saw nothing notable. I was just turning away, when I thought I heard a groan. In a flash, I turned back, aiming my light in the direction of the sound.

Oh, dear Lord, what now? Show me what is going on.

I shined my flashlight into the ditch and then farther away. Its beam was picking up something, but it was too far away to distinguish any details through the fog.

It was the size of a large person or maybe an animal, but as unsure as I was, I wasn't inclined to go any closer. I strode back to the car and shifted its position so that my headlights shone on the area. I still couldn't see much, but I could again hear a soft moaning. Or was it the wind?

Oh, why, didn't I grab my cell phone? Drew was always chiding me for never having it when I needed it, and after this, I would find a way to wear it around my *neck.* I hurried back to the house and rushed inside, to find that the dogs had let themselves in the front door, which evidently hadn't been closed all the way. My first thought was *there goes the heat bill.*

I hurriedly dialed 911. "This is Makkie Yeats, out at the Kellogg place on Primrose Lane. I think I just hit someone with my car. Please send someone to investigate as soon as possible."

After a restless few minutes, I heard a car pull into the drive. I stepped out onto the porch, shivering, wishing he'd pick up the pace.

The sheriff's deputy, second-in-command, Salvatore Hughes, stepped out, slammed the door, and stood beside his unit.

"Makkie, you called? What happened? Dispatch said you hit someone with your car?"

I blinked. Since I had last seen him, Sal, a husky man in his late forties with dark hair and eyes, had grown a black cookie duster mustache and looked suddenly very furry. I couldn't help but smile as he reminded me of Charlie Chaplin.

Running now, I jumped into his car, while he just stood there, looking confused. I opened the car door and yelled out. "Sal, what on God's green earth are you waiting for? Get in. I'll show you where it happened. Hurry up, will you? Someone is hurt—maybe even dying."

Moving in what seemed like slow motion, he finally slid behind the wheel, started up the car and backed down the drive, still looking dazed. It didn't take but a second to reach the all-too-familiar spot.

I shouted, "Here! Stop here."

Looking around, I pointed. "Shine your light right there. I heard someone groaning over there."

He shined the large flashlight slowly over a wide area, but its beam was as ineffectual as mine had been.

"Sal, turn your car so the headlights shine over there."

He quickly maneuvered his unit into position and shone his headlights onto the area.

"Do you see anything?" he asked.

"I see something, but I can't tell what it is in all this fog. Do you have a flood light?"

He flipped open his trunk lid and pulled out his light. I walked to the edge of the road and thought I heard another groan, but he had left the engine running, so I couldn't be sure.

"I'm going over there," I said, feeling desperate to do something.

He put his hand on my wrist to restrain me. "You aren't going anywhere. You have no idea what you'd be getting into. It could be a rabid animal or something. I'll call for backup, and we'll go there properly equipped. You stay put." His eyes glinted with steely determination as he said it.

I rolled my eyes as he got on his radio, calling for backup.

After he hung up, I argued. "But Sal, whoever that is could be dead by the time help arrives. I'm going."

He grabbed me by the shoulders and turned me to face him. "I repeat, you have no idea what you're getting into over there, and I will not allow it. Do we understand each other?"

I frowned. Another macho male with an attitude.

He glared at me. "You never answered me. What's it going to be?"

"Give me a break, Sal! I'm still here, aren't I?"

"Yes, and I'd like to keep it that way."

I sank down on the protruding bumper of his patrol car and sighed. Why could I never get anyone to cooperate with me?

The second unit was certainly taking its sweet time. Nearly frantic by then, I began to pace beside the road's edge. Within five minutes, two more sheriff's vehicles approached and shined their lights on the area in question. By then the fog had lifted a little, and what we saw was horrifying.

A man lay on his side, covered with what looked like blood, and from my vantage point, I couldn't tell whether he was alive or not.

"Listen, Sal, I'm an R.N., and I need to get to that man and see what I can do."

"No way, Makkie. We need to wait for the EMS unit. We're not equipped to handle this."

I frowned. "What are you talking about? Police go the aid of injured citizens everyday, starting CPR and giving basic life support. I know you do, because I even lobbied the city to get special respirators for each squad car. Now where is it?"

Looking chagrined, Sal knew he had messed with the wrong guy—me. He pulled the respirator from the glove compartment, and I grabbed it, yelling as I broke into a run. "Now, let's see some action over here! Come on."

I led the way to the man and leaned over him. Sal handed me rubber gloves, which I quickly donned. The man's eyes were slits, and I knelt to feel for a pulse and breathing. His heartbeat was thready—barely palpable and his respirations shallow.

I met Sal's gaze. "Did you call the EMS unit yet? We need them yesterday."

"They're on the way. How's he doin'?"

"Not good. But these injuries didn't come from being hit by my car or anyone else's. It's clear he was badly beaten before I ever came along."

I took the penlight out of my pocket and shined it on the back of his head, where there was obvious blunt force trauma. He appeared to have a depressed skull fracture, about two inches square on the back of his head, which meant there was no way on God's green earth he would make it without being flown to a trauma center, better equipped than our little town ER.

Abruptly, I yelled, "Sal, radio for a Life Flight, or he's not going to make it."

His mouth twisted into a grimace.

"Listen, I'm not sure about this. Life Flight is prohibitively expensive, and from the look of things, it may already be too late." I knew Sal had heard one too many lectures on fiscal belt-tightening.

My ire flared. "What kind of an attitude is that? Listen, Sal, I don't know about you, but I tend to listen when scripture addresses an issue. It says in Hebrews thirteen, verse two: '*Do not neglect to show kindness to strangers, for by this some have entertained angels without knowing it.*' Now, you gonna call for a Life Flight, or are you going to stand there and argue with scripture?"

He grudgingly made the call. I was not hopeful, since our victim was clearly critically injured. A compression fracture of the skull can put pressure on vital brain centers, cutting off oxygen and causing certain brain death. But he wasn't dead yet, and I've learned you never can discount God's part in the equation.

In fact, I had seen some pretty miraculous stuff in my lifetime, things that are out of the scope of human capability, where even the docs have no explanation.

Because I didn't dare to move him much, I log rolled him with my excellent support staff, ie, reluctant deputies, just enough to make sure he had a good airway.

It took about ten minutes for the air ambulance from St. Kat's in KC to set down in the field, and I was a wreck by the time it finally arrived. I wasn't sure how much time he had left, but I quickly reported what I knew, as they bundled him up, preparing to transport. Relief and fatigue washed over me as I sent them on their way with their new patient.

Sal looked at me, then at the deputies as we walked toward our cars, their floodlights still illuminating the night. "Anybody ever seen him before?"

The deputies all shook their heads, and after a beat, I said, "Thanks guys, for coming down. Sorry if I gave you a hard time."

Sal's second in command, Mick Franklin, a congenial thirty-year old with blonde hair and expressive brown eyes, looked at Sal and gave him a wry wink, then turned to me. "Listen, Makkie, when we get a call and you're involved, we expect to get chewed up and spit out if we don't do the right thing."

"Oh, yeah?"

"Word's out." He grinned, and they all burst out laughing. Not a minute later, I sat in Sal's unit, where I flipped on the heater full blast, trying to thaw my frozen limbs. After I helped complete his report, Sal dropped me at my place.

"Thanks, Sal."

"Listen, kid. You stay out of trouble—hear me?" His eyes glinted with merriment.

"Good night, Sal," I said dourly.

EIGHT

I slept fitfully, waking at the slightest sounds, my senses heightened after the events of the evening.

When I woke at seven, the dogs were ready to go out, so I donned warm clothes. Air cold enough to see my breath blew in as I opened the door.

A damp chill penetrated my heavy coat as I walked toward the accident scene, but I wanted to inspect it in the light of day.

I jumped the ditch, and the dogs followed. I could see the outline where the man had lain, about twenty feet from the road. His blood was everywhere, now turned a rusty brown. The dogs sniffed the area, and I frowned, as I wondered why Sal hadn't cordoned it off. It was a crime scene of sorts, wasn't it? So as not to disturb anything anymore than it already was, I stood still, surveying the area.

Something black and glossy caught the morning light as the weak winter sun glinted through the trees to the west, and I knew immediately, I had found his leather wallet. I went as close as I dared, pulled out my hanky and picked it up. I carefully surveyed the rest of the area, assuring myself that there was nothing more to see.

When I got back to the house, I opened the wallet and looked for identification, but it yielded nothing but a ten-dollar bill. It looked like someone hadn't wanted him identified. I carefully extracted the bill and frowned. The front of the bill had been defaced with a name and phone number scrawled in black ink. I copied the name and number on my hand, then dialed the sheriff.

"Makkie," said Duffy Murdock, when he picked up, "is this you again? Where is that husband of yours? Does he know how much mischief you get yourself into when he's not home?"

I huffed, "Duphraitis Murdock, would you just listen to yourself?" I paused, trying to calm down. I didn't want to start anything I couldn't finish when it involved the long arm of the law. "Now please, let's be professional about this, okay?"

"Okay, I guess." He paused before sniping, "So what do you want now?"

I sighed then said evenly, "Did you hear about the man I found out by my place last night?"

I waited a long moment before he finally said, "I heard about it—so what?"

I had had it up to here. "Well, hey, maybe I should just get my mother involved. What do you think, Duffy?"

He gave an audible sigh. "No need, no need. Now what do *you* need?"

"Well, I found a wallet in the field where we found him, when I was out walking this morning. I thought maybe you'd want it."

He sounded annoyed. "And just what exactly am I supposed to do with it?"

"Well, I was thinking, you could contact St Kat's, and they might be able to get the wallet back to him.

Or maybe it has some fingerprints on it. I was really careful not to mess up any evidence."

"Makkie, you know as well as I that that man probably never even made it to the hospital. So why should I go to the trouble of returning a wallet? Was there any ID in it?"

I hated to admit it. "No, none. There was only a ten-dollar bill inside."

"And you want me to jump through administrative hoops to return a wallet and a ten-dollar bill to an unknown John Doe who's probably in the morgue? Now who's being unreasonable?" After a beat, he added, "Listen, as far as I'm concerned, you deserve the ten-spot for reporting it. Do what you want with it. Give it to charity if it makes you feel any better, but do me a favor, and leave me out of it, will you please?"

He was really on a tear now. "You civilians have no idea how much time and paperwork a stupid, empty wallet can cost our office. You've done your duty as a citizen, and now I'm going to forget this call ever happened. See ya." He hung up on me.

I was seeing red when I called Mom and filled her in regarding the injured man. She asked me to describe him and promised to have someone check out the missing persons database.

I had calmed down a little after our visit, but still felt like there had to be something else I could do. While it was fresh in my mind, I wrote down the man's description, and studied the information on my hand. It was definitely calling my name.

I dialed the number, and a computerized voice asked me to leave my message at the tone. I did, asking Will Holmgren to call me, adding my number slowly, and repeating it again at the end. Who knew if he'd even call me back?

I hadn't heard from Drew since he left, and I found myself at loose ends. I had gone into this marriage knowing, in my head, at least, that it could be like this. Reality, however, was much harder to handle.

I had never asked how often he would be whisked off to who knew where, but now I wished I had.

The house felt empty without him. I hated to cook for one, and in fact, had only recently begun to get into cooking for two. Now I was losing motivation, and I could see the handwriting on the wall, *peanut butter and banana sandwiches for the rest of your dreary little life, unless you take steps to prevent it.*

I dug a couple of chicken breasts from the freezer, that I had precooked for just such an occasion and pulled a cookbook down from the cubby over the stove, inciting an avalanche that caused multiple bruises and great annoyance.

After picking up the mess, I thumbed through, but was puzzled. What on earth is a chicken croquette? It sounded like a brutal yard game. Scanning the recipe, I thought it sounded revolting, so I kept flipping pages, until there were no more chicken recipes left.

I carefully pulled down several more cookbooks and flipped through the chicken recipes, including chicken cacciatore, fricassee, ala king, Kiev, Divan, and tetrazini, all of which sounded complicated, and not even vaguely appealing for all that work, especially hating casseroles the way I do.

I got out my pencil and some recipe cards, jotting down ingredients that went well with chicken. My list included, not necessarily in combination, rice, broccoli, lettuce, tomato, tortillas, diced celery, Mrs. Dash, Parmesan cheese, grated mozzarella, ranch dressing, and onion and garlic powders, with salt and pepper to taste. There, that gave me a jumping off place at least.

Back in my early sweaty, menopausal, premarital days, I had begun collecting recipes for a cookbook I was compiling, called *Recipes for Hot People*.

If the recipes in these cookbooks were anything, they were labor intensive, and definitely not for hot people, who prefer to cook by microwave at five in the morning, to keep from heating up the house, to say nothing of themselves. This is one subject I knew up close and personal. After giving it some thought, I decided I'd have to check the Internet to see if there were any websites dedicated to Hot People.

I took out another recipe card and wrote: *A Chicken Salad Recipe for Hot People* and began jotting ingredients and directions onto the card. *One large, boned chicken breast, fully cooked and diced. To that, add one-fourth cup chopped celery, two tablespoons low fat mayonnaise, one half diced tomato, a handful of shredded lettuce, and place all ingredients on a large warmed tortilla. Season with onion and garlic powder, salt and pepper. Spread with Parmesan and grated mozzarella, and top with ranch dressing and a dollop of low fat sour cream.*

I had my mouth full of Chicken Azalea, as I had named it, when the phone rang, jolting me out of my reverie. I grabbed my water glass, and hurriedly swallowed, then picked up the phone.

"Hello. Is anyone there?" I heard someone say.

"Oh, uh, yes, excuse me, I'm here. Who's speaking please?"

His deep voice replied, "My name is Will Holmgren. Is this the party who left a message on my machine?"

"Oh, yes. Thanks for returning my call."

"Now what can I do for you, Miss uh, Yeats, is it?"

"Well, last night, I found a badly beaten man in a field not far from my home. I saw to it that an air rescue unit evacuated him to a Kansas City hospital. This morning, I was walking the area, to see if I could learn anything more, and found a wallet, completely devoid of identification, with only a ten-dollar bill inside. But on the bill I found your name and phone number, and I thought perhaps you might be his next of kin."

"Well, what exactly did this man look like?"

I picked up my clipboard, on which I had jotted notes. "Now you have to remember I saw him lying in a field, in the darkness, using only floodlights, so I'm not sure how accurate this will be."

"Miss Yeats?"

"Yes?"

"Please go on."

"Okay. He was about forty to forty-five years old, approximately six feet tall, I think, with short graying, dark brown hair. He had a small scar on his chin, if I'm not mistaken."

"Was the scar in the shape of an arrow, by any chance?" he asked in a tremulous voice.

"You know, I think it might have been. Do you know…"

He interrupted, "Tell me—what you think happened to him."

"From what I could see, he had been badly beaten, with a compressed skull fracture, which is why I was so worried about him. His breathing was shallow and his heart rate thready. Other than that, I can't tell you much."

"Well, just how did you happen to find him in the dark?"

"Oh, yes, well, there was a slight chance that I hit him with my car, sort of."

"Sort of?"

"Well, I was driving slowly, looking for my missing dogs, when I felt a thump, and got out to see what I hit. I spotted him in a field about twenty feet from my car and had to use a flashlight to search for him. I didn't mean to hit him, if I actually did hit him."

"I believe you, Miss Yeats, but it sounds as though you think he was already injured before you hit him. Is that right?"

"Yes, I was only going about ten miles an hour, so I can't understand how…" After a pause, I added, "Actually, there's no way I could've hit him. He was too far away from the road to have been hit. I guess I have no rational explanation for any of this. All I can tell you is what I saw."

"And where did you say they flew him?"

"To St. Kat's in Kansas City. At least that's where the air ambulance came from."

"Thank you for your help, Miss Yeats. If you could give me your address, I would like to reward you for your assistance."

"That won't be necessary, but I would like to know his name."

"I'm sorry, but I'm afraid I can't do that. It might put him in more danger than he already is." I hung up, puzzled. How could my knowing his name put him in further danger?

NINE

I cleaned up the kitchen, then let the dogs out into another unusually mild afternoon, with the temperature in the low fifties and no wind. I took my book out to sit on the patio, in the sunshine, hoping to deter them from running off again. I was able to detach from everything around me long enough to lose myself in my mystery for a time, before clouds drifted in, and the wind picked up.

Because I needed to begin writing again, I gathered up the note cards on which I had jotted *Recipes for Hot People*, wondering just how many hot people there were. I would have to investigate.

I turned on the computer and was going online, when the ring of the phone interrupted my wool gathering.

Mom said, "Makkie, dear, what are you up to? Am I interrupting anything important?"

"Yeah, Mom." I said, shaking my head. "I was just coming up with the cure for cancer."

She laughed. "I knew it had to be something like that. I got a call back from Gertie, at the police station. She looked up your missing person from last night, to see if she could find a match and found one that might be promising. His name is Manley Andreason. Was your guy between forty and forty-five? I wasn't sure."

"I think that's about right. So who is this guy, and where is he from?"

"Gertie said he is a pharmaceutical company researcher, with Smith, Darden and May, or something."

"It's March, Mom. Smith, Darden and March. Go on," I urged.

"Well, it seems his company filed a formal complaint against him, alleging he was stealing company secrets. You know—as in industrial espionage."

"Good grief. This sounds more like a Kinsey Milhone mystery all the time."

"I hadn't really thought of that, dear, but you may be right. Scary that these things are really happening in our little corner of the world, isn't it?"

I sighed. "Boy, you can say that again."

"There was a warrant out for his arrest when he disappeared."

After a beat, I asked, "Did she say where he's from?"

"St. Louis. Do you suppose Smith, Darden and March have offices there?"

"I have no idea. What else did she say?"

"Gertie asked me something odd. She wanted to know if he has a small scar on his chin in the shape of an arrow."

My chin dropped involuntarily.

"Mom," I said quietly, "that has to be the same guy. There was an arrow-shaped scar in the cleft of his chin." I paused and rubbed my right temple with my fingers in deep thought.

Mom said, "I wish I understood what was going on."

"Remember when I said I found a name and phone number on the ten-dollar bill in the wallet? Well, I left a message for that person to call me, and he returned my call a little while ago."

"So you already knew all this?"

"No, he refused to divulge the injured party's name—said it might put him in more danger than he's already in."

"That's an odd thing to say, isn't it?"

Once again I sighed. "That's what I thought. I've been puzzling over it ever since."

Mom said, "Gertie wanted to know where they took him for treatment."

"Now that should have been in Sal's report, for sure. Don't the sheriff's office and the police department share information? It was an air ambulance from St. Kat's in Kansas City that came for him. I'm sure of it."

Mom was quiet for a moment before she said, "You know, dear, I find it odd, but it seems as though mysteries have made a habit of falling at your feet. In fact, the whole town is talking about it."

"Oh, for heaven's sake. They must be really bored to be talking like that."

I hung up with no more insight than before, when I received a call from Drew.

"Hello, my love," he said brightly. "And how are you?"

I answered, pouting, "Lonely, that's how I am. Where on God's green earth are you anyway?"

"I'm in Clearwater, Florida. Should be back in about two days. Anything exciting happening there?"

I rolled my eyes involuntarily, snuggling into the corner of the sofa. "You wouldn't believe it if I told you."

After a pregnant pause, he sighed. "Makkie, what are you talking about?"

"How much time do you have?"

"Enough for this," he said sternly.

I explained the events of the previous night, and his only comment was, "I knew it wasn't good to leave you alone."

"What do you mean by that?" I asked with a frown. "I lived alone for the better part of thirty years and did all right."

"I didn't mean it that way, love. I just meant that I have never seen anyone get into so much mischief. And always in my absence."

I shook my head in frustration. "You think I'm asking for this stuff to happen, or causing it in some way?" After a beat, I added, "Excuse me, but to be honest, I feel like trouble is always shadowing my steps, and it makes me very nervous."

In a soothing tone, he said, "Now calm down, honey. It's no reflection on your character that these things happen, but my point is, I feel that I should be there for you, and I'm not. Do you see what I mean?"

I did. "I'm sorry, Drew. I'm tired and upset and feeling frustrated that I don't have the faintest idea what to do next."

"Look, I'll get into our data banks and see what I can find out, okay? And I'll call tomorrow when I get the chance. So hold the fort until I get there, all right?"

I hung up, missing him all the more. I wondered if there were female agents on the Clearwater detail. I had to give that thought to the Lord in a big hurry.

After eating a bowl of Cheerios, I turned my attention to the Internet, and searched baby boomer statistics, shocked to see there are immense numbers of us in the Overheated Generation, as I call it. I was guessing, from my own experience, that there are hundreds of thousands of women, and even some men, who are overheated all the time. I logged off and opened a blank document, beginning work on *Recipes for Hot People*, in earnest.

I worked through suppertime, not realizing it had come and gone, but the dogs were antsy, ready to go out, so I took a break.

The sky was clear, and a crisp, damp chill nipped the air, but thick clouds were looming on the horizon, as though ready to dump a foot of snow.

About ten, Neely called to chat, and I couldn't contain my curiosity. "So did you go back to work today?"

"I did," she said, "and do you know what? Mrs. Hakes wanted them to fire me because I didn't call in while I was being held hostage. Can you believe that?"

"Actually, I can. When I went to the school looking for you, she was very cool, and not at all helpful. Besides that, she had made herself right at home in your library, at your desk, as if to replace you."

"She did?"

I sighed. “Oh, sorry, I didn’t mean to gossip. It’s just that she made me so mad, sitting there pretty as you please, as if she had moved right into your job. If I weren’t a believer, I might’ve given her what for right then and there, I was so angry.”

She sighed aloud. “It sure is a dog-eat-dog world, isn’t it?”

“Apparently, but tell me. Did she actually have the nerve to say that right in front of you?”

“She did, but thank God, the principal backed me to the hilt, so as you can imagine, she’s none too happy with me right now.”

“Well, I’m happy. I’m grateful to have you back in one piece.”

The dogs and I were curled up in bed within ten minutes, and Quinn snuggled by my neck. They seemed to sense it when I was alone, and rushed to fill the void in my life. It wasn’t the same as having Drew beside me, but I was grateful for the company.

TEN

At eight, we woke to freezing drizzle of sorts, dreary and miserable, and awfully early in the season for such crummy weather. I was hoping it wouldn't last. That our Indian summer would stick around a little longer.

While I was in the middle of whipping up a breakfast of peanut butter toast, Zoe called. "You've made yourself pretty scarce lately."

"Zoe? How are the wedding plans coming?"

She had come to me, wanting advice about six weeks earlier. She asked what she should do to start the ball rolling in a relationship, said she had her eye on a chemistry professor, who didn't know she was alive.

I suggested she join him in the elevator and start a conversation, simply to gauge his interest. She did, and apparently the elevator chose that moment to get stuck between floors for twenty minutes. As hard as it is to believe, she denies any part in that little incident, but it apparently gave them time to talk, and from what she says, they've been talking ever since. The nuptials are scheduled for Thanksgiving weekend, and I am to be the unfortunate matron of honor.

She was in rare form. "I'm so excited about the wedding. The reception will be at the University Club, where all the bigwigs hang out. Can you imagine?"

I wasn't glad to hear it. I frowned. "Why are you doing that?"

"Well, why not? Bryce's parents are loaded, and they want to have it there since he's their only child. They're paying for it, so by rights, they can have it wherever they want."

After a stunned pause, I asked, "You two are in your fifties, and Bryce's parents are paying for the wedding?" I had never heard anything more ridiculous.

"Listen, I never want to look a gift horse in the mouth. And besides—what's it to you anyway?"

Help, Lord, I need chocolate. Zoe knows exactly which of my buttons to push to make me absolutely nuts. She knows I can't stand snobbery, which is one of the reasons we don't hit it off. She boasts a social climbing gene that's perpetually and wildly out of control.

I sucked my index finger, a habit I thought I'd given up years ago, and only resort to involuntarily—when Zoe makes me crazy.

Pacing now, I ventured, "Zoe, I hate that scene, so what say I just attend the wedding and skip the reception?"

"No way!"

I could see it all now—Me, standing beside Zoe, in front of a carved ice sculpture of a half naked mermaid and tables covered with pate' and crab legs, smoked salmon, and caviar, and no doubt, surrounded by an abundance of snobs. *Gag me with a tablespoon, please.*

She continued, "What's the big deal? I've noticed you have no trouble doing whatever you set your mind to, so I don't think it's too much to ask that you swallow your pride and do this one thing for me. I mean, how often have I asked you..."

"Give me a break, Zoe. I'll be your matron of honor, because we're sisters, but I don't have to like hobnobbing with the mucky-mucks you hang with, so don't even go there, okay?"

When she said nothing, I continued, "Now, do you still want me for a bridesmaid or not?"

"I do."

I sighed. "Then you'd better fill me in on the details."

"The wedding is set for Saturday, November twenty-fourth."

"What does my dress look like?"

"Oh, don't worry. It'll be a knockout."

I persisted, annoyed. "Zoe, what does my dress look like?"

"I haven't quite decided yet. I'm still narrowing down my choices."

"Well, give some thought to my preferences, will you?"

Testily, she said, "Don't you think I have any taste?"

I chose not to answer that, unwilling to open up a whole new can of worms.

I asked, "It's still being held at the Fellowship of God in Primrose, right?"

"No. We're having it at All Saints Community Church in the city."

"What? When did that change?" I asked, appalled.

"Well, Bryce's parents go there, and it's large enough to hold a crowd of a thousand give or take, so it should work out better than the Fellowship of God building."

"A thousand? A thousand what? People? You must be out of your mind." After a brief pause, I asked, now irate, "Zoe Webster, what on earth are you doing?"

"What is your problem?" Her voice rose with every word.

"Let me get right to the point. Does Bryce know the Lord or doesn't he?"

"He's been attending the Fellowship of God Church for three years now," she said defensively, her voice bristling with attitude.

"That's not what I asked. Now, I repeat, is Bryce a Christian, born again, or not?"

"We haven't actually discussed it, and I don't know why it should be such a big deal, so just drop the subject, will you?"

"I can't, Zoe. I cannot let you knowingly marry an unbeliever without warning you about it."

"Give me a break, you goody-two-shoes." She was right. That last sentence hadn't come out as well as I'd hoped.

"Zoe," I said, trying to calm my rapidly beating heart. "I'm going to pretend you didn't say that. And I'm going to hang up now, before one or both of us says something else we might regret."

I gently replaced the phone and sank into the nearest chair. I shouldn't have been surprised. My sister has done very little living of her Christianity, if she does, in fact, have any. I felt frustrated and didn't think I could just let this issue go. It was too important. Would I be able to stand up with her, knowing she was marrying an unbeliever, or were they really unequally yoked if she wasn't living the life in the first place? I knew this was a question I'd have to answer, and yet I knew she'd never forgive me for refusing to stand up with her. In fact, I was certain I'd hear about it for the rest of my natural life. Maybe that was what the scripture meant when it talked about persecution, but you scarcely expect it to come from your own sister.

Feeling upset, I dug in the cupboard until I found a tiny box of Stover's Chocolates, with caramel and nuts, and ate the whole box, all six pieces, without a shred of guilt. Talk about emotional eating.

I was so upset that I turned my attention to house cleaning. I fished out the bucket that held cleaning supplies and gathered and shook rugs out the door in the sleet, and then had to hang them up to dry. Then I proceeded to vacuum, moved and polished furniture, rearranged the living room, emptied trash, cleaned the kitchen and bathroom, and washed the inside of every window in the house.

The place sparkled when I finished, but by then, I could scarcely move for the fatigue. Pulling a quilt over me, I slept almost instantly.

At lunchtime, I let the dogs out, then built a fire against the damp chill of the afternoon. I picked up *I is for Innocent*, starting where I'd left off the other day.

I must've nodded off, because the phone rang, sending the dogs into spiels of whining and barking. Mom's voice weighed heavy with concern, and I thought I knew what was coming.

"Makkie," she said, quietly, "I just got off the phone with Zoe, and she's very upset. She thinks you don't want to stand up with her. What on God's green earth is going on?"

"Did she ask you to talk me into it?"

"You know me better than that. Even if she had, it's not my place to be your conscience, is it? I just want you to tell me what's going on."

"Mom, she just dropped the bombshell that they're getting married in the All Saints Community Church, instead of at the Primrose Fellowship of God. Now I know it's no sin to be married elsewhere, but that isn't the point. The point, as I see it, is that she's marrying an unbeliever, and there is a definite command against it in scripture."

After a pregnant pause, she asked, "Do you really see this as an unequal yoke, dear?"

"That's what I want to know. I hate to put on my fruit inspector's hat and start judging Zoe, but honestly, I can't tell whether she has a relationship with God or not."

"Well, that should be your first clue right there. You can see it as clear as the nose on your face, as can I, that there is no relationship with God."

I blinked in confusion at her words.

She paused, then continued, "When Zoe was small, I taught her the very best I knew, about salvation and the reality of heaven and hell, but met resistance from the first. I knew early on, that she would have to go through the fire to be convinced by God's Spirit, of the things she had heard with her ears. So far, she gives no indication she has any interest in spiritual things, which is probably one of the reasons the two of you don't get along."

I felt like I'd been shot. "Mom, why haven't you told me any of this before now?"

"I guess I was hoping she might come around, especially when you have such a powerful and visible relationship with God, which even Zoe can't ignore."

I sighed. "Well, that puts a lot of things in perspective, doesn't it? What she sees in me makes her hate me even more than she ordinarily would."

"I know, dear, and I'm sorry. I know she makes your life…well, shall I say miserable?"

My laughter sounded slightly hysterical. "Sure Mom. Miserable is the perfect adjective."

Mom laughed. "You know, don't you, that I've always felt much closer to you than to her, no matter how impartial I try to be? Well, it's because of our mutual relationship with the Lord."

"I know, Mom, and I treasure our closeness more than I can say." I paused. "I guess I'm in shock. I really never knew before that Zoe had rejected the Lord."

"Maybe that will help you decide whether or not you want to stand up with her. What do you think?"

I huffed, "That's not the only reason I would like to say no. She knows how much I hate that social climbing thing, and so what does she do? Hold the wedding reception in the Mecca of social snobbery, with me as her matron of honor." I grumbled, "Some honor."

"Well, maybe we should pray over this situation. You know, dear, this may be the Lord, prompting you to do something you're not crazy about, to show your sister love, when it would be easier not to. We'll just ask the Lord to give you wisdom—show you what to do."

After a beat, I said, "Mom, you know as well as I do what I have to do. I just need prayer for the right attitude and the grace to do it, so pray that in, will you?"

"You know I will, my dear. You have a kind heart, and I'm proud to be your mother."

"Oh, Mom, don't," I murmured. "I can't stand it when you go all gooey on me."

"Okay, dear, I'll stop. Let's pray, shall we?"

"Go for it."

"Lord, this is a tough one. We have to be made willing sometimes, and this is one of those times. We need You to pour out Your Spirit on Makkie and even on me, for grace to do the hard things, regarding the wedding. We want Zoe to accept Your gift of salvation, but only You can place that desire in her heart. Until then, give us grace to love her when she's a pill, and we'll give You the praise in Jesus' name."

I had to laugh. "Mom, I wonder if God has many requests dealing with *pills.*"

"Speaking of pills," she said in a distracted tone, "I need to go give Snooky his pills with his hot chocolate before he falls asleep sitting in his chair, poor dear."

"Bye, Mom. Give Snooky a big kiss for me."

ELEVEN

It was getting dark early these days, and by 5:30, though I knew it was all in my mind, I felt sleepy. It's one of those jet-lag kinds of things that happen every time we either *spring forward*, or *fall back*, and I hate it.

Drew phoned as I was fixing a gooey, toasted cheese sandwich and canned chicken noodle soup. I turned off the burner under the sandwich, as I picked up the phone.

"Hey, there, hon, I thought I'd be home tonight, but the freezing drizzle is so bad here in Chicago, where we had a layover, that they're grounding all flights out. Just wanted you to know." After a pause, he added, "Are you guys all right?"

"We're fine. I hate it that you have to sleep sitting up in an airport terminal, but better safe than sorry, right?"

"No kidding."

I said, "Well, take care of yourself. And don't forget to eat and drink, okay? I just heard them say on television that it helps with jetlag."

"Okey dokey, chief. I love you."

We hung up, and I ate my solitary supper with a feeling of contentment that came from merely hearing his voice. *Am I in love or what?*

The dogs and I watched the news and later, I snuggled to read in bed, where the quilts were piled high, until I could no longer keep my eyes open.

By morning, the sun was out, but a white dusting of snow blanketed the ground, as slick as the dickens. I stood and stared, shading my eyes from the glare. Every winter, I stand in awe of the first snow. No matter how many times I've seen it shimmering in the sun, I'm dazzled by its brightness and the way it turns the world into something magical, beautiful.

I laughed as Duke and Fred gingerly made their way to about an inch off the patio and did their business before scurrying back into the warmth of the cottage.

I looked at Duke, who stood there, his massive, hairy body shivering.

"Hey, I thought you were a Newfoundland hound, able to brave the elements, at least as well as the US Postal Service." I laughed when he cocked his head and looked at me as if I'd lost my mind. Hoping to take the chill off the room, I built a fire and put on a Christmas DVD.

After making us breakfast, I felt like baking and did up a fragrant batch of chocolate chip cookies. I must've accidentally doubled the recipe, because I ended up with five-dozen, three of which I stuck in the freezer. Feeling generous, I threw a piece to each of the dogs, before realizing it was a mistake. Duke wretched it up within a minute. Nuts, and on my clean floor too.

I chopped vegetables and chicken breast and put together a thick savory soup to simmer in the Crock Pot.

Today was my quilting day, but before I had given it any thought, Freezia Harcourt called. "Makkie, we're canceling today, since it's slicker than a banana peel out there. No use us old ladies takin' the chance of breakin' a hip for the sake of a quilt, right?"

"You're right, Freezia. Keep warm," I said.

"Say, while I have you on the line, I want to run something past you, okay, Makkie?"

Oh-oh. "And what's that, Freezia?"

"Well, remember when I told you I was getting into Tuppermaid?"

"Sure. How's it going?"

"Not too good, actually. It sounds like the entire world is up to its elephant ears in Tuppermaid."

"You mean the market is flooded?"

"Sure sounds like it. Unless someone melts something in the dishwasher, very few people have a need for more. But that's not why I'm calling. I wanted to let you in on a wonderful new business opportunity."

I hesitated, not knowing what to say. There was no way I'd be involved in any of her crazy schemes. But I said quietly, "Let's hear it."

"I knew you'd be excited. Okay, well, by a chance happenstance, I ran across a jobber who bought a truckload of amazing closeout items and resells them to far-seeing individuals like me. He's letting me in on the deal of a lifetime. I'm buying 25,000 Tuppermaid Popsicle makers for a dollar and a quarter each. They sell for $3.95 each." After a beat, she added, "You do the math, girl. I won't be able to spend that much money in a lifetime. I'll be in tall cotton." She giggled like a schoolgirl in love. "So what do you think?"

"Um," I hesitated. "I don't suppose you told the man you'd sleep on it, did you?"

She plunged on. "I'm so excited about this. I think it's a very savvy move on my part. So can I count you in for...say...ten thousand Popsicle molds?"

"Um, no. I don't think so."

"Makkie, I'm making you the deal of a lifetime. Can't you see that?"

"Listen, Freezia, did you consult Mamie about this before jumping in with both feet?"

"Oh-oh. I should've seen this coming. You always get out your trusty hatpin and pop a hole in my bubble, don't you? What is it with you? You just get a kick out of doing that? Is that it?"

"No, Freezia. That's not it at all."

"Then what is it?"

"We've discussed this before."

Freezia huffed. "I know, and you never seem to learn from your mistakes."

My mouth dropped open in shock. "Me?"

"Well, okay. Say no more. I'll take my deal of a lifetime and find another investor." *You mean another pigeon.*

"I'm hanging up now, Freezia. I hope it works out for you." I hung up, shaking my head.

Several hours later, I heard the Bronco in the driveway and threw open the door, to take Drew's duffel, while he pulled off his coat and hung it up.

He grinned, swept me into a warm embrace, and kissed me soundly. "Hey, gorgeous. How's my best girl?"

"Missin' you." I smiled and kissed his cheek.

He looked at Duke and Fred. "So has she been behavin', guys?"

I laughed, as Drew threw himself on the floor, tussling and playing tug of war with the dogs. Even Quinn stopped washing herself long enough to watch.

I said, "Do they expect you back at the office today?"

"Not on your life. The Bronco was like a pig on ice just reaching home. No way I'd risk driving all the way to the city in this. Besides, they owe us comp time for having to sit in that awful Chicago terminal. So what've we got to eat around here?"

"How about chocolate chip cookies?" I laughed. "I got carried away."

"That sounds good, but…"

I put up my hand. "I'm kidding. I have homemade vegetable soup in the Crock Pot."

I began setting the table as he disappeared to shower and change, and I couldn't help but laugh when he emerged wearing oversized sweat shorts and a short-sleeved sweatshirt. The soup was bubbling when Drew set the table, while I made toasted cheese sandwiches.

"Mmm…just what the doctor ordered. I'm starved. Can you believe that after being stranded, the airlines still give you peanuts and soda to tide you over on the flight home?"

I set the plate in front of him and he smiled. "This looks great. I hope you've got more where this came from."

He ate like a lumberjack while I watched.

"Didn't you eat at all while you were gone?"

"We could only eat what we could capture, and there wasn't much in the way of wildlife in the airline terminal. Oh, let me rephrase that," he said with a twinkle in his eye. "I did see a few squirrels, but not the edible kind." He paused. "Actually so many people were stranded that the concessions stands ran out of food by the end of the first day, so I'll bet there are a lot of folks chowin' down big time right now."

I filled his soup bowl a second time and set the crackers in front of him, adding a short stack of cookies to his plate.

Smiling, he said, "There's simply no place like home. Do you know what I mean, love?"

"I do, but I have to admit, home isn't very homey when *you're* not here."

He finished his meal, while I stoked the fire. While I washed dishes, he wiped the counters and table, though I knew he had to be exhausted.

"Thanks for the help," I said, as he pulled me into the circle of his arms and tossed the dishcloth into the sink.

He smiled. "I should be thanking you for the great meal. I think you just saved me from starving to death."

He gave me a playful kiss on the lips and cocked his head. "So what's been going on in my absence? Anything exciting?"

"Hmm...well, Freezia called. She's upset with me, because I wouldn't jump into her latest *deal of a lifetime*."

"Oh, no." He shook his head. "What's that fruitcake up to now?"

"Honey, please."

He held up his hands in surrender. "Okay, okay."

"Well, she found a jobber who made her a great deal on Tuppermaid Popsicle molds."

"On what?"

"Popsicle molds. They're plastic, made by Tuppermaid."

He glared, wide-eyed. "I'm familiar with Tuppermaid. You didn't take her up on this deal, did you?"

"Are you serious? With a history like hers? Well, anyway, she bought 25,000, and offered me 10,000 of them at a dollar and a quarter apiece. She said they sell for $3.95 each. And as she so blithely put it, 'You do the math. I'll be in tall cotton. Won't be able to spend that much money in a lifetime.'"

Drew laughed, shaking his head.

I continued, "The only thing is, the reason a jobber got them as closeouts in the first place is that the crackerjack sales force at Tuppermaid can hardly give them away. And it's not encouraging that you can buy them for a dime at a garage sale nearly any weekend during summer."

"Well, I'm glad you didn't let her talk you into anything."

"And here I thought she'd found the perfect occupation. I had no idea she could get into so much trouble just selling food storage products," I said, shaking my head.

We snuggled in front of the fire and talked, until the magnet of kissing was too much to withstand. He smiled. "I can't tell you how much I miss the small stuff being away."

I couldn't help asking, "I was wondering—were there any women agents on this detail?"

"Yup, three. And as usual, they were tough to get along with and not the least bit appealing. Is that what you wanted to hear?"

"If it's true," I answered honestly.

His look was wistful. "My love, how can I convince you? I have never been more sincere about anything in my entire life."

"Glad to hear it," I said, as he kissed me and nuzzled my neck. I was getting pretty good at this nuzzling thing myself.

I must've fallen asleep a while later, because he tapped my shoulder and took my chin in his palm. "Hey, sweetie, you need to get to bed. You'll freeze out here."

I felt comforted by his warmth as we settled under the pile of quilts and slept, with the sound of freezing rain tapping on the windows.

At seven, I awoke to the sounds of banging metal from the kitchen. The smell of bacon and eggs filled in the air.

"Oh, rats." I had never told him about Zoe's ritual bacon and egg breakfasts while we lived at Mom's. Unfortunately, she had ruined bacon and eggs for me forever.

I pulled a robe around me and headed toward the kitchen.

"Hey, babe, thought I'd whip us up a gourmet delight, bacon, omelet and toast. Does that sound good?"

I smiled. I hated to break his bubble, so I sat down to the plate in front of me and nibbled the bacon.

"Did you let the dogs out?" I asked.

He laughed, gesturing to the hearth, where the dogs lay snoring. "Those two are like pigs on ice. Won't even try going farther than necessary to do business."

"I know," I said, yawning.

"You know," he commented absently, "I think I saw a bag of Ice Melt up in the shed. I should probably bundle up and go clear the driveway and patio."

He stood and picked up his plate. "Sure do love you, babe," he said, as he bent down and kissed my cheek.

"Thanks for the breakfast."

I knew it was a guy thing to want to work out of doors in winter, and it really did need to get done. I'm not all that fond of the outdoors, except when the weather is perfect. I just do what has to be done, and most of that with gritted teeth.

Drew bundled in layers of fleece and headed out the door, while I cleaned up the kitchen. He was out there for several hours, and finally came in when I yelled out the front door, "Are you ready for a break yet?"

I had made him hot chocolate with those little marshmallows, mostly for the nostalgia factor. Comfort food; what life was all about.

He divested himself of his layers and took off his boots, setting them on the hearth. "So, did you see how much I got done?" he asked, looking hopeful.

"I did, and it looks great. *We* women folk really appreciate your hard work," I said with a smile.

He had cleaned the ice and snow off both vehicles and cleared the patio, spreading Ice Melt on the slickest spots. It was going to be mighty handy having a man around to do the guy stuff.

The sun came out a little later and began melting the ice, on what turned out to be a beautiful day. Drew came in and asked, "Hey, how would you like to go into the office, so I can teach you how to shoot?"

"Really?" I asked, smiling. "I'd love it."

"Great. As soon as I finish up this paperwork, we'll head out. The roads will be soupy, but at least passable."

I was excited at the prospect of learning to shoot. Having grown up in an academically inclined family, I had missed the joys of camping, hunting, and fishing, things that other families took for granted.

I was hoping against hope, as a non-athlete, that maybe I could excel at target shooting.

Walking into the cavernous, dimly lit indoor shooting range, just outside downtown Kansas City, it felt like we'd stepped into another world. The place was deserted. A half-wall separated the shooters from their targets, with an electric pulley system that allowed the shooter to hang a target and then examine it later.

Drew gave me some earphones, heavy and not particularly comfortable, then showed me how to wear them, as if I couldn't have figured *that* out for myself. Then he explained the weapon, a smaller version of his massive handgun, helped me get a grip on the thing and placed my fingers where they should go. He explained how to load it and how to stand and aim.

Why is it that men feel the need to go into so much detail? Most of what he said was a little like computer language. I heard it, but since it wasn't my world, I didn't really assimilate much of it. But I was clear on the high points, able to repeat them back when quiz time came.

I wanted to watch while he demonstrated, then have him help me shoot the first time. He made it look easy when his first shot hit slightly to the left of Targetman's heart. Of course, Drew had been doing it for thirty years.

When it was my turn, he stood behind me and positioned me, urging me to bend my knees. He put his hands over mine, aiming. He let go just long enough to reposition my earphones, then covered my hands with his. He said, *squeeze* just loud enough. Hesitantly, I squeezed the trigger, but was too scared to look, and closed my eyes.

He must have sensed it, because he laughed, took the pistol from me, and removed my earphones. "What happened? Get scared?"

"I don't know if I can do this," I said doubtfully.

"Sure you can. Just try it again, and remember what you've learned."

I did, only this time I kept my eyes open and watched the target. I hit about four inches from dead center, but Drew seemed thrilled. "That's great for your first time. Can you loosen up a little? Try rolling your shoulders. You're way too tense."

"What?" I said, frowning, "I shouldn't be tense my first time shooting a gun?"

He laughed then nodded. "Go ahead and try it again."

My second shot hit the target low on the torso, still not very close, but Drew seemed tickled that I was trying. The pistol was becoming heavy in my hands by now, and I could feel my shoulders and arms shiver with fatigue. He wanted me to try one more time, but I argued, "I'm too tired. I won't have good control."

"Try anyway, okay? Just one more time, and then we'll call it a day."

I aimed and shot, but my hand shook with fatigue, so I hit way off the mark.

"That's okay, sweetie. We'll just have to work on upper body strength. Then it won't seem so hard."

"Oh-oh," I said with an exaggerated sigh, "that sounds a lot like exercise."

"I'll get you some two-pound weights, and you can just do a few lifts whenever you feel like it. You'll be doing better in no time."

I made a face. "Maybe you would've been better off marrying Wonder Woman."

He laughed. "Maybe, but it wouldn't have been this much fun."

Because we weren't far away, he took me to Dayton's Treat, a darling 1950s diner he had introduced me to only a couple of months before. It was a scene right out of "Happy Days", with pink and blue fluorescent lighting, roller skating waitresses, and the most outrageously delicious junk food ever. They even played fifties music. It was like walking back in time.

Drew got a call on his cell as we were pulling out of the parking lot. After a brief pause in their conversation, I cringed when I heard him say, "But Marty, we were supposed to have at least one day off. No, I can't just jump a plane. I've got my bride in the car with me. Look, talk to the Red team—they haven't been out for nearly a week." He listened for a minute, and then said dejectedly, "Listen, I'll call you when I get home."

He flipped the phone closed, frowning in annoyance. "You know, one of these days, I'm going to toss this thing right into the river. Something's up in Denver. He didn't say what, but for some reason, Marty seems to think the Blue team is indispensable. He wants us to fly out today."

When I said nothing, he said, "I told him to call the Red team. We need a break."

"But you'll probably have to go, right?"

"I'll have to call him when we get home."

We were quiet, until I asked, "You know, I was wondering how often you get called out. Is this normal?"

"It isn't usually quite this often. About two to three times a month is normal, for a couple of days at a time, but this is nuts."

He picked up the phone as soon as he hit the door, dialing Marty. In spite of myself, I was beginning to like Marty less all the time.

Drew came to find me in the bedroom, where I was tugging on my house slippers. He took my hand. "I guess the Blue team has to roll on this one, but only for a day or so, so don't miss me too much, you hear?"

Tears filled my eyes, and I hurriedly brushed them aside. He kissed my damp cheeks, and looked sad as he drew me into his arms. "I'm really sorry, babe. I sure hate to leave you again so soon."

I caressed his cheek. "Don't mind me. It's just that I've grown accustomed to having you around."

"Hey, I like the sound of that," he said, chuckling.

I tried to memorize the sound of that laughter, knowing it might have to last a while.

As he laid his clothes in the duffel, he said, "Sure am gonna miss you, babe."

He held me tightly before leaving, and I whispered thickly, "Be safe, sweetheart, and come back soon."

"Count on it. Oh, and don't you go getting into any trouble now, hear me?"

I watched him pull out of the drive and felt sad, realizing that my worst adjustment would be his constant coming and going.

It was only a quarter of four in the afternoon, but the day already seemed long, when I noticed the huge pile of laundry sitting next to the washer. I started a load. I'd have to hustle to keep this traveling man in clothes.

Drew has great taste in clothes, and I wondered if it was something his mother had inspired. He favors muted pastel solid shirts and a few classic plaids. He has some beautiful ties, but doesn't wear them often, which suits me fine. Although I have to admit he really is a hunk when he dresses up, I can't say I blame him for preferring a casual style. I'm not the formal type either.

Zoe phoned me just before suppertime and acted like we had never had the big tiff of two days ago.

"Hey, Makkie," she said with a giggle. "You'll never guess where we're going on our honeymoon."

I said nothing.

She sounded miffed. "Well, aren't you going to guess?"

"Zoe, you know I hate games. Just tell me if you want me to know."

"Okay, party pooper. We're going to Switzerland, skiing."

"Wow," was all I could think of to say.

"So what do you say to that?"

"You don't ski."

"Is that it? You sure know how to throw a wet blanket on my excitement. I mean, can you imagine a more romantic place for a honeymoon?" She paused and then said with irritation, "Do you do this on purpose or what?"

"Zoe, I'm happy for you, but I am glad it's you and not me." After a beat, I added, "I'm sure you'll have a wonderful time."

"You're only saying that because I made you."

I couldn't win for losing with her.

She hung up on me, I supposed, because I wasn't giving the right answers to the questions. I sighed, wishing things could be different, but at this late date, it wouldn't pay to hold my breath.

I dug in the fridge, where I found some boiled eggs and whipped up egg salad, which I spread over lettuce and tomato. I ate it in front of "Unsolved Mysteries" for the company, forgetting my vow not to eat in front of the television.

I was so bored and bummed, since Drew was gone, that I went to bed at nine, falling into a dreamless sleep, until later, when the nightmare began. Fighting the bedcovers and rousing the dogs, I screamed and wept, trying to get away from my pursuer. Finally I awoke and turned on the lights. It was only after drenching myself in Psalms that I finally fell back to sleep several hours later.

I was up by six, in the pitch dark, and got busy organizing *Recipes for Hot People* on computer. I was able to lose myself in it, until the phone rang about 8:30.

TWELVE

"Hello," a masculine voice said. It sounded vaguely familiar.

"Is this Makkie Yeats?"

"It is," I said. "Who's speaking, please."

"Will Holmgren. We spoke the other day. Do you remember our conversation?"

"Of course, Mr. Holmgren. I've been wondering how your friend is doing. Is it okay to ask?"

"He's in a deep coma and not likely to improve any time soon."

I sighed. "I'm sorry to hear that."

"Thank you. Listen, I wondered if you could answer a couple more questions for me."

"I don't think I can be very helpful, but I'll try. What is it you want to know?"

"Did he say anything at all while you were near him?"

"Nothing at all. He was unconscious. I thought I mentioned that when we…"

He interrupted. "Did he give you anything, or did you find anything besides the wallet with the ten dollar bill?"

"No, that was all. But I could send it to you if you'd like me to."

"I think that would be helpful. Send it: care of me, P.O. Box ten, St. Louis." He gave me the zip code, thanked me and hung up.

I sighed. I had an overwhelming feeling that Mr. Andreason, the mysterious man I had found, wasn't going to go away any time soon.

I let the dogs out, into a gray but balmy November morning. There was no wind, but the ice that had thawed the day before had once again frozen overnight, making everything very slick.

With no more excuses, I finally sat down and worked on book two. After losing myself in my story for four solid hours, the dogs nudged my jean-clad leg to let me know they wanted out. I spent the rest of the day reading my mystery and working on *Recipes for Hot People*.

Late the next morning, as I was standing out on the patio in the sunshine, in my robe and slippers, the phone rang. I hurried inside. The Shady Acres Social worker was on the line. Oh, no. *High pressure sales*.

"Hey, Makkie, how's it goin'?" asked Marla Kelly, a little too cheerfully, I thought. I poured a cup of coffee and leaned against the counter.

"Hi, Marla. I'm fine. What's up?"

"Well, I need to schedule transportation to Kansas City for Sturgess Claymore. You do know Sturgess, don't you?"

"Yes," I said, not committing to anything.

"Well, he has an appointment at the wound center in Kansas City a week from today, at ten, and I need you to transport him."

I hesitated. Sturgess is not a friendly sort, not at all. More like a *sturgeon*, ornery and withdrawn. Of all the people she could have asked me to ferry, Sturgess had to be my least favorite. And I knew he felt the same way about me.

She was waiting for my answer.

I said, "Let me ask you this. What's the appointment for? Exactly how long are we talking here?"

"Well, he needs a small skin graft, so it might take several hours."

I took a breath before asking, "So you're asking me to take Sturgess for a good part of the day on a seventy mile round trip for six-fifty an hour?"

"I guess I am," she admitted feebly.

I mused aloud, "Hmm…Well, you know, I guess I'd like to renegotiate my rates right about now. Either that or you're welcome to try to get someone else to take him."

"Hmm…" she murmured into the phone. "If we were sending him on the Senior Mobile Service, we'd be paying a lot more…" I knew she was wishing she had kept her big mouth shut.

"Like exactly how much?" I asked hopefully.

"We can't pay you that much, of course…"

"And why is that?" I asked stubbornly. "Now don't forget they're being transported by a registered nurse."

"You don't have to tell me—I know."

"Well," I said succinctly, "my time, gas and TLC are certainly as valuable as the Senior Mobile Service's, aren't they?"

"But Makkie, that's not the point. It's just not in the budget."

"Well, Marla, why don't you just schedule Sturgess on that Senior Mobile Service then? Or better yet, drive him yourself?" I knew how well that suggestion would go over.

"They're booked up way ahead, and…oh, man, we pay them $26 an hour."

"So that's what I'm worth, too, right?" I asked, feeling hopeful.

She said grudgingly, "I suppose we can come up with the money from somewhere."

Marla hung up, having just given me a more than 300 percent wage increase, which I knew she would bill to Medicare anyway. And besides, she doesn't have any paperwork to do when I do the transportation, and I thought that should be worth something.

With the phone still in my hand, I wrote it on my calendar and resigned myself to spending my entire next Wednesday in Kansas City with Sturgess the sturgeon.

My mind was wandering as Duke and Fred chased each other in circles around the kitchen, tugging on the ten-foot long phone cord. I took a step and, too late, realized it was wrapped around my legs. I fell, crashing to the floor; cracking my left foot on the edge of a chair, and banging my head. Great, just what I needed.

I'd disengaged myself with a great deal of effort and tried to stand, when a lightening bolt of pain rushed up my left foot and leg and made me gasp. It would bear no weight at all.

I thought I recalled seeing a pair of crutches in the closet, from an old injury of Ernie's, so I hobbled, hopping from one piece of furniture to the next, until I made it to the closet, where I fished them out. They were about eight inches too long, so I sat on the bed and unscrewed the sections, shortening them to fit me.

Hey, I brightened at the thought—*maybe I can get out of Zoe's wedding after all.* I knew it was wishful thinking. With my luck, it would only be a sprain.

I sat down on the sofa and examined the foot. It was swelling rapidly, already discolored on the inside of the ankle, and tender to the touch. I pulled an Ace bandage out of the kitchen drawer, and gingerly wrapped it, swallowed eight hundred milligrams of Ibuprofen, and pulled out a Ziploc storage bag to use as an ice bag.

I hadn't even had my shower yet, and here I was, handicapped, to some degree. I'd never tried showering with crutches and wondered how hard it would be. I finally settled for a sponge bath and struggled to put on my clothes. Still not admitting defeat, I found my mystery book, marked at page 123, and propped my foot on a pillow, to read. Usually a fast reader, I was getting way behind.

A couple of hours later, the pain and swelling seemed worse instead of better, so I broke down and called Arlo, who's been my doctor for years, as well as my friend since we were small. His office is located in the emergency room of the Memorial, which is convenient. Besides, he answers his own phone if you have his private number.

When he heard my voice, he said, "Makkie, what's going on?" He's been on alert since I've been so prone to accidents the past seven months.

"I fell and hurt my foot. Do you have time to see me?"

"Don't drive. Call Jane or something. I'll fit you in when you get here."

I called Mom, and she and Snooky drove me to the hospital, where Arlo looked at my foot and shook his head. "I think it's broken. Let's get an X-ray."

Upon seeing me, Shirley, Arlo's nurse said, "Nice to see you again," a little sarcastically, I thought. She wheeled me around the corner into X-ray and doggoned if the thing wasn't fractured. She handed me the X-ray folder, and I handed it to Arlo, when we got back to the room. With his red head bobbing, he surveyed the films.

"You just don't do anything halfway, do you, Makkie?" He looked more like Dennis the Menace than ever when he teased me, eyes twinkling.

"What do you mean by that?" I asked, surprised.

"Well, by the looks of this picture, you've broken not one, but two bones in your foot. One is a hairline crack. See?" He pointed to the X-ray. "Here, let me help you up on the table. We need to cast this."

"Rats," I said, adding, "I should've taken a shower this morning, crutches and all, since it looks like it might be awhile till I get another."

"You got that right," Arlo said dryly. He paused, with a bewildered look on his face, "What is it with you, Makkie? Do you have a death wish or something? I've never seen a woman your age who gets herself into so much difficulty, unless she's married to an abuser, which you definitely are not."

At least he hadn't said *mischief*.

I turned away just then as tears burned my eyes, but not before he noticed. After I'd collected my emotions, I said, "Listen, Arlo, how long is this cast going to be on anyway?"

"Why, got a hot date?"

"No, but I'm supposed to be in my sister's wedding in less than two weeks."

He shook his head. "Forget that. This thing won't be off for at least six weeks, maybe longer, depending on how fast you heal."

"Will I be able to get a walking cast soon?"

"That will be at least three weeks away, so get used to those crutches. Keep the foot elevated for the next couple days. And stay off the ice. Crutches and ice don't mix." He made a face when he said that.

I stuck out my tongue. "You wouldn't kid me now, would you, Arlo?"

"Where's Drew?" he asked, noting his absence for the first time.

"Out of town. Can't plan on him to be here for life's little emergencies."

He had finished the cast and turned to wash his hands, when he laughed and said brightly, "Right. That would be a full time job."

I playfully slugged him on the arm.

"Now," he added, ruffling my hair, "I need to see you in three weeks. Put it on your calendar."

Mom and Snooky drove me home, and I sighed, knowing I'd be housebound more often than not, doing the crutch thing in winter. I wondered if they had spiked crutch tips you could add for icy weather.

Mom and Snooky stayed to visit, and Mom fixed supper for the three of us.

Just as they were leaving, Snooky pulled me into a hug. "You know, Makkie, you might want to think about getting one of those cordless phones. It'd be a lot safer, you know."

I laughed. *A safe phone. Now there's a new thought.*

I was dreading it, but I had to make the call. I knew Marla Kelly wouldn't be happy when I said, "Listen, Marla, I've got bad news. I broke my foot today, so I won't be able to transport Sturgess to Kansas City next Wednesday."

She took an audible breath. "You what? Could you please repeat that? I must've misunderstood."

"I said you'd have to find someone else to transport Sturgess. Sorry."

I couldn't believe it when she said in a nasty tone of voice, "You do this stuff on purpose, don't you?"

"Excuse me?" I asked, frowning.

"I think you hurt yourself when you want to get out of doing something distasteful."

"Oh man. Get real. I'm hanging up now, Marla." I did. *The nerve of some people.*

Drew called a couple of hours later, and I told him about my new cast. He muttered, "I knew I shouldn't have left you alone."

"You don't have to keep repeating that, you know."

"I just can't understand how you can get into so much trouble when I'm not around."

I didn't know what to say. I was getting a complex. I felt like people were picking on me.

Drew said he'd be home in three days and asked if I could manage till then.

"Three days? I thought it would only be one or two."

"Well, that was my hope, but as usual, the best laid plans…"

"Well, I'll miss you."

"The question is, will you be okay by yourself now that you're handicapped?"

"I can only say I'll do my best."

"Please try to stay out of trouble, love," he said, before hanging up. The conversation hadn't done a thing to help my complex.

I tried to get interested in my mystery, but found that pain was distracting me, so I swallowed more Ibuprofen.

The real problem, when I finally zeroed in on it, was that I needed to talk to Zoe, and was not up to the task yet.

I called Mom for moral support. "I need to tell Zoe I'll be on crutches and in a cast for the wedding. Do you think she'll have a problem with that?"

Mom sighed. "What doesn't she have a problem with these days? Zoe can be a real pill sometimes."

I'd never heard Mom talk this way about her before, and I said, "Mom, you're making me really nervous. Why don't you call and tell her for me?"

"No, it needs to come from you. Just say it. What can she do about it?"

I frowned. "Well, she can yell and scream like she always does."

She laughed. "You live through that, though, right?"

"Just barely."

Then I asked, "What's going on between you and Zoe anyway? I can tell something's up."

After a long beat, she admitted, "She bought my mother-of the bride dress, and you should see it."

"Why? What's wrong with it?"

"You can't imagine. It's cut down the front practically to the navel, in black satin. Can you imagine me, at eighty-one years old, in a dress like that for my daughter's wedding?"

"What on God's green earth could she be thinking?"

"Not much, I'm afraid. I've always wondered how someone so bright could be so dense about certain things." Then she added, "Forgive me, dear, I shouldn't talk about my own daughter like that, but she just makes me so mad sometimes."

I laughed. "Welcome to the club. At least I'm not the only one who has a problem with her."

Mom huffed, "Makkie, it's not funny. What am I going to do?"

"Exactly what you should have done in the first place. Buy your own dress, and wear it to the wedding."

"Have you seen yours yet?"

"Oh, rats. Don't tell me. What am I wearing?"

"You'll have to see it to believe it, that's for sure."

Now I was really upset.

Mom said, "Oh, I almost forgot. I'm sending Snooky over with a cordless phone. Maybe it will make your life a little easier."

"Oh, yeah, a safer phone. Thanks."

After Mom hung up, I phoned Zoe. Jumping in before I chickened out completely, I said, "Hey, Zoe, I just wanted to check in with you and see how the wedding plans are coming."

"Things are moving right along, I'm happy to say."

"Well, I have something to tell you that you're probably not going to like."

"Oh? And just what is that?"

"First let me say I didn't do it on purpose, so don't get mad."

She sounded exasperated when she asked loudly, "Exactly what did you do?"

I sighed and plunged in. "I broke my foot. My ankle, actually. It's in a cast, and I have to be on crutches for the next six weeks."

"You what?"

"I'm sorry, Zoe, I know it's not the ideal wedding scenario, a bridesmaid sauntering down the aisle on crutches."

"I'll be right over. I was going to bring your dress by anyway," she shouted, and then she was gone.

I usually have no trouble with anxiety, except when Zoe is around, when it goes sky high. So of course, I was thrilled with the idea that she would be on my doorstep within fifteen minutes.

It only took ten. I noticed she was unaccompanied when she stalked in with a dry cleaner's bag draped over her arm, chin in the air. She glared at me and seemed shocked to see my cast propped on a pillow.

"I thought you were joking." Her voice was louder when she added, "I thought this was a joke. You really did go and break your foot just in time to hobble down the aisle at my wedding?"

I could feel a headache coming on. *Lord, I need chocolate.*

As she tossed the bagged, floor-length dress into my lap, I took my first good look at it. It was brilliant red satin, off the shoulder, also cut very low in the front, with a slit up the side about two feet long. It was gross.

I sighed and bit my lip. She slumped into a chair across from me.

"You know," she said, her eyes flashing fury, "I think you do this stuff on purpose."

"That's ridiculous," I said. I didn't mention the fact that she was the second person to bring it up that day.

Her face puckered in a frown of disdain. "Look, I bought you this beautiful dress, paid big bucks for it, or rather Bryce's Mom did, and now this! How are you going to look on crutches?"

I said miserably, "Listen, I'm sorry. But there they are. Propped against the end table." I gestured at them, looking at her out of the corner of my eye.

She scowled. "Don't they have anything more fashionable than those?"

I laughed out of nervousness and tried to cover it by saying, "Well, I hadn't actually checked into it yet."

She studied my cast, before looking up with a wide frown. "Well, I can't have you in my wedding wearing a dress with a slit up the side. Your cast will show. And those awful wooden crutches are definitely out."

I encouraged her, saying, "And that means…?"

"I'll just have to find someone else to stand up with me and wear this gorgeous dress."

Yes! Zoe stood suddenly, picked up the dress and stalked to the door, where she turned in fury to meet my gaze.

"You know, you've just ruined my wedding, and I'll never forgive you for it as long as I live." Oy. This wasn't going well. Without another word, she turned and slammed the door on her way out.

I sighed and shook my head. There are no words to describe her. None whatsoever. She makes me so nuts.

I was still shaken when I called Mom and said with false gaiety, "Mom, I've been severely chastised and *thrown out of the wedding.*"

She gasped. "She threw you out of the wedding?"

"She brought the dress over and threw it at me, saying I couldn't be in a cast and on crutches in her wedding, especially in a dress with a slit up the side."

I could feel myself begin to relax. Laughing, I added, "Actually—I feel like celebrating."

She repeated, "She really threw you out of the wedding?"

"She sure did. She said she'd never forgive me as long as she lives, for ruining her special day."

"Oh-oh, that doesn't sound good." After a long pause, she added, "I wonder how I can get thrown out of the wedding." We both broke down in giggles.

"Mom, you were right about that dress. It looks like a hooker's outfit. There's no way I could've worn that, no way, Jose'."

She sighed. "It's great that you don't have to wear yours, but now you need to help me figure a way out of wearing mine."

We talked a little longer, and just before we hung up, we agreed Zoe needed to find herself a whole new family, preferably one that was a little more chic.

Snooky knocked on the door a few minutes later and came in, package in hand.

"I think you need this," he said smiling, as he tugged out a cordless phone and plugged it in. I gave him a hug, and he said seriously, "I never anticipated how exciting life could be with you Yeats girls. Never a dull moment, that's for sure." His eyes twinkled as he waved before exiting stage right.

I went to bed at ten, and for once, skipped the book. My ankle was still smarting every time the pain med wore off, so my sleep was restless and disturbed. But better that, I thought, than dreaming.

THIRTEEN

The dogs woke me the next morning, wanting out, and I opened the door to see an ominous-looking front coming from the north, with dark clouds that looked ready to dump something at any second.

The dogs didn't stay out but a minute, giving me only enough time to try to start a fire. The trouble is, on crutches, you can't carry anything, your arms being otherwise occupied. My only option was to shove the logs into the fireplace with my good foot, perched somewhat precariously on my new crutches. *No one ever said I had good sense.*

I had a toasty fire going in no time and sat down, planning my next move.

I had taken to carrying the phone in a bag suspended from my neck, since getting up for it took forever.

It rang just as I let the dogs in, so I fished it out of the bag.

Suse Reilly said, "Hey, Makkie, haven't seen you in a coon's age. What's been happening in your neck of the woods? Thought I'd see if you wanted to meet me for lunch."

I told her about my unfortunate accident, and she volunteered to bring lunch to me. I agreed. One more meal I wouldn't have to worry about.

"What would you rather have—Chinese, or Verlene's taco salad?"

"Surprise me, will you?"

She arrived within the hour, her pregnant belly protruding visibly. She made a gorgeous pregnant lady, her wavy hair shining and her fair complexion radiant.

She handed me my carton of sweet and sour chicken. "Fork or chopsticks?" she asked, laughing like a hyena. I personally didn't see the joke until she stuck the chopsticks under her arms in an imitation of crutches. I rolled my eyes.

When she'd finally settled into her chair, I asked, "So how's everything with you and the baby?"

"Great. We had an ultrasound. It's a girl, and her name is going to be Rachel Dawn. What do you think?"

"I love it, but I can't believe you guys are really doing this."

"Like we have a choice?" she asked, smiling wryly. "My doctor says I'm about the oldest natural mother he's cared for in all his years of OB."

"Was that supposed to be a compliment?"

"No clue. But he says we're doing remarkably well." After a beat, she continued, "You should see Elvee. It's like he's got this new lease on life. He's even *acting* younger. Been out playing Frisbee with the neighbor kids when the weather is nice. They even come to the door now and ask, "Can Elvee come out and play?" She shook her head. "I can't remember the last time he jumped so high."

We burst out laughing at the thought.

"He's already gotten the crib out and set up, with the mobile hung over the bed. He painted the room and even put up a cool wallpaper border. Hey, did I tell you he actually gave up his den for a nursery?"

"Wow. That's really sweet of him."

She shook her head. "Well, he either had to give up his den or his home office, so it's not really quite as sweet as all that."

"So what does the room look like?"

She smiled. "He painted the room kind of a pale purplish gray to match that same Peter Rabbit themed border he found at the paint store in Primrose. The border matches the crib set I told you about and it looks fabulous. Very high-end." After a beat, she added, "Elvee told me I didn't have to help since I'm already doing my part." A sudden laugh bubbled up inside me.

She continued, "The only trouble is, he's not as young as he used to be, and hanging that wallpaper, standing on a ladder just about did him in. He came out of that room looking like he'd been rode hard and put up wet."

I hadn't laughed like this in a long time. It felt good.

I asked, "Have you seen Neely lately? I really need to call her. I don't want her to feel left out."

"Well, if you're worried about her doing another chat room thing, I think she's terrified of the idea."

"Good, that's what I was hoping for. I hope they put that guy away for good."

After a brief pause while we nibbled our food, she asked, "So how are Zoe's wedding plans coming?"

I swallowed a bite of chicken. "Well, I'm probably not the person to ask."

"I thought you were her matron of honor."

I could hardly keep from laughing. "Not anymore."

She frowned and set down her fork. "What do you mean? What on God's green earth happened?"

"When I finally got up the courage to call and tell her I'd broken my ankle, she rushed over to show me the dress." I sighed. "Suse, you wouldn't believe the dress."

"Tell me," she urged, using hand motions to press the point home.

"The thing is full length, fire engine red satin, off the shoulders, with the neckline cut down to here and a twenty-four-inch slit up the side."

"You're kidding, aren't you?"

"Girl Scout's honor," I said, putting up my hand.

She laughed and shook her head. "You were never a Girl Scout."

I shrugged.

"Then what happened?"

"Well, she looked at my cast and said, 'I thought you were kidding about the cast.' Then she said she couldn't have me in her wedding in a cast, wearing a dress slit up to the hip, and I said, '*So that means'*," and she said, 'That means I'll have to get somebody else to wear the dress.'"

Suse looked wide-eyed with shock. "You mean she actually threw you out of the wedding?"

"She sure did. And not only that, she said I had ruined her wedding day, and she would never forgive me as long as she lives."

"Bummer," said Suze, adding, "I'd sure hate to be in your shoes, messing up her plans. She can be one vindictive woman."

"Tell me about it," I agreed.

Suse left an hour later, after cleaning up the lunch mess, picking up the house a bit, and letting the dogs out for me.

I called Freezia Harcourt, our quilting group coordinator, to let her know that I was incapacitated and wouldn't be at quilting unless the weather was dry and fair, which would be surprising this time of year.

She said, "Makkie, I was going to call you anyway. I want to pick your brain about something."

"Really?" *Oh-oh.*

"We quilters decided we should do something in January, like an all-church rummage sale and ham and bean dinner or something, to help break up the winter. What do you think of that idea?"

I was thinking, *Are you crazy*, but of course, I couldn't say that. Instead I mused slowly, "Well, it's certainly something to think about."

"Good," she said confidently, "I knew you'd be crazy about the idea."

I shook my head. *How do I get myself into these messes?*

I had just hung up with Freezia when I heard someone at the door. Emily Keating stood, waiting to be admitted.

"Oh, Em, it's been so long. How have you been doing?"

I gestured to a chair, and she sat down.

"I heard you've had a long streak of misfortunes, and now I can see it for myself. What's the deal with the foot?"

"Oh, I got tangled in the phone cord and broke my ankle."

"Looks bad. Does it hurt?"

"Are you crazy? Of course it hurts!" After a brief pause, while I flushed in embarrassment, I added, smiling, "Sorry. So what's going on with you?"

"Well, I wanted you to know about the latest project Freezia has cooked up. She hasn't told you about it yet, has she?"

"Actually, I just got off the phone with her."

"So she told you?"

"Told me what? About the all-church rummage sale and ham and bean dinner?"

"It's not only that, but she thinks we should redecorate the inside of the entire church this winter. By that I mean wallpaper every wall."

I wrinkled my nose. "What? Why would we do that?"

Wide-eyed, Em continued, "Personally, I think she has entirely too much time on her hands. And can you imagine how the church would turn out if she were given free reign to redecorate?"

"Ooh, I hate to say it, Em, but you've hit the nail on the head exactly. The church might resemble her house, which is fine for her, but maybe just a little gaudy for the Lord."

She shook her head. "Have you been to her house lately?"

"No, why?"

"Well, her brother-in-law just bought into a paint and wallpaper franchise, and he lets her have everything that doesn't sell for pennies on the dollar. She's gone crazy with it." After a beat, she explained, "Her dining room is now sporting black wallpaper with massive purple and white flowers on it.

"And if I remember right, her bathroom is done in a 1970's era gold and red-flocked paper, which is bad enough, but the bedroom is worst of all. She found some plaid wallpaper that sort of tilts on its axis, in a pattern where the lines aren't exactly plumb—you know the kind I mean. It affects me like a sideshow mirror. Totally wipes out my equilibrium."

I could picture it. My mouth must've been open, because she gestured and said, "You can close your mouth now." I did.

I asked, "Goodness, Em, what are we going to do?"

She sighed. "That's why I came over. I thought we could brainstorm. I thought that maybe, with a little encouragement, you could come up with one of your scathingly brilliant ideas."

I chewed my lip in deep concentration for a few seconds before I said, "Hmm...Well, maybe the pastor and the board could gently decline."

She gave an audible sigh. "Listen, I've already consulted them, and they won't touch this with a ten foot pole."

"Really?"

She went on, "I never thought I'd see the day the pastor and the board would duck issues like this, but they dumped it right back in my lap, as pretty as you please."

"Hey, Em, if we can't stop her, what if we could change her course? You know—sort of channel her good intentions in another direction?"

"Explain..."

"Well, I can think of at least four or five elderly widows around town who would absolutely love to pick out a wallpaper, and let Freezia and her merry band paper their little hearts out. It would be a ministry, and at the same time, get us off the hook, wouldn't it?"

"Oh, Makkie, you never fail to come up with something brilliant. Where do you get this stuff?"

I shrugged. "Beats me."

Emily left, gushing with enthusiasm for the new plan, saying she was going to share the idea with Freezia as soon as possible and get back to me.

When she left, the house seemed entirely too quiet, with the fire dying down, and the animals curled up sleeping. I thought about working on my book, but Arlo had ordered me to keep my foot elevated for a couple of days, and I couldn't, for the life of me, figure out how to sit at the computer with my foot elevated.

I turned on the television, nearly always my last resort these days, and found that the movie *An Affair to Remember* was on. That sounded okay, but flipping channels, I came across a more recent remake of the same movie—*Sleepless in Seattle*, one of my all time favorites, and sat through two hours of that.

By the time the credits rolled, I was sick of being parked on the couch, looking at approximately the same view of the room for entirely too long. *Listen, Lord, if I have to be an invalid at any time in my life, please let me be in a coma, so I won't care one way or the other.*

I wasn't sure that was exactly the way I should've worded that, but it was exactly how I felt.

When you can't get around, even simple things like going to the bathroom can be daunting. I was acquiring a whole new set of empathies in spite of myself.

Not long afterward, I got excited, when I heard the Bronco pull up a day early.

Drew flew in the door, covered with snow, and I frowned in confusion. "I didn't know it was snowing out."

"Well, now you know." Frowning at my cast, he said, "You really are laid up, aren't you, love?"

He came over, squeezed onto the sofa beside me, resting my leg over his lap. He patted my cheek with his icy fingers, before realizing it and stuffing both hands under his arms to warm them. "Listen, honey, I'm sorry I couldn't have been here when this happened."

Tears filled my eyes. "Why? So you could've laughed all the way to the emergency room?"

He gave me a look of chagrin. "Oh, honey, no. Not at all. I know it has to be a struggle, getting around. Accomplishing the smallest things must be terribly frustrating. I just wish I'd been here."

"Me, too," I said, swallowing tears.

He smiled and changed the subject. "I sure missed you. But listen, tell me all the latest news. I feel like I've been totally out of the loop."

I hated to admit it. "Well, first, I'm no longer a bridesmaid in Zoe's wedding."

His eyes widened in disbelief. "No kidding? What on God's green earth happened?"

I laughed. "You sound like a real homeboy now."

"Give," he said, taking my chin in his hand.

"Well, I called to tell her I'd broken my ankle. I even apologized, but she flew over here to show me the dress." I made a face. "Drew, you wouldn't have believed the dress."

"Tell me."

I gave him the rundown.

"You're kidding, right?" When I shook my head, he said, "That seems a little over the top, even for Zoe."

"That's not all, either. Zoe bought Mom's mother of the bride dress, and it's black satin, cut down to never-never land and off the shoulders. Can you picture Mom in something like that?"

"What, no slit?" We burst out laughing at the picture that conjured up. "You know, I really think your sister is one sandwich short of a picnic, at least in certain areas."

I couldn't argue with that.

Drew said, "Listen, I brought you something. Close your eyes. Let me up for a minute, and I'll be right back."

A minute later, he came back and resumed his seat. "Okay, you can open."

He handed me a square box, wrapped in gold foil paper and tied with a shiny red satin ribbon. I took off the lid, and saw a musical Christmas snow globe. He wound the key, and it began playing *While Shepherds Watched their Flocks by Night*, as the shepherd and the little lambs inside moved around in circles in the meadow, with snow falling all around them.

I blinked back tears, as he smiled. "I know how much you love Christmas, and I thought you'd enjoy it."

"Oh, Drew, it's beautiful. Thank you."

I gave him a long, slow kiss, and since he hadn't shaved for a while, my face was sore and scratched afterwards. He hurried to apologize, then went to shave, and put on my favorite cologne. I felt bad that I couldn't doll up for him, but he didn't seem to notice. The rest of the evening passed in a lovely blur, except that my dumb cast kept getting in the way.

FOURTEEN

Drew had gotten it in writing that he could have two days off with a guarantee of no interruptions. Since I was pretty much confined to the couch, he went to Primrose and brought home a video of *The Enchanted Cottage*, as well as a stack of others.

Over a lunch of his special Southern fried chicken and potato salad, we watched *The Enchanted Cottage* together, and he enjoyed it as much as I did, once more agreeing that there is nothing wrong with seeing each other through a lover's eyes.

While he was outside shoveling a while later, with snow still falling, I got a call from Emily, who said Freezia was in seventh heaven, listing ten ways from Sunday, those she wanted to bless with her new ministry.

When I got off the phone, Drew looked at me with interest. "So what was that all about?"

I filled him in on Freezia's idea for redecorating the church and our plan to head her off. He laughed until tears slid down his cheeks. Then I mentioned the January all-church rummage sale and ham and bean dinner, and he grunted, saying, "I hate ham and beans. Don't those women have enough to keep them busy? And knowing you, they'll have you roped into chairing the thing before you know what hit you."

A short time later, Drew took the dogs out for a romp, since they were getting squirrelly and restless from being cooped up for so long. They were gone a long time, and when they got back, the dogs shook snow all over the room.

"Honey," Drew said, taking off his coat. "We were over in the field where you found that man, and Duke dug this up."

I looked to see what was in his hand. It was a DVD in a plastic cover. Surprisingly, it looked none the worse for wear.

Drew looked at me and then at my foot. "I don't suppose it would be a good idea to have that foot down yet, so we'll look at it in the morning, okay? That way we can do it together."

"Oh, did I mention that the guy whose name was on the ten-dollar bill called back while you were gone?"

"He did? What did he want?" he asked, furrows of worry etched between his brows.

"He had a few more questions. He wanted to know is if the injured man had said anything or given me anything."

Drew looked me seriously. "And you said no, right?"

"Of course. What else could I say? It was the truth as far as I knew at the time."

"I would say the DVD changes everything now, wouldn't you?" he said quietly. I didn't answer.

He looked pensive before asking, "Did you give him our address or any way to contact you?"

"Nothing but a phone number. Why do you ask?"

"I'm leery of this whole scenario, though I can't say exactly why." After a brief pause, he said, "I don't want you calling strangers or giving out any more personal information. Do you hear me?"

I turned away when hot tears burned my eyes at his harsh words. He frowned in dismay when he saw them, and put his arms around me. "I'm sorry. Really. I'm just worried about your safety. I didn't mean for it to come out like that."

For supper, Drew fried up some of the frozen catfish from the freezer. He dipped it in egg and milk, coated it with a blend of cornmeal combined with commercial breading, and I couldn't remember when I'd tasted anything so good. After tidying the kitchen, he built a fire, and then went out at twilight, to clean the snow and ice off the cars and patio, coming in all rosy-cheeked and happy. I felt myself flush with joy just watching him.

In the morning, the sun was out, gloriously reflecting on the snow and beginning to melt everything. He made me French toast and cappuccino, and we lazed around, until he remembered the DVD. I gingerly made my way to the computer, where he put an extra chair next to his and propped my foot on a stool.

He inserted the DVD, and we both watched in wonder as it opened with a commercially produced promotional pitch. The scene was the drug company, Smith, Darden and March, its exquisitely sculpted grounds and a state of the art glass and steel building in the background. Next came a tour, showing the latest in technical advances, and a carefully worded plaudit, portraying the company as a sappy, philanthropic father figure. As if money had nothing to do with it.

The picture was cut, rather inexpertly, and a wide-eyed, jumpy-looking man appeared on the screen, saying his name was Manley Andreason. He had bushy brown hair and intense, deep-set brown eyes clad in gold wire rimmed glasses. Dressed casually in tan chinos and a golf shirt bathed in sweat that also glistened on his brow, he said that he had proof the company was involved in the development of biological weapons of war.

My eyes opened wide in shock, as I laid my hand on Drew's arm. "Honey, that's the guy I found in the field. Is he talking about germ warfare?"

"He is. Listen."

We turned our attention to his voice, as he explained in a rapid discourse, how the company had been producing massive quantities of hemorrhagic smallpox virus, to which the world's population, specifically those under forty years of age, was terribly susceptible.

From what he said, the country paying for its production was spending billions, and the company would go to any lengths, including murder, to prevent being exposed. He said his life was in danger, and he needed whoever found the DVD to make sure it got to the proper agencies for investigation. The proof was in a locked safety deposit box at the First National Savings and Trust in St. Louis. The key was in the hands of an attorney, also in St. Louis, who would be willing to cooperate in the investigation. Drew was taking notes by now, his attention riveted to the screen.

The man said he needed our help to get the disc to the Centers for Disease Control (CDC) and the FBI, since he didn't believe he would live long enough to insure its safe arrival.

The tape ended abruptly, and I asked, "So somebody really did want him dead, didn't they?"

"Sure looks like it," he agreed quietly, patting my cheek, looking concerned.

I couldn't believe it had fallen into the hands of an FBI agent. I mentioned it to Drew, who said this was the best possible outcome—and that he would take the ball and run with it.

"Drew, it's possible that anyone involved is also vulnerable, so please, be careful, okay?"

"And that goes double for you, love."

He was on the phone a minute later, talking to the St. Louis attorney and shortly someone from the D.C. office, who cleared him to fly out the next morning. He booked a flight for ten, saying he had to get to St. Louis and collect the evidence before flying to D.C.

I phoned Mom, to fill her in on the latest and to let her know Drew was leaving town again, giving up his only days off. I was trying to understand, but still hated to see him go.

When I awoke the next morning, he was gone, and a note on his pillow said, *Pray for me, I'll be in touch. Love you.*

I did. I prayed, *Lord, I don't know if I can keep letting him go, running off to his job, knowing he's involved in such a dangerous occupation. Please keep him safe, and then strengthen me to deal with whatever comes.*

I made myself get up and let the dogs out, before hobbling to the kitchen to start a pot of coffee. The crutches were making my underarms and shoulders very unhappy.

As I opened the blinds on the living room window, I noticed a strange car parked down the road at the place where I had found Manley Andreason. I closed the blinds and watched at the edge of the window to see what would happen. A few minutes later, the car drove away, in the opposite direction, so I never did get a look at its occupants.

If this had happened a few months earlier, I might have made an effort to investigate, but now that I was handicapped, I couldn't help feeling nervous. Why did this always seem to happen when I was alone and vulnerable? Stuck in the boonies on crutches, I was a sitting duck if someone wanted to isolate me here.

I poured myself a cup of coffee and made a piece of toast, then set my crutches against the wall and sat on a chair to pour dog and cat food into their dishes, praying for wisdom. Should I try to get out or stay? Was I in any real danger from my contact with Andreason or not? I couldn't decide.

I asked the Lord for a scripture and He gave me Isaiah forty-one, verses thirteen and fourteen: *For I am the Lord your God, who upholds your right hand, who says to you, 'Do not fear, I will help you.' I will help you," declares the Lord, and your Redeemer is the Holy One of Israel.*

As soon as I knew they'd be up, I phoned Mom and told her about the strange car. She said that they would be out first thing to spend the day with me.

They arrived just as I was struggling to make the bed. They each took a side and the bed was made in no time. She began making what she called a substantial breakfast, then eagerly tidied the house, chattering the whole time. Probably to keep my mind occupied.

With a cup of coffee in hand, Mom sat down beside me. "I almost forgot to tell you. I found a dress for the wedding. It's pale lavender, with a jacket, very conservative and flattering. When I told Zoe about it, she said she wished I wasn't her mother. Can you imagine?"

"Oh, Mom, that had to hurt."

She continued, "At this point, I'm not too surprised by anything she says. But to be honest, I'm not sure if she even wants me at the wedding. I'm dying to see what Bryce's parents look like. I know they're probably younger than I, but I can't imagine anyone over seventy wearing anything as outrageous as that black dress, can you?"

"When will you be meeting them? Are they having a dinner or something to introduce you?"

"Not that I know of. You know, dear, I think Zoe is ashamed of me."

"I can't imagine anyone being ashamed of you." I reached over and put my arm around her, watching sympathetically as tears slid down her cheeks.

"Oh, Mom, I'm so sorry about all this."

Snooky gave her a tender look and was shaking his head.

I hugged her. "We're going to make it, Mom. We really are."

She answered the phone on its second ring a minute later. Freezia had tracked her to my place, and I could tell from the conversation that she was trying to recruit Mom for her new wallpapering ministry.

Mom listened for a long time, then said in her most long-suffering voice, "Freezia, dear, I'm going to have to beg off. I have my plate rather full with my new husband, my new job as mayor and my involvement in Fair Oaks. I'm sure you'll find plenty of support from the church ladies and the quilting group. Good luck, dear."

Mom was laughing after she set down the phone. "She's so funny, thinking I'd want to help hang that disgraceful wallpaper she's so crazy about." After a beat, she added, "Do you suppose taste is inherited?"

Snooky had been getting up, at intervals, to look out the corner of the window, and had always come back and sat down quietly. This time, he didn't come back, but said, "Makkie, do you own a pair of field glasses?"

I looked at him, puzzled, and he said, "The car is back. It's a gray blue sedan. The same one?"

I nodded and pointed to the end table, where he took out the binoculars, and returned to the window. He watched for quite a while before speaking. Then he looked at me. "Do you think you could take a look?"

I grabbed my crutches, pushed them under my sore armpits, and headed toward the window.

"Here. See what you think," he said, gesturing down the road. I looked and saw a burly man in a barberry coat and muffler. He had parked the car on the far side of the scene, so I could see him crouching, putting something into a bag with gloved hands. He stood up, and it looked like he had tried to get all the dried blood off the ground, because quite a lot of it had filled the gallon-sized Ziploc, along with some dirt. That was odd. Why would anyone try to remove the blood?

It suddenly hit me—it was an attempt to erase any evidence of the incident.

I said, "That's the same car I saw earlier."

I was getting tired, and Snooky picked up on it, took the binoculars from me, and said, "Go ahead and rest, sweetheart. I'll watch for a while."

Mom looked at him with a question in her eyes. "Snooky, is there someone we should notify about this?"

I frowned. "Mom, remember what a fuss Duffy made when I just wanted to give him the wallet?"

"You're right, dear, but I think he still needs to know."

Snooky set down the binoculars and was about to pick up the phone when Mom said, "Oh look, the car's leaving," as she peeked through the shade.

Snooky shook his head. "Why would anyone want the crime scene obliterated?" Then he gave an ironic smile. "I guess I answered my own question, didn't I?"

Mom queried, "But why would anyone go to all that trouble?"

Snooky stroked his chin, looking thoughtful. "To cover up the fact that it ever happened."

Mom nodded. "We know there's a company who has a lot to lose over this, especially if they know he made a DVD, exposing their activity. What I want to know is, will they be looking at Makkie, thinking she has the DVD?"

I sat there, getting more nervous as she spoke. She looked apologetic as she finally said, "I'm not trying to upset you, dear, but Snooky and I are worried about your safety while Drew is away. We think you should come and stay with us."

She paused to wait for my answer. I shrugged. "Pack me a suitcase. I'll leave Drew a note."

"No, don't do that," Snooky exclaimed. "We'll telephone. Don't leave any indication of where you've gone."

"Snooky, you're scaring me," I cried.

"I'm not trying to scare you, my dear. I'm just being cautious." After a pause, he looked at Mom. "Dear, why don't you pack her things?"

Mom found my duffel in the closet and filled it with my things. We packed up the animals and hurriedly loaded everything into the car. The sedan in question had not returned by the time we left a half hour later.

I shook my head. When had my life gotten so complicated? Maybe a better question was, why? Was I really looking for trouble like so many people insinuated?

Once I was situated at Mom's, she patted my hand. "I feel so much better when I know you're okay.

Snooky and I like nothing better than looking after our daughter."

It was as if a parade had started by late afternoon. Neely stopped in after school to visit, cheerful and upbeat, rattling on about things I barely heard. Then came Aster and Zenia, the ninety-year old sisters from down the block. They seemed tickled to see Duke again, and it looked as though the feeling was mutual.

Zenia said, "Now, Makkie, as soon as you get that cast off, you come and swim in our pool. It's heated, you know. It could even be quite therapeutic."

Not long afterward, Libby Peters stopped by, holding out her signature peach cobbler. She hugged me. "It's been a month of Sundays, girl, since I've seen you." She was shocked to see my cast, and had to be filled in on the latest.

Mac and Blanche Finchley rang the bell only minutes later. I wondered if Mom sent out invitations to this reception, but when I asked her about it, she shrugged. "You know how the grapevine works around here, dear."

It had clearly been working overtime. Behind the Finchleys came Suse and Em, followed by the entire quilting group. Mom whipped up some snacks and passed them around. Someone pulled out Magic Markers, and the cast signing got underway.

I tried to remember what day it was. *Saturday*. Oh, that explained everything. In Azalea, Saturdays in November can be boring in the extreme, unless someone holds an auction, which is a rare occurrence. My new cast was apparently the latest curiosity. *Lovely.*

In spite of my misgivings about the whole thing, I started to relax, circulating and hugging my friends. I finally realized they were all trying to show support.

Everyone had left by suppertime, and Mom whipped up her famous fried chicken and twice baked potatoes and broke out a pint of home-canned green beans, which she fixed with chopped onion and tomato. *Hmm...I could get used to this.*

I sat with my leg propped on the couch, and for the first time in a month, watched "Who Wants to be a Millionaire?"

Mom and Snooky are avid fans and usually get most of the answers correct. The first contestant was at the $32,000 mark when he got stumped. With audience help, he made it to $64,000 and then zoomed his way to the $500,000 mark. We were all rooting for him, hoping he'd win the million.

The last question, however, was very obscure, and even Mom and Snooky weren't sure, but after some discussion, we finally agreed on one answer. The contestant played it smart and left with his half million, and we cheered and gave high fives when we found our answer had been correct. For their age, these two are pretty sharp.

I was too tired to stay up to watch Robert Stack and "Unsolved Mysteries", though the pull was strong. The two programs had swapped time slots. His had been our favorite show back when Zoe and I moved to Mom's.

During a commercial break, Snooky remembered to call Drew's cell and filled him in on the events of the day. Drew said he'd already reported to the proper authorities and would fly out in the morning. I was elated at the news.

FIFTEEN

I woke at seven, to my favorite Christmas music, playing softly on the stereo. Mom and Snooky were talking quietly in the kitchen, and I could smell the fragrance of Mom's cinnamon coffeecake, as I got hold of my crutches. For some reason, my toes seemed uncomfortably tight in the cast today, and as I looked down, I noticed they looked a dusky purple.

Mom must've heard the racket of crutches, because she came and stood in the doorway. "Is there anything I can do to help, dear?"

"I need to get to the bathroom, then do a sponge bath." After a beat, I said, "Mom, do my toes seem a little discolored to you? The cast feels awfully tight today for some reason."

She knelt down and took my toes in her warm hand. "Oh-oh, your toes are cold, and the nails don't blanch. We need to get to Arlo's ASAP and get the cast cut off before you lose function in that foot."

I frowned at Mom, whose eyes read my face. "I know, dear, one more frustration. But perhaps you could just look at it as an opportunity to feel God's grace, instead of seeing it as another obstacle."

"I'll try." But once again I squelched tears that threatened.

Arlo saw us coming and held the door open. Mom explained, "We think her cast is too tight. Take a look, will you, Arlo?"

He glanced at it and threw a wheelchair under me, lifting the leg piece into the horizontal position. "How long has it been like this?" he demanded, with a look of concern.

"I just got up a little while ago and noticed it for the first time."

Frowning, he asked, "It didn't look like that yesterday, did it?"

I said sarcastically, "No, Arlo. The reason I noticed it in the first place was that the cast felt too tight when I got out of bed this morning."

He hurriedly grabbed the plaster saw and rushed to remove the cast. My leg felt oddly weightless after the plaster clattered to the floor. He examined my foot and pressed on my toenails.

"Usually, this happens within the first twenty-four hours after a cast is applied. It's almost never seen this late in the game, but then you don't generally follow anyone's textbook picture, do you, Makkie?"

I grimaced and said nothing, fuming in embarrassment at his words. *What on earth is my problem?*

Again he pressed my toenails and smiled. "Well, it looks like we caught it in time. Let me apply another cast."

Suddenly I had a scathingly brilliant idea. "Hey, Arlo, what would you say to me hustling into the shower while I'm here, before you apply the new cast? I sure would like to wash my hair and get cleaned up."

He looked thoughtful for a few seconds before he spoke. "Whatever, just make it snappy. That cast needs to be back on ASAP. And don't put any weight on that foot for any reason."

I grimaced. "Don't say it. Don't even…"

Mom wheeled me down the hall to the staff locker room, where we peeled off my clothes, so I could get in the wide tile shower. She helped me with my crutches and looked up as Shirley entered the room carrying a walker. Shirley said, "I think a walker might make things a little easier. You can hold on with one hand and wash with the other. Okay?"

"Thanks, Shirley."

Mom adjusted the water temperature, and I scooted under the spray and tipped my head back, letting its exquisite warmth run over me. "Mmm…it feels like heaven," I said, sighing.

Mom grinned and stripped her clothes off, doing a funny little dance that made me laugh.

She draped her clothes over a chair and stepped toward the shower. "I'm not going to let you have all the fun. Besides—you need help. I don't know of anyone who can wash her hair with one hand and do a good job. Move over, will you?"

I grinned as she slipped in beside me and poured shampoo into her hands. Nothing had ever felt as exquisite as a shower and a shampoo, and I knew I would never take it for granted again.

Shirley poked her head in a few minutes later. "Hey, you two. Arlo thinks you've taken long enough." She couldn't stifle a grin when she shook her head. "Isn't that just like a man?"

"Tell him we're hurrying," I said, as I finished rinsing my hair and reached for a towel.

Mom wrapped a towel around her middle, helped me dry and dress, and set me back in the wheelchair. "Do you think you can get back if I open the door for you? I can't go out like this."

I chuckled. "It would be good, Mom, if you put your clothes on before making an appearance."

"You don't have to tell me," she said, giggling. "I'll be out in a minute."

I wheeled myself down the hall and maneuvered into the casting room. Arlo said, "Feeling better, are we?"

I grinned. "We definitely are."

Mom showed up with Snooky and Drew in tow a minute later. Drew bent down to hug me, then lifted me onto the casting table at Arlo's suggestion.

"I saw the car in the parking lot, and I knew it had to be you. What's going on?"

"The cast was too tight, cutting off circulation to my foot. But Arlo was kind enough to let me shower before applying the new one. The hot water felt like heaven."

Drew's brow furrowed in concern as he turned toward Arlo. "Is her foot going to be all right?"

Arlo nodded. "No lasting ill effects, thankfully. They got here just in time."

He looked at me and added with a mischievous grin, "I knew it was getting way too quiet around here."

Everyone but me thought that was uproariously funny.

Shirley put the hair dryer to the cast before we left. Then she handed it to me, and I dried my hair with it.

When we got home, Mom said to Snooky, “You should see the underside of Makkie’s arms, dear. They’re awfully bruised. Isn’t there some way to pad those crutches?”

Drew picked up a crutch, eyed it and pressed on the hard rubber top. “This thing is about as soft as a leather riding saddle. Surely we can figure out something to soften it up.” He and Snooky took the crutches with them and could be heard digging around in the garage, then the basement, and finally clattering up the stairs, with thick strips of egg crate foam duct-taped over the crutch arm pads. Snooky handed them to me. “They may not look that great, but they’re sure a lot softer. See what you think.”

They watched as I stood, but two inches of padding had raised their height, so they no longer fit under my arms.

“Sit back down, Makkie,” said Snooky. “I’ll adjust one crutch, and Drew can do the other.”

The relief must have shown on my face, when I put my weight on the pads, because they all laughed.

“Thanks, guys.” I said, with a huge sigh of relief.

Mom said, “Well, I can certainly take care of their appearance. Let me scrounge through my sewing room and see what I can find.” Shortly, she had tacked some soft navy velour to each crutch, hiding the unsightly duct tape and foam.

Drew and I stayed for lunch, then he and Mom packed my duffel. He made several trips to the car with the pets and their paraphernalia and then came back for me.

"Ready?" he asked.

I hugged Mom and Snooky, and they promised to keep in touch and to pray.

We still didn't know how to gauge the danger of living at the cottage, but Drew was confident. That is, until he unlocked the door and saw the entire place in disarray. Nothing was damaged, but things hung out of open drawers, and odds and ends covered the floors. They had even unzipped the sofa cushions and searched inside.

I felt shaky and upset, nearly paralyzed, as I surveyed the mess. Someone had violated our space, and I shook my head, uncertain whether I could ever feel safe here again. After glancing around, I said, "Honey, how do you suppose they got in?"

"By the looks of it, they probably used a credit card and opened the front door. Thankfully, they didn't do any real damage."

I frowned and burst into tears. "What do you mean they didn't do any real damage? I don't think I'll ever feel safe here again."

"Now, honey," he said, pulling me into his arms, "I'm here now. You're safe."

"But Drew, you aren't here most of the time. What do I do when you have to fly off, on the spur of the moment, in the dead of night, leaving me alone?"

He helped me to the couch, took my crutches and sat down, taking me in his lap, propping my new cast on an old towel.

"Oh, honey, I didn't think about how frightening that must be for you. You always used to be so strong. You never let this kind of stuff get to you before."

"Well," I said, with tears trickling down my cheeks, "I'm sorry, but I don't feel strong anymore. I don't."

He pressed my head against his shoulder and let me cry, caressing my hair. "You have every right to feel violated," he said, "but don't forget that the Lord is with you when I'm gone."

I knew he was right, but that wasn't a lot of comfort right then.

He said, "I'll do whatever I can to make you feel more secure, honey." After a beat, he added, "I'm hearing you, Makkie. I am."

He finished putting everything to rights a short time later and once again sat down beside me.

"How about watching a videotape with me?"

I nodded. Anything to take my mind off my fear.

We had never returned the videotapes he had rented, and he held one up. "Maybe I'll just offer to buy them. Do they let you do that?"

After starting a fire, he turned on the VCR, and again stuck in *The Enchanted Cottage*. He fished out Ernie's ratty old wire popcorn popper and made some popcorn over the fire, then snuggled with me on the sofa, offering me some from a giant glass bowl.

As though he didn't know better, he regularly tries to feed it to me, but I always decline, not fond of popcorn. As usual, more popcorn fell on the floor than made it to his mouth, but Fred took care of the fallen ones, snatching them out of midair and making me laugh, in spite of myself.

The Enchanted Cottage was somehow comforting, and I fell asleep before it ended.

It was dark outside when he said, “Hey, Sleeping Beauty, I’m going to whip up some linguine and garlic bread. Do we have any lettuce for salad?”

I couldn’t remember one way or the other. He smiled. “Well, maybe I’ll have to go get some.”

He must’ve seen fear in my eyes, because he gave me a gentle smile and squeezed my hand. “Or we could open up some of the home-canned veggies from the garden—yeah—let’s do that.”

I was having trouble imagining how I would stay here while he was away for any length of time, now that someone had broken in.

He tilted his head, studying my face. “Listen, babe, I called Ronny at Ace’s while you were sleeping, and he said he’d be out to install deadbolts on all the doors and windows in the morning. Okay?”

“I appreciate it. Thanks.”

He tried to make small talk while we ate, but I barely heard a word he said as I toyed with my food.

The phone rang, and Drew handed it to me. “It’s for you.”

“Is this Miss Yeats?” the familiar male voice asked.

“It is. What do you want?” I asked anxiously.

Drew picked up on my tone and flew to grab the extension.

Will Holmgren said, “We know you have the DVD. Now where is it?”

"So it was you who searched the house…"

"Yes, but we didn't find the DVD."

I sighed. "I thought you were his friend."

"That is neither here nor there," he said caustically.

Drew jumped in. "Listen mister, the DVD is now in the hands of the FBI and the Centers for Disease Control in Atlanta, so why don't you just surrender to the authorities, because the game is definitely up."

Instantly, the line went dead.

My nerves were shot, and Drew must've seen the strain on my face, because he said, "Listen, honey, there's no reason for them to come after us now, because we no longer have the DVD."

"But they have to know we looked at it."

He put his hand around the back of my neck, massaging it. "You're really stressed, aren't you?"

SIXTEEN

It was barely light when I woke to pounding on the door that threw me into a sudden panic. Drew shrugged into his robe and found Ronny Grimm standing there, a bag full of hardware in his arms, and a tool pouch hanging from his shoulder.

He opened his mouth in surprise. "Gee, did I wake ya?"

I sighed. It would take me an hour to calm my wildly racing heart.

Drew laughed. "No, Ronny, we're always up by 7:10 on a Monday morning. Come on in." Drew closed the French doors to our room, and I heard Ronny say, "Did I hear right? You want deadbolts on every door **and** window?"

"That's exactly what I want. Can you do it?"

"I can do it, but it's gonna cost you a pretty penny."

"Don't worry about that. We're good for it."

From the other side of the door, Ronny sounded flustered and embarrassed.

"Oh, dear—that's not what I meant. I know you're good for it. It's just that no one has ever had me install deadbolts on both doors and windows before."

"Well," said Drew matter-of-factly. "Just think of this as your lucky day, then, why don't you?"

I sat on the edge of the bed and pulled on a thick terry robe, before making my way to the kitchen, where I poured myself a cup of coffee.

"Hi, Ronny." He gave an embarrassed wave, as if he'd never seen anyone in a full-length terrycloth robe before.

The phone rang, and Emily Keating said, "Makkie, I just had to ask how your foot is doing. I heard about Arlo having to cut the cast off yesterday. Boy, you sure have the luck, don't you?"

She went on to say that she had been trying to talk Freezia out of the ham and bean dinner scheduled for January, since nobody in town likes ham and beans, and the turnout is always lousy.

Em continued, "But Freezia was adamant when she said stubbornly, '*Well, I like ham and beans, so we're having ham and beans whether you like it or not!*' How do you like that?"

I frowned. "You're kidding. That doesn't sound a bit like Freezia. I know she's a little eccentric, but she's always been more or less cooperative." After a beat, I added, "Emily, we need to talk to Mamie, see what she thinks. Maybe something's going on with Freezia that needs to be checked out."

She agreed, but said she nominated me to do the follow up thing, since I am the one with the nursing degree.

There was too much noise to hear over the din of Ronny's drill, so I decided to call Mamie after the din was past.

While Drew took the dogs out for a run, I went in, made the bed as best I could, carefully picked up laundry, balancing on my one good foot, and stuffed it in the bag I carried around my neck. I threw a load of whites in the washer and turned it on just before locking myself in the bathroom.

Drew came in just after I had applied makeup for the first time in a week. He smiled. "Wow, you look great. What's the occasion?"

"Nothing, I just thought it might be nice to feel like a human being today."

"Well," he laughed and bent to kiss my forehead, "you definitely have my approval."

He made up a batch of pancakes with warm maple syrup and bacon, which made my stomach growl. Even Ronny turned to sniff the air. Drew offered him a plate, and I could see him toying with the idea.

He finally said, "Listen, thanks, but I had three glazed donuts before coming here, and I know Dad'll have a cow if I don't hustle. I've got three more good-sized jobs to do before four, so I'd better say no. But thanks for the offer."

He left before we finished eating, and Drew went to put in "A Fresh Aire Christmas". He knows exactly how to handle a stressed woman—pancakes and Christmas music.

I tried to phone Mamie Harcourt at Shady Acres, but her roommate informed me she was out playing poker with the card players who came in once a week. *Poker?*

Mamie called me back a while later. "Makkie, I'll bet my roommate told you I was playing poker. Did she?"

"Well, she did mention it."

"I knew it. I just knew it. She's always trying to get me into trouble. I think she's jealous of me, though I can't imagine why. I hope you know I'd never play poker. It's against everything I believe in. I was playing Pitch."

After a pause, she said, "So what's up, girlfriend?"

"Mamie, I want to ask you something."

"Shoot."

"I'm worried about Freezia. She seems to be acting strangely. You haven't noticed any odd behavior lately, have you?"

She hooted. "And how's a body to know that? She's been acting strange since the day she was born. I should know. I'm her mother."

"But you haven't noticed anything unusual lately?"

"Not that I can recall, but I'd sure like to hear what you think."

I related the incident of the ham and bean dinner, and Mamie said softly, "Well, maybe there is something wrong with her. She's always been strange, but I've never known her to be pushy or obnoxious. What do you think we should do about it?"

I said, quietly, "Do you think you could talk her into seeing a doctor?"

"Are you kidding? She has absolutely no use for doctors. In fact, I've heard her say they'll have to carry her there, before she'd darken the door of a doctor's office again."

After thinking about it for a time, I said, "Hey, Mamie, what about this? What if we asked her to accompany you to the doctor, for a neuro exam? Maybe you could refuse some exam, and Arlo could say to her, "Let's show her how it's done,' or something like that. What do you think?"

After a beat, she chuckled. "Well, I do declare, you are the cleverest thing. You must've gotten straight A's in nursing school, my dear."

"I don't know about that, Mamie, but what if I make an appointment with Arlo for you, and fill him in, and you can ask Freezia to take you to see him?"

"Sounds like a plan to me. Let me know when you've nailed down the details, okay?"

We hung up, and I called Arlo, whose first reaction was, "Are you okay, Makkie? What's going on?"

"I'm fine. I need to talk to you about someone else, for a change."

"Well, that's refreshing," he said with a note of sarcasm.

To which I replied, "Put a lid on it, Arlo, and listen."

I filled him in and he said he thought next Tuesday would work out. He'd have his office call Mamie, to confirm the appointment date. He said he'd do a neuro exam on Mamie, making up some story, and then when Mamie refused, he would engage Freezia's help and do it on her. I thought it might just work.

I called Mamie and explained the plan, and when I hung up, Drew was laughing out loud. "I see the queen is ruling her kingdom from afar…"

I gave him my best scowl, but it turned into a silly giggle.

He said, "You know, I don't think this town could run without you."

"That's bit of a stretch…"

A short time later, Drew led me on a tour of our newly lockable apertures. He jiggled the first one and said, "A person would have to break glass to get in here now."

Looking chagrined, he realized he had said the wrong thing.

"Sorry." He sighed, grimacing. "If I help you get dressed, how's about we break outa this joint?"

The ice had pretty nearly melted when I hobbled to the car, where he stowed my crutches. We headed to Verlene's where, as predicted, crowds of friends and acquaintances gathered to comment on my injured leg, sharing lots of hugs and plenty of sympathy, before we had a chance to finally order our meal. I was amazed when people emerged as if from the woodwork to sign my cast, passing around an iridescent purple marker.

It was a half-hour before people left us alone so we could eat our now tepid food. Drew looked at me and I at him, rolling our eyes. That we'd have to eat in Primrose or the city from now on was tacitly understood.

Another round of freezing drizzle hit as we drove home, making me very nervous, since I'd be skating from car to cottage, even if only a distance of thirty feet. Thirty feet on ice looked more like ten miles.

With Drew's hand on my arm, steadying me, we made it to the door just as the fine mist turned into noisy sheets of heavy, sloppy sleet. I was never so thankful to be on terra firma. I had seen photos of people kissing the ground and might have done it myself had I had two good legs.

A glance at my caller ID told me Zoe had left a message on my machine. I decided to dispel the rising strain by immediately facing the music.

"Hey, Zoe, what's up?" It was the least provocative phrase I could come up with on the spur of the moment.

She was not happy. I could feel the tension vibrate over the phone line. Biting my lip, I waited, but not long.

"Was it you who suggested Mom buy her own dress for my wedding? I want to know who to blame, now that she's refusing to wear the one I chose."

I hesitated. How could I put this diplomatically?

"Well, I thought she should wear something she'd feel comfortable in." I thought it was a good answer.

Electricity nearly arced through the phone line as she spoke. "So if she would've felt comfortable in sweats, then that should be allowed too, on principle. Is that correct?"

Oy vay, this wasn't going well at all. I took a deep cleansing breath, trying to relax. "Well, I don't think I'd be comfortable in that dress if I were eighty years old, either."

"Who asked you? And how can you say that—you haven't even seen her dress."

"Well…she described it to me briefly."

"So you two discussed it behind my back?"

I couldn't win, and I knew it, so I said, "Zoe, is there something in particular you called for, or was it just to fuss and yell?"

She screeched, "How dare you?"

I shrugged my shoulders and with a big sigh and ended my conversation with an all too frequently used phrase: "I'm hanging up now, Zoe. Bye."

I put on "Nat King Cole's Greatest Christmas Hits", trying to de-stress. It was already 9:30, and my life on crutches felt like a marathon, wearing me out before I'd accomplished anything. Rats.

I felt safer with Drew at home after dark. I couldn't remember how I managed to feel safe living alone for all those years. I guess I didn't know any better.

He stoked the fire and settled into his chair to read the paper, while I got into my flannel nightgown, suddenly freezing.

I felt my anxiety rise in my sleep, as the dream began. Day Barclay was standing in the open front door and began to chase me, intent to kill. I woke, in a sweat, anxious and trembling.

Drew turned on the lamp, pulled me into his arms and caressed my wet cheeks. "It's okay, babe. Open your eyes. You're safe now."

"Oh, Drew, that dream is so real." It was like my shuddering frame had a mind of its own. I was soaked with perspiration, but the terror of the dream was already fading in the light.

"Honey," he said, as he pushed the hair from the back of my neck, "you're drenched. Even your hair is dripping wet. You need to get into warm, dry pajamas before you freeze."

Within minutes, he had helped me change, put on clean sheets, and replaced my damp pillowcase.

"Thanks, honey. I'm sorry I woke you."

"It's okay, love," he said, as we crawled into bed, and he leaned against the headboard, brushing the hair from his beautiful blue eyes. He scooted me into his arms and held me, gently pushing my head against his chest. He was toasty warm, and his steady heartbeat reassured me.

He patted my back. "Close your eyes, sweetheart. I'm right here." Some time later, I sighed as he settled me back under the covers.

A loud noise startled me awake in the complete darkness some time later.

"Drew, what was that?" My heart pounded in my ears, as I snuggled closer to him.

He struggled to waken and tried to turn on the lights, but to no avail. He pulled on a robe and went to look around, while I pulled back the curtain and looked through the window. A huge sycamore had fallen within centimeters of the cottage, weighted down by several inches of heavy ice and nearly gale force winds, which were still blowing.

When he came back, he said, "A tree pulled down the power lines, which means we have no furnace either. Let me see if I can contact the power company." After a beat, he asked, "Hon, where's the flashlight?"

"In the kitchen drawer, to the left of the sink." I heard him bump into something and exclaim in pain, and I could only wish I had two good legs, so I could've helped him search.

"I found it," he said, and then added, "It's pretty dim. Do we have any spare batteries?"

He had things in good shape within minutes. The phone lines were down as well, probably on the same pole, so our options were limited. The cell towers must have been affected by the ice storm, because we couldn't get even a minimal signal.

I pointed him toward our polar fleece sleeping bag, which he positioned on the couch, just before opening wide the French doors to our room, then stoking the fire. He said, "I'm going to sleep out here so I can keep the fire going. Will you be all right?"

"Sure, coach, I'll be fine. Remember the stovetop is gas, so you should still be able to use that if you need to. And if you want to make coffee, there's an old tin pot under the sink on the left side."

"Well, Annie Oakley lives," he said with a delighted chuckle.

"Listen, I can't take credit for that. It was Ernie's."

I drifted off to sleep, to the sound of the crackling fire. I knew it was a God thing that Drew had thought to bring in plenty of dry firewood the day before. We Missourians are used to ice storms, but we don't plan on them until at least January.

SEVENTEEN

I woke to the sound of Drew stoking the fire. It felt nice and toasty in the house, so I knew he must've been up frequently during the night to keep it going.

When I made my entrance, he was sitting at the kitchen table with his head in his hands.

"Are you okay, honey?" I said, hugging him with one arm.

"Be careful," he said, pulling me into his lap. The dark circles under his eyes were deep, so I suggested, "Why don't you sleep a while, and I'll keep watch and finish reading my mystery?"

"Are you sure you don't mind?"

I stroked his hair. "Go back to sleep, honey. I'll take my turn watching the fire."

I didn't have to ask twice. He was out like a light, and I sat by the fire, with a flashlight in my hand and a kerosene lamp burning next to me. It took both to illuminate the page enough for me to read.

The thick oak logs he added burned for two hours before I had to wake him to add more. By then, we were both hungry, and I felt like cooking, so I made us oatmeal, and French toast. We ate by firelight, and it was amazingly romantic.

Drew was wide-awake by then, and threw his sleeping bag on the floor in front of the fire, where he lay down to watch the flames darting and dancing. "Come on down, why don't you?"

"Okay," I said, smiling. It was toasty there, and he began kissing me hungrily, and caressing my neck, until one thing led to another. He never ceases to amaze me with his endearing expressions of love. Later he pulled a quilt over us, and we slept.

The fire had died to embers when we woke, and he was frantic. Jumping up, he threw more logs on the grate.

I said, "Honey, it's okay," just in time to see a spark land on the quilt only inches from my nightgown, where it started smoking.

"Drew, the quilt is on fire!"

He grabbed his shoe, the closest handy object, and beat out the flame. At least this quilt was a five-dollar garage sale purchase, and not the $880 wedding ring quilt he had given me as a wedding gift. The old quilt was still usable, with only a small hole in it, about the size of a dime.

He sank down and again put his head in his hands, not a gesture I had often seen.

"Are you okay, honey?" I asked, smoothing his hair.

When he looked up, I saw tears in his eyes. He sat up, wearing a distressed frown. "I had such high hopes of protecting you when we married, but I can't seem to protect you from anything."

One of his tears dropped onto the quilt. Scooting closer, I put my arms around him. "What are you talking about? Of course you've protected me. You've been the only thing keeping me going lately. Don't you realize that?"

"Really?" he asked as his eyes widened in surprise.

"Would I kid you about a thing like that? When I'm by myself, and things are hard, the Lord reminds me that I have you in my life, and that thought is enough to keep me going, whether I feel like it or not."

He sighed, his eyes sparkling with unshed tears. "I've missed so many great years waiting for you. I wish I could have them all back."

"I know, but maybe it's better this way. Maybe we'll appreciate each other more."

We slept again and woke later to a knock on the door. Drew opened the door, and Snooky appeared, looking like a furry, fat snowman. The sun was out, but a frigid wind blew in with him. "Your mother was worried when she couldn't get a hold of you, so she sent me to see if you're okay."

I laughed and hugged him. Drew pulled out the tin coffee pot. "Hey, there, Snooky. What say I make coffee? You're definitely the man of the hour."

Snooky had just peeled off his third layer of clothing, when the first drops of sweat began forming on his brow. "Whew, warm in here."

I laughed. "We like to think of it as toasty."

Snooky smiled. "Okay then—plenty toasty." He looked from one to the other of us. "That big sycamore take out the power and phone lines?"

I said, "It did, with a huge crash, barely missing the house. Drew kept the fire going all night."

"Well," said Snooky, "If you have your cell phone handy, I'll phone the utility companies." The cellular signal was, by then, restored, and after calling, Snooky hugged us and took his leave, telling us to call if we needed anything.

Within a half-hour, the electric company crew arrived and began sawing the tree in our yard, and putting things to rights. Drew, doing his guy thing, bundled up and went out to watch, taking the dogs with him, using the excuse of cleaning ice off the patio and cars.

Shortly, I was relieved to see the lights flicker and stay on.

After starting laundry, I made some toast just because I could. I was still in my robe when Drew invited the three-man crew in for hot chocolate, and they took him up on it. Seeing them enter, I tightened my robe around me and flew into the bathroom, gazing at my reflection. The Bride of Frankenstein had nothing on me.

I ran a comb through my hair and made myself presentable. I arrived just in time to see their exit.

"They were getting overheated," Drew explained.

"Were there any lines down in town? I forgot to ask Snooky."

He smiled and shook his head. "Not many. They were called out, planning for lots of downed lines, and—no action. In fact, they said they were actually grateful for a diversion from the boredom of poker playing."

I laughed. "Well, let it never be said that we aren't accommodating."

Drew seemed to have recovered his good humor. "One of the guys thought I might like to read the KC Star newspaper. Said they were through with it. Wasn't that thoughtful? Why don't you lie down on the sleeping bag, and let me read the comics to you, okay?"

I parked my frame on the floor, and he slid down next to me, kissing me on the forehead. He smiled. "You're the peanut gallery, so listen up."

I called Suse Reilly after lunch, just wanting to hear her voice. She said, "Makkie, I'm so glad you called. I need to ask you if it's normal to be spotting at seven and a half months."

"You're spotting?"

"Just started this afternoon. What should I do?"

"Is anyone there with you?"

"No, Elvee won't be home for hours yet. Do I need to worry?"

"No, don't worry, but lie down and elevate your feet, and I'll have Drew call Elvee and 911. We'll have Elvee meet you at the hospital, okay?"

"Oh, Makkie, 911? Is my baby going to die?"

"Now, that's not what I'm saying at all. I just think it's time Arlo took a look at you and checked out the baby, okay?"

"Okay, I've got my feet up."

I covered the phone and said to Drew, "Call 911 for Suse Reilly on your cell phone. Then call Elvee's office and tell him to meet her at the hospital."

I said to Suse, "I'm going to stay on the phone with you until the ambulance gets there, okay? And Drew is using his cell to call Elvee."

I covered the phone again and said to Drew, "Tell them she's spotting at seven and a half months. They'll know what to do."

I said, "Suse, I am going to pray right now, okay? You just hang in there." I prayed, "Lord Jesus, You said where two or three are gathered, You are with them, and we come to You, asking for wisdom and protection, both for Suse and this precious baby. Surround them with Your comforting presence and Your peace. And we give You all the glory, in Jesus name." After a beat, I asked, "Suse, are you having any pain, any contractions?"

"Not really."

I could hear the siren through the phone line, when Suse said, "The ambulance is here, Makkie. Do I get up to let them in?"

"Is the door locked?"

"No, we never lock it."

"Then just stay put, and they'll find you, okay? Love you, Suse."

When she hung up, I broke down. "Oh, Drew. She's spotting. She could lose the baby."

He put his arms around me, and pulled me close, where I rested my head on his chest, looking up at him.

"Now let's not jump to conclusions, okay?"

"But I'm frightened for her."

"I know you are, honey, but don't you think you can trust that the Lord will take over now? You asked Him to, you know."

He got up to toss another log on the fire as I took a deep breath, trying to relax. "I know, you're right," I looked at him, pleading. "but could we go to the hospital?"

"In this ice storm? With you on crutches? That's too much of a risk. Remember, Arlo said crutches and ice don't mix."

"Please honey. Suse is like my sister, and I really need to be there for her."

"Makkie." He sank down next to me and turned my face to look in his eyes. His voice was gentle when he said the words I dreaded hearing.

"Listen to me. I really think you should just keep in touch by phone, at least for today, okay?"

I turned away as my eyes filled. I had no words. I'd been my own boss for so long that I never imagined I would have to take no for an answer to something so important. If he hadn't been here, I would've gotten there by hook or crook. But he had said no, and I didn't know how to respond. So I said nothing, just prayed for the right attitude.

Elvee called about an hour later from the emergency room, where Arlo had examined Suse, pronounced her and the baby okay, but said she needed to be on modified bed rest until the baby came.

My first thought was *this is perfect; I'll go over and help Suse*. But I would need good weather for that to happen. I called Mom, caught her in the middle of exercising, bicycling with her feet in the air. When I told her the news, her response was, "Well, how about this? On nice days, I'll come and get you, and we'll both go over, and on the other days, Snooky and I will go."

"Thanks, Mom. I know they'll appreciate the help." Here she was at eighty, still ready to serve when the need arose. Suse had no family nearby, and her parents were long deceased.

Mom asked, "How are you holding up, dear?"

"The power and phone are back up, but I was sure wishing I could be there at the hospital with Suse."

"I know," she said, "but we'll just have to wait in the wings and pray, won't we?"

The rest of the evening dragged by, with me desperately wishing I was mobile.

After Drew left for work the next morning, I decided there must be a way of cleaning up the house. I resorted to crawling, stowing items in the bag I hung around my neck: newspapers, dirty laundry and socks, cups, a pen, my book, and the ibuprofen bottle, which was wedged between the sofa cushions. I frowned in annoyance. Hadn't I just deep cleaned this place the other day?

It took a second trip to drag the quilts to the bedroom. How humiliating. My back and hips were killing me by the time the living room was finally in order, and I decided that life must be a lot more work for quadrupeds.

Zoe called at nine, saying she really wanted me in the wedding.

Apparently, she wasn't above begging. "Isn't there some way you could go without the cast and crutches for one day?"

I couldn't stifle a laugh. "Zoe, in spite of what you might think, I'm not wearing a cast for the fun of it.

My ankle is broken in two places, so there is no way I can put weight on it for at least six weeks. Can't you understand that?"

"That's ridiculous," she huffed. "You just did this so you wouldn't have to be in my wedding. I really think you could do it if you'd just stop acting like a self-centered, spoiled brat."

After a pause while I counted to ten, I tried to explain that I didn't have a choice in the matter. But for some reason, she refused to understand that I couldn't just rise and walk for her wedding day. She angrily hung up on me, and I wondered if the real reason she was so upset was that she couldn't find anyone else who could fit that wretched dress.

Mom called, saying she and Snooky were going to Suse's just before lunch, and would do whatever she needed. We talked for a few minutes, and I filled her in on Zoe's latest phone call.

Mom gave a sudden surprised giggle. "She said what?"

"She thought I should be able to forego the cast and crutches just for one day, for her wedding...that I could if I would simply stop acting like a spoiled brat."

Mom laughed until she cried, related the story to Snooky who took up the laughter, and Mom said, "I really don't think she was switched at birth, but sometimes I can't think of any other explanation for her wacko behavior."

I spent the rest of the day on the computer, catching up on my writing. During a break in the action, I e-mailed Drew a love note at work, and he sent one back.

I really hate the heat of summer, but I have the same feeling about the gray overcast skies of winter, though for a different reason. It makes me so melancholy, I want to crawl into a hole, and pull it in after me. I had heard there was a light bulb, described as full-spectrum, which could imitate the sun's light and was known to help those of us with seasonal affective disorder, also known as SAD.

Each day, I could feel myself slipping a little deeper into depression, but today after Drew left for work, I had a brainstorm. I surfed the web, for electrical supply houses that stock full-spectrum bulbs, and ordered several with my credit card right over the Internet. Just that tiny proactive motion was enough to improve my mood a little.

The sun still did not materialize by noon, so I turned on every light in the house, trying to mimic the light my brain was starving for, and then I turned on Christmas carols and stirred up some hot chocolate. *Please, Lord, I need sun.* Well, He did say we wouldn't receive if we didn't ask.

Drew called, to ask how I was doing, and I told him about Zoe's phone call. When he finally stopped laughing, he said, "I love hearing her latest escapades… it's fodder for coffee breaks—gives me and the guys a good laugh."

I frowned, not sure how I felt about him laughing with strangers at Zoe's expense. She was odd, but she was still my sister. I hung up feeling upset by the call. *Lord, help my attitude.*

A short time later, Suse called, raving over what wonderful help Mom and Snooky were. She hadn't had any more spotting, which was a good sign, and Arlo said she could try being up a short time each day, in a chair, instead of the couch. It still sounded horrid to me, after being laid up, but she seemed thrilled, so who was I to rain on her parade?

Neely called on her break to report that her kidnapper had been sent to a mental hospital for the criminally insane, and she had gotten rid of her chat room capability. I was as relieved as she was to hear that he was off the streets.

I had just started browning sirloin for swiss steak when I had an odd call.

The woman said, "Is this Makkie Yeats?"

"Yes."

"Well, this is the social worker at St. Kat's Hospital in Kansas City. We need you, as the next of kin for Mr. Manley Andreason, to tell us how you want to proceed with burial arrangements."

"Excuse me?"

"Do you really want me to repeat that whole spiel again?"

"No, I just don't know why you would be calling me."

After a beat, she asked, "You are his next of kin, aren't you?"

"No. I'm no relation at all. I just happened to have found him injured in a field near my home. Until a few days ago, I had no idea who he was."

"Oh. Well, I'm sorry to have troubled you. Someone wrote down your name as his next of kin."

Before hanging up, I got a contact name and number in case I should come up with anything later.

Afterwards, I phoned Drew at work, and asked what, if anything, he had dug up on Andreason. He had accumulated a whole file on him by then, and said he would call the hospital and see what he could do.

When Drew called back a few minutes later, he asked if I was sure it had been St. Kat's hospital who called, because they had never heard of anyone by the name of Manley Andreason, nor was he listed anywhere in their data banks.

Am I losing what little I have left of my mind? Oh, nuts. I hate it when that happens. I had thought the mystery was a dead issue, but here it was, rearing its ugly head again.

Several days later, Mom called, wanting to know if she could take me out to lunch. Since the ice was melting in the morning sunshine, and I was dying for Chinese, I jumped at the chance.

Mom helped me fill my plate at the buffet, which is one more thing you can't manage easily on crutches. Only nine more days until I could get a walking cast. We handicapped folks, I have learned, eagerly anticipate the smallest strides toward progress.

As we were eating, Mom said, "Makkie, I've hesitated to bring it up, but I'm worried about you. Each day, I see you becoming more and more depressed. I know winter always gives you trouble, but I wonder if you might need to see Arlo about getting an antidepressant."

I met her gaze and saw that she was serious.

I sighed. "I wondered why Snooky didn't come with us."

She said, "He's worried about you. We both are. You've had so much on your plate for the last what... eight months now, that it seems to be sapping your spirits. Am I correct about this?"

"You are," I agreed in a shaky whisper.

Mom gave me a compassionate smile. "Oh, my dear, you're such a wonderful caretaker of others, but I think sometimes it empties your bucket more than is good for you. Is this making sense?"

She continued, "Well, I think we should go see Arlo about this. I hope its okay. I took the liberty of making an appointment for you, but you don't have to keep it. It's up to you."

Resigned, I agreed. "I'll go."

In Arlo's office an hour later, he said to me, "I thought I'd noticed you on the verge of tears a lot lately." As soon as he said that, the tears started falling, as if to prove his point.

After a brief physical exam, he handed me a prescription, then squeezed my hand. "Do you have any questions?"

I whispered, "Not really, but this just feels like one more failure."

His eyes narrowed in surprise. "What do you mean —this feels like failure?"

"Taking an antidepressant. Needing one in the first place."

He put his arm around my shoulder and hugged me. "Makkie, you're allowed to be human, you know. You've been through tremendous stress lately, not just once but several times, and had major life changes that are all stressful, even though they're positive—like getting married, for instance. You simply can't label this a failure."

"Well, I do."

"Okay, well, maybe I should refer you to a therapist. What do you think?"

I shook my head. "No. No. I can do this by myself." Mom's frown let me know she disagreed, though she said nothing.

Arlo looked perplexed as he held me at arm's length and looked at me. "Makkie, I need to ask you—why won't you talk to someone about this?" He and I have been close friends since pre-kindergarten, so he gets in my face about things sometimes.

I hesitated a long minute before I sighed. "Please don't force this on me. I promise I'll take your antidepressant. And then we'll go from there, okay?"

"Okay, kid," he capitulated. "I'm not going to force you to do anything you don't want to do, but it kills me to see my usually lighthearted buddy so low."

"Thanks, Arlo. I appreciate it.

"I'll want to see you in two weeks, so we can decide if the med is helping, okay?"

With that, he looked at my cast, and bent down to check the circulation in my toes. "Good return blood flow. Glad to see it."

He hugged me briefly at the door. "Take care, Makkie. And don't forget to come back in three weeks, so we can X-ray that ankle."

Mom dropped me off at home and handed me the mail she'd retrieved from the box. First things first, I decided, as I opened the medication bottle, and let one capsule fall into my palm. What did I have to lose?

I was sleeping when Drew walked in, and I woke as the dogs stirred next to me. He came in and kissed me. "So how's my sweetheart today?"

I smiled. He said, "Hey, I stopped up at St. Kat's after I talked to you, and checked seven ways from Sunday, but they claim they never admitted anyone by the name of Manley Andreason. I even showed them his picture, a company ID thing I had from his file, and there is no sign he was ever seen or admitted there at all." He frowned, shaking his head. "I just don't get it."

Drew looked toward the kitchen and sniffed. "Mmm...something smells great. What's cookin?"

"Swiss steak."

He said, "Just tell me what to do, and I'll get it on the table."

He whipped up a salad and garlic toast, and a few minutes later said, "So did you see the doc today?"

When I gave him a perplexed look, he said, "Jane said she was going to talk to you about it. So what did Arlo say?"

I was fried. "So you and Mom had a little powwow about my mental health, huh?"

He frowned. "Honey, we were worried about you ...you haven't been your normal cheerful self lately. Your Mom brought it up, because she can't stand to see you suffering this way."

"Well, next time please just talk to me about it. I don't like to be discussed behind my back. And just for your information, Mom didn't exactly have to drag me into Arlo's office kicking and screaming, you know."

"I'm sorry. I never thought she would," he said quietly.

We finished the meal in silence, and Drew pulled out a pile of paperwork and began to work, after donning his reading glasses.

I was sure hoping the medication would kick in soon, because even I wasn't too crazy about the person I had become. *Help Lord.*

EIGHTEEN

I did a lot of sleeping for the next several days, only getting up to take my pill, let the dogs out, and do the essentials around the house. Zoe's wedding was only two days away, and I couldn't have cared less.

Mom checked on me by phone and dropped by to stock our refrigerator. She was quiet when she walked in, as though she knew I was upset that she and Drew had conspired against me. We both knew that as soon as the antidepressant kicked in, I would bounce back, and I think we were all ready for that. But in the meantime, it was all I could do to keep my eyes open.

On the tenth day, it was like a minor miracle had occurred. I woke, without feeling hung over, actually glad to see a new day dawn, especially since the sun was shining, and it was dry outside. I had to check the calendar to see what day it was. I had missed Zoe's wedding entirely, but I wasn't regretting it much, though I knew I'd never hear the end of it. Drew had been out of town for several days on assignment.

I realized for the first time that I had completely slept through Thanksgiving, as evidenced by a plate of sliced turkey breast and other holiday side dishes stacked in my refrigerator. Oh, well, I wouldn't have been good company anyway.

Today, however, I felt like I could lick the world. The calendar said I had a ten o'clock appointment to see Arlo, and hopefully, get my walking cast. I drove myself, just for the sheer triumph of it.

After a new set of X-rays, Arlo announced that my fractured bones were looking good, and a walking cast was definitely the order of the day.

He asked me how I felt, and I said I was starting to feel a glimmer of hope. He smiled, patting my hand. "Just hang in there. You won't believe how much better you feel as you go along." Glancing around, he frowned. "Where's Jane? Isn't she chauffeuring you?"

"No, I thought I'd give her the day off." He frowned again, and then suddenly smiled, as if understanding we had a breakthrough here.

After approaching the car on my own two feet, I tossed the crutches in the backseat and headed to Shady Acres, to see my old buddies.

There were hugs all around, and Mamie Harcourt said, "Where have you been, girl? You know you're about the best pipeline we have, and it's absolutely dead around here without you, no pun intended." Everybody laughed, before she added, "We heard about the cast, though, so we've decided to forgive you."

I laughed. "Thanks, Mamie."

Bitsy Keller had a twinkle in her eye when she asked, "So how are the newlyweds?"

"Great, Bitsy. I don't see much of him, sometimes, but I like being a married lady."

Her eyes lit with mischief, Pansy Barclay said, "Say, you haven't heard the latest, have you? Well, you know Sturgess Claymore had that appointment at the wound center in KC? We heard the rumor that you were supposed to take him. Is that right?"

I nodded, and she said, "Well, if you want my opinion, I'd say you broke your ankle just in time. Marla was seeing red, having to spend a whole day up in the city with that grouch. I even heard some rumblings about it as I wheeled past the office that morning. Well, she must've said something to get Sturge really riled on the way up there, because he smacked her upside the head with his newspaper from the backseat, and she's filing charges against him."

"Oh, no. Poor Marla." I couldn't stifle a laugh and covered my mouth. *Assault with a deadly weapon.*

She continued, "Sturge is now looking for another place to live, if anyone will have him." She gave a low chuckle. "Fat chance after pulling a stunt like that."

Shuggie Heinz stuck out her hand and patted me on the shoulder. "Are you okay, honey? You're so quiet."

"I'm fine, Shuggie."

Maybelle Steadman was heading toward us with her walker, smiling like a Cheshire cat. "I was thinking you might just pay us a visit. You always come on cinnamon roll days, don't you?"

I smiled as she stuck her hand in her pocket and pulled up a squished ball of plastic wrap.

"I guess it might look that way. Why, what've you got for me?"

"What do you think, dearie?" She thrust the roll at me. "I wrapped it up real good, so it wouldn't dry out."

I hugged her. "You guys are just the best. Do you know that?"

Dabney Franklin, croaked from the outer edge of the circle. "Cheez, it's the cops." Everyone turned to see the administrator heading in our direction. In a defensive move, the group enveloped me even more snugly.

"Hello, Makkie," said Bonnie Hunt with little more than a sneer. "Don't think I can't see you."

I turned my head away with a grimace that made the seniors laugh. When I looked back, Bonnie was eying them suspiciously.

"Don't you people have somewhere to be?"

Shuggie innocently met her gaze, shaking her head. "No, Ma'am, not me. Besides, we enjoy visiting with Makkie."

Maybelle piped up, looking Bonnie straight in the eye, and asked rather brazenly, "But shouldn't you be getting back to work, dear?"

I thought Bonnie would do well to make herself scarce, but she continued to stand there, getting red in the face, glaring at the lot of us for an uncomfortable length of time. However, we knew this was our shootout at the Okay Corral, so we made our stand, united.

Finally, she turned and stomped away, while a subdued cheer went up from the group.

Shaking my head, I said, "You know, guys, it's not good to bite the hand that feeds you."

Dabney smiled, meeting my gaze. "You know, my granddaddy used to say that a lot back before he died in 1935, and I never did know what on God's green earth he was talkin' about."

"Me either," came the chorus of cherubic innocents behind him.

"Hey, Makkie," said Maybelle, with a cagey grin, "did you know that Dodge Prentice is in the hospital, and he'll be moving here shortly?"

Looking like a schoolgirl in love, Shuggie added, "He sure is. And we can't wait till he gets here." She batted her eyelashes. "He's about the most beautiful man I've ever seen in my life."

Both women nearly swooned with delight at the mention of his name. He was over eighty, but very spry, so I asked, "What's he been in the hospital for? And why is he moving here?"

Shuggie said, "Oh, he fell off a ladder putting up storm windows, and broke a hip a week ago Sunday, so his stay is strictly until he recovers. He needs therapy for a couple of months, and then he'll return home, but we girls won't be letting any grass grow under our feet while he's here, that's the ticket."

I smiled. "I suppose not. So you've got a time limit to catch the big one, huh?"

"Yup," they said simultaneously. With a wide, mischievous grin, Maybelle said, "Nothing like a little friendly competition to liven up a mausoleum like this."

On my way out the door, Mather Gillette caught me. He was a tall, lanky man with thinning white hair and thick glasses.

"Makkie, I just wondered, do you have any idea how a person can get transferred to one of those assisted living units? I really don't like it here. I'm way too young and spry to be here. But for the life of me I just can't get anyone, even my sons, to listen to me. What do you think?"

Mather was a relatively new admission, a lifetime resident of Azalea, who I could tell had slowed down considerably, though I couldn't see any obvious physical reason for institutionalizing him. But what did I know?

"Well, which one did you have in mind?"

"Cedar Creek in Kansas City looks quite good. I've seen their ads on television, and thought I might really like it there. Of course, I would've liked it a lot better if you hadn't gone and gotten yourself married to that guy." There was an unsavory sparkle in his eye when he said it.

Without thinking, I made a face. "What?" I gasped, dumbfounded.

"I've had my eye on you for years, girl, from one vantage point or another. Though I've never let on, I've always thought you were a knockout."

I frowned. He was seventy-five if he was a day.

He laughed. "I can see I've taken you by surprise."

"That's the understatement of the year."

"Well, I guess I didn't play my hand soon enough. Actually I've been out of it for a few years—living in Primrose with my son. I guess I just assumed you'd be available when I was ready to declare myself."

He came closer, getting in my face, so I backed up a step.

"You afraid of me, girl?" he asked quizzically.

"No…I…just need to get going. I have an appointment shortly."

"Well, I suppose there's no use kicking a dead horse, is there?"

"I suppose not," I said, looking to exit stage right.

"Still, if you figure out how I can blow this joint, I'd be mighty glad to hear what you have to say on the subject."

"Okay, Mather. I'll keep that in mind." Like I'd get within fifty feet of the man now.

With that I gave a tiny wave and exited the front door. What was it with men these days? Was everybody crazy? Or was it me?

From there, I headed for the school library, where I found Neely with an arm full of papers.

A beautiful smile lit her dark eyes when she saw me. "Hey there, Makkie. You doing any better? You sure look better. Everyone's been worried about you."

I laughed. "Yeah, I heard I've been the talk of the town for some time now."

She said, "I can take a break. Got time?"

I followed her down the hall to the faculty lounge, where she poured me a cup of their signature strong, bitter coffee. I cringed involuntarily at the first sip.

She turned to doctor her coffee. Without making eye contact, she asked, "So what's been happening in your life these days?"

"Oh, nothing very exciting."

"Come on. That's about the only thing I don't believe about you. Your life is an amazing array of drama and comedy. Never a dull moment, from where I stand."

When she looked up, I gave her my most annoyed frown. "Get a grip, will you?"

"Okay, well, I'll bet if you thought about it, you could tell me something interesting that happened today. Even within the past hour, isn't that right?"

"No," I said succinctly, lying through my teeth. As if I would tell her *anything* now.

"Well, then, you're not being honest. I know, because I always hear later, due to the excellent workings of the grapevine, what's up. Now, you want to try again?"

"No way."

"Okay. So let's talk about something else. You go first."

I could think of nothing, so I shrugged and kept my mouth shut.

"Okay, well…then I'll go first. Um…Hey, those cats of yours have sure livened things up at my place."

"You mean those cats of *yours*," I said, chuckling.

"Right. Well, they're so precious—I can't believe I lived this long without them."

"They do keep things lively, don't they?"

"I had to learn the hard way not to leave food sitting on the counter," she said, shaking her head. "Hairy ate a whole stick of butter, and oh, what a mess."

"He always did like his saturated fats. What did he do, throw up all over your antique brocade sofa?"

"Well, actually he hit the throw on top of the sofa back, so I just tossed it in the wash, but believe me when I say I won't make that mistake again."

"I'll bet."

She had to get back to work, so I said, "I'd better head out. I want to stop and see Suse before I head home. Hey, I think my new cast is dry enough now—want to be my first signature?"

"Sure, but only if you let me use my chartreuse marker. I want my name to stand out."

"Cool," I said, hugging her. Her yellow/green John Hancock was at least twice the size of the one she had signed on my old cast. She was feeling better.

"Tell Suse hey for me." She waved, smiling.

At my knock, Suse yelled for me to come in, and I frowned as I made my way to where she rested on the living room sofa.

"You sure are some kind of trusting soul. What? You just yell come in to any old Tom, Dick or Harry who comes to the door?"

"Pretty much, and well…at this point, after spending endless hours on this miserable couch, I can say I'd welcome a visit from any of the above, just for the novelty of it."

"Well, I'll try to send you some business."

I paused before saying, "Have Mom and Snooky been here today? I didn't see their car."

"No, Elvee has most of the chores caught up, so we told them to take a couple of days off."

"Well, listen—is there anything I can do?"

She smiled. "Your timing is perfect. You can help me get lunch ready. I'm eating for two now, and I'm starved."

"So have you had anymore bleeding or contractions?"

"Nope," she said, patting her round belly, "we're right as rain as far as Arlo can tell. He's working with my OB in the city, keeping tabs on us."

"Glad to hear it. So what's for lunch?"

"I'm in the mood for a French dip. I had Elvee get stuff from the WalMart deli last night. Does that sound okay to you?"

I gave her a wide grin. "Need you ask?"

I fixed lunch and we ate in companionable silence, until finally she said, "You may not realize it, but I've been worried about you." After a beat, she added, "You look like you're feeling better now. Are you?"

"Mom and Drew conspired against me, when all they would've had to do was ask me."

She wiped her lips with a napkin, catching an errant drop of au jus that trickled down her chin. "To do what?"

"To see Arlo about an antidepressant. He started me on it ten days ago, and this is the first time in months I've been glad to see morning come."

"Wow," she said with a sigh. "That must've been hard."

"Let's just say I feel a lot like that frog that was put into a pan and the water heated up slowly. It kind of just crept up on me until I was nearly paralyzed. I won't let it happen again, I'll tell you that."

After lunch, she motioned me to follow her down the hall. "Come on, you've got to see the baby's room. You're gonna love it."

"Oh, Suse, it's wonderful," I said, admiring its grandeur a minute later.

It was indeed, another world, with Peter Rabbit and his friends cheerfully inhabiting the space.

"Elvee did all this? I'm impressed."

"He sure did. For some reason, he's really excited about this baby. As I recall, he wasn't particularly interested when the others were born. What is that, do you think? Male menopause?"

I shrugged. "He probably feels he missed out when the others were born. Maybe he wants to make up for lost opportunities with Rachel. You are still calling her Rachel, right?"

"We've called her that for so long now, it's like we've known her all our lives. I guess that doesn't make a lot of sense, does it?"

"It makes perfect sense to me."

She sighed. "The last few weeks get so long. I remember when the other kids were on the way, I felt like they'd never get here."

I hugged her. "Well, you just let me know what I can do to help, okay? We'll be good for one another. Think of all the cash we'll save on therapy bills if we just talk."

I left then, telling her I'd keep in touch.

I drove to Mom's, and she smiled and hugged me as I walked through the door. "Well, it looks like you're your old self again."

"Mom, I feel so much better, I've been celebrating. Seeing all my old buds. But, hey, you've got to tell me all about the wedding."

She handed me a cup of coffee and joined me at the table. "You got your walking cast?"

"I did. Want to sign?"

She added her signature, in her trademark bold, curvy script. She smiled. "I'll bet you're glad to be shed of those crutches."

"You can say that again."

She sighed. "Well, dear, if I could've gotten out of attending the wedding, I would have. It was one of the hardest things I've ever done."

"Why? What happened?"

"Well, Zoe called me the night before the wedding and said they weren't going to assign the bride's and groom's friends to separate sections at the church, that people could just sit wherever they wanted. She said Bryce's parents and their friends were going to sit in the front rows, so we'd just have to find our own seats. Have you ever heard of such a thing?"

I shook my head. "I can't even imagine such rudeness."

She sighed. "Well, I guess when you have the kind of money they do, rudeness is allowed, sometimes even elevated to an art form."

"What did Snooky think?"

"Well, you know Snooky. He's very longsuffering, but his comment was, 'What on earth is the world coming to when your own daughter treats her mother like a common street person?'"

"So he was angry?"

She snorted, "As a hornet."

"Can't say I blame him. I'm glad I wasn't there. Oh, who gave her away?"

She shrugged. "Nobody. They don't do that anymore in polite society."

"Really? I had no idea."

She sounded sad when she said, "I'm beginning to see why you despise that *society gene* so much."

"Well, I think the Lord hit the nail on the head when He said not to give the good seats to the rich and consign the poor to sit on the floor in the back."

She twisted her wedding ring on her finger, clearly upset. "I've never felt so humiliated in my whole life."

I held her until she collected herself a moment later. "You should've been at the reception. You'd have thought the President himself was in attendance."

"What do you mean?"

"Oh, they all do this back-slapping, hugging thing that is just so shallow, it turns my stomach. The women even give each other air kisses."

"Well, was the food good?"

She made a face. "I think some of that stuff must be an acquired taste. I'm not fond of liver pate' or smoked salmon," she said, cringing. "I tried a little bit, but didn't care for it much. I can't, for the life of me, see what the attraction is."

"Was the place impressive?"

"Hmm…well, they have these huge crystal chandeliers at the University Club, so it's very grand, but I thought it noteworthy that except for the bride wearing a fancy gown, you'd have thought it was just another society fundraiser."

"What was Zoe's dress like?"

"About what you'd imagine. Off the shoulder, in the palest pink satin. With a slit up the side, and the neck cut down to you know where. Honestly? I thought her auburn hair clashed with the pink."

"Other than the dress, did she look nice?"

"Oh, I suppose. But she was so cold, I hardly recognized her."

"That doesn't surprise me a bit." After a beat, I said, "I wish I could've been a mouse in the corner, but I'm sure she'll show me the album when she gets it."

Mom held up an index finger. "You'll be interested to know that they had an ice sculpture of a mermaid, which was really intriguing. A little riske', but intriguing."

"I knew it. And I imagined pate' and salmon, crab legs and caviar."

"Well, you weren't too far off. They had pheasant under glass, and Duck al Orange, or something. I had no idea what it was, and it looked disgusting to me, so I didn't eat much of anything. The cake looked okay, but by then, people were so pushy and rude that I finally said to Snooky, 'Let's get out of here.' I doubt that Zoe even missed us when we left. And I wouldn't be surprised if she never speaks to me again."

"In some ways," I said, "it's sad, but in another, I think it might be a relief."

"You're right about that. I think my blood pressure has probably dropped thirty points since the wedding."

"Did you get to meet the groom's parents?"

"Yes. When we realized Zoe would never do the honors, we walked up and introduced ourselves." After a beat, she gave me a forlorn look. "I wish we hadn't. They looked at us like we were bugs in their soup."

"They did?"

"Yes. His mother acted like she wasn't sure if it was safe to shake my hand. Was that rude or what?"

"Well, what are they like?"

"You even have to ask that question after what I just said?"

"I'm curious. Is his mother gorgeous, and his father handsome in a tux?"

"Well, his father looks like a stuffed goose, like he might have been wearing a corset to fit into his tux. As if he didn't dare breathe. Little short guy, not that there's anything intrinsically wrong with that, but there is if you have to pretend to be something you're not."

"What do you mean?"

"Oh, he wore those tall, elevated shoes that are so obvious. I don't think he was actually much taller than Snooky, if you want to know the truth."

"What about Bryce's mother? Is she pretty?"

"Pickled is more like it. Her face has been stretched so many times, she looked positively poached, if you get my meaning."

"I got it, Mom, and I'm sorry you had such a miserable time."

After a brief hesitation, I said, "You never mentioned who Zoe got to wear the dress in my place."

She looked at me wide-eyed. "No one. There were no bridesmaids or groomsmen at all." After a hesitation, she frowned. "Do you think they could've alienated their last friends?"

"I hate to think so." I sighed.

Mom said, "Wonder what the chances are of Zoe coming to know the Lord now that she's living in a world where *things* are elevated to god status."

"Well, you always told me where there's life there's hope, where the Lord is concerned, remember?"

"I did, but I also told you it's easier for a camel to get through the eye of a needle than for a rich man to enter heaven—remember?"

"We'll just have to pray," I said and she agreed.

I got home about four, and felt more alive than I'd felt in years, interested in life for the first time in I couldn't remember when. I saw the answering machine blink, and pushed the play button.

The first message was from a giggly Freezia, who said, "Makkie, I just wanted to tell you how much I'm enjoying my new ministry. The girls and I just finished decorating Candace Green's house. You know her, don't you? She's eighty-four and an invalid. Anyway, we gave her four brand new walls to look at, and she's thrilled. So if you're ever bored, come join us."

That will be the day.

The second message was a shock. An unfamiliar man's voice said, "My name is Manley Andreason. I am the man you found in the field. I've made a full recovery and need to speak with you regarding the whereabouts of the DVD. Please call me at this number."

He recited a number, which I quickly jotted on my palm. My heart instantly jumped into a staccato rhythm that thudded in my ears. Anxiety gripped my heart at the thought of having anything more to do with him, and I didn't know whether to believe he was alive or whether someone had assumed his identity.

I decided the issue would have to wait until Drew came home from work.

I started supper and was actually hungry by the time he walked in the door. He looked surprised to see me up and about. He smiled and wrapped me in a warm embrace. "It looks like I've finally got my girl back."

I greeted him with a hug and kiss. "It's really me. I feel like I was lost somewhere for a long time, if that makes any sense."

"Well, I'm glad you're back, love. I can't tell you how much I've missed you." His eyes lit up in a grin. "So what did you do with this new found energy surge?"

I filled him in on my day, telling him about Zoe's wedding, my visit with Suse and my stop at Shady Acres. He gave a delighted laugh. "No wonder you enjoy spending time with those old guys. They sound like a blast."

"You haven't heard the best part yet. Mather Gillette told me he had set his cap for me years ago, and just didn't make his move fast enough to beat your time, mister. He seemed surprisingly disappointed."

Drew laughed. "Well, first come, first served, I always say."

"Hey!"

I remembered the note on my palm and extended my hand for him to see.

"What's this?" he asked, shaking his head in confusion.

"It's from a message on the machine. Just listen."

I rewound it and played it for him.

"Good grief. Isn't that man supposed to be dead?"

"He is, Drew. So what on earth do we do now?"

He held up his finger, while swallowing a mouth full of carrot he'd snitched from the vegetable bin. "First we eat and think this thing over. This is one time I don't think we should do anything in a hurry."

We finished eating, and he made a phone call to his contact in D.C., where he'd turned over the evidence. It seemed odd that we hadn't seen anything in the news exposing the illegal manufacture of biological weapons. Surely the feds had had enough time to ferret out the truth and bring it to light.

After he hung up, I asked Drew about that, and he said some things take more time to uncover than others. He assured me that he had complete confidence in the team he'd entrusted with the evidence, but he didn't sound all that certain. I wondered whom he was trying to convince—me or himself.

NINETEEN

I woke early the next morning and realized it was the day Freezia and Mamie were supposed to see Arlo for Mamie's imaginary neuro complaint. I was dying to hear the play-by-play, hoping Arlo could determine whether Freezia had some organic reason for her recent bizarre behavior.

I took the dogs out, and we walked for a while in the chill morning air, getting back just in time to find Drew shaving. He wiped his face, set the towel down and reached for me. "I hate it when you're gone when I wake up."

I smiled. "I know exactly how you feel."

"Touche'."

He kissed me, saying he would be going out of town on a detail in a day or so. When he searched my face, I found myself saying, "I'll be okay. Don't worry."

"Well, if you get nervous, you can always go to Jane's."

"I will, but please—don't forget where you live."

With a dazzling smile, he said, "How could I possibly?"

I laughed as I went in and got busy with laundry, which had somehow gotten away from me. Again.

Emily Keating called to say hello within the hour, and asked if we could meet for lunch now that I was mobile, and I eagerly agreed. I was thrilled with everything and had energy to do it all.

I dressed, doing my makeup for the first time in ages. I looked pretty good, even a little thinner, I thought. Stepping on the scale, I saw that there were five pounds less of me. I could live with that.

I met Em at Verlene's, where we had taco salad, heaped with tomatoes and cheese, and I ate slowly, savoring every bite.

My cell phone rang as we finished our lunch, and I could hear loud noises, talking and confusion on the line.

Pansy Barclay was nearly drowned out by background noise.

"Pansy, is that you? What's going on? I can hardly hear you."

I knew it must be bad for her to call my cell phone.

"Oh, Makkie, we need you over here right now. Something's happened to Bonnie Hunt."

After donning my jacket, I hugged Emily, who said, "Keep me posted, will you?" I bounded out the door and parked in the nursing home parking lot in no time.

Outside the building, pandemonium ruled. Police cruisers and ambulances with lights flashing sat out front with engines still running. I ran inside and was eagerly greeted by my friends, who all rushed to talk at once.

Accompanying me down the hall, Pansy said, "Makkie, they found Bonnie's body. Her office was locked, and we all assumed she had gone home, but Gina Henning needed some paperwork out of the office, and started screamin' like a banshee when she unlocked the door."

I was stunned. Things like this just didn't...well, at least they didn't used to—happen around here.

I could see the body slumped over the desk, still sitting in her chair. I could see no blood or other obvious signs of violence. The police had strung their crime scene tape across her office door, and behind it, I could see a coffee cup tipped over in its saucer, but nothing else appeared to have been disturbed.

I turned toward the guys. "Did any of you notice anything unusual here today?"

"Not really," said Pansy.

Maybelle said, "I don't know if it's anything important, but her son was here today. I'd never met him before, but when she walked him to the door, she introduced him to me as her son, Ellis. I didn't think much of it at the time, but she showed me a necklace she was wearing and said, 'Look, he gave me this for my birthday today.' She seemed really pleased about it."

"Did you mention this to the police, Maybelle?"

She gave me a doubtful look. "I don't think they see us as credible witnesses. Not one of them has seen fit to ask us a single question. Listen, I've watched enough of Perry Mason in my lifetime to think they'd want all the help they can get. But no," she whined.

"Listen, I'll make sure they know about the son. What did you say his name is? Ellis?"

"Yes, I'm just sure that's right."

I turned to the others. "Did anyone else see anything?"

Dabney Franklin scratched his balding head. "Well, I was sittin' out front when he left, and I think I remember him tossin' somethin' into the ash can by the front door."

I hugged him and smiled. "You guys are really sharp. I'm awfully proud of you."

A minute later, I sought out police chief, Ace Grimm. "Hi, chief. What have you found?"

He frowned. "What are you doing here, Makkie?"

"These people are my friends, and they called me." After a beat, I added, "You know, they see a lot living here that people don't give them credit for. I think you might want to get their input."

"Why? What did you hear?"

"Bonnie's son visited her today."

"So? Is that unusual?" he asked, running his calloused hand through thinning gray hair.

I shrugged. "No one around here has ever seen him before, in all the years Bonnie has worked here."

"Oh, yeah? And how would you know that?"

Annoyed, I said, "Listen, Ace, I just told you these seniors are sharp, and they know exactly what's going on."

He glanced doubtfully at the small mass of humanity, huddled in the hallway behind me. "Well, just who is it you think I should talk to? Surely you could narrow it down for me?"

He threw me a pen. "Write down their names please, and do it on paper, if you don't mind."

"I don't have any."

"Dale, throw Makkie here some paper." Under his breath, he muttered to himself, "Won't do me a bit of good to have to copy it off her hand."

Dale tossed me a tablet over the yellow ribbon that surrounded the scene. "Now," said Ace, "I want to know the names of everyone you talked to."

I listed their names and turned to smile at them as I handed the tablet back to Dale and prepared to leave.

Maybelle gave me the thumbs up sign. "We'll put him on the right track, Makkie. Just leave it to us."

I patted Maybelle's hand. "Just make sure nobody messes with the ash can out front. Actually one of you should probably go and guard it until Ace gets around to checking it out."

"I'll keep an eye on it, Makkie," Mamie offered before wandering toward the front door.

"Thanks, girlfriend." I turned to Dabney, "And make sure you're the first one he questions, so Mamie doesn't have to sit out front for hours, okay?"

"No problem, boss." He gave me a delighted smile.

I waved. "Call me if you need me, okay, guys?"

Standing beside the front door, I checked out the ash can myself, not touching, just looking to see what Ellis Hunt had dropped. It looked like a Band-Aid wrapper to me. From her chair by the door, Mamie waved. "I'm on the job, chief," she said, wearing a proud smile.

"Mamie, you're wonderful." I smiled and patted her shoulder.

Drew was at home, tossing clothes into his duffel, and I hugged him around the middle. "Are you on your way, honey?"

His voice radiated annoyance. "I sure am. For some reason, they couldn't give us even one day's notice, though they knew this was scheduled. I just don't get it."

With a jerking motion, he zipped it shut and headed for the refrigerator. "Couldn't even get a decent meal before leaving."

I took two apples and a banana from the fridge and dropped them in a bag, along with a package of corn chips and a Snapple. He was closing the bag, when I said, "Wait, let me throw in some baby carrots and yogurt. Oh, and you'll need a spoon."

"I can't take too much, or I'll have every agent on the team begging it off me."

He flew out the door, kissing me on the run. "I'm late already, but I'll call when I can. Love you."

I picked up my jacket and hung it up, listening to the Bronco peel down the driveway. I hadn't even had a chance to tell him about Bonnie Hunt.

I fed the dogs and let them out, and went to scrounge up my own dinner, a big salad with lots of tomato and green pepper.

A little later I noticed the message light blinking on my machine. It was another message from the guy calling himself Andreason. I couldn't believe the man I found in the field could have completely recovered from such a severe head injury. From my experience, it seemed highly doubtful.

After settling down in front of my computer, I worked on book two until the screen blurred before my eyes.

I snuggled under the covers with my furry friends, who had once again claimed Drew's side of the bed in his absence. Duke always ends up on the floor, overheated, after a bit, sometimes waking me with a thud, but I was grateful not to be alone.

The new morning dawned bright and clear. It was still bitterly cold, but the sun shone brightly, a welcome sight. I opened all the curtains and let the sunshine in, finding myself drawn toward sunlight.

I called Mamie Harcourt, wanting to know how the investigation was coming. A wellspring of information, she said, "That new police chief—well, at least he's better than the old one. I really think he started to listen after you talked to him."

"Did he check out the ash can?"

"Finally. Sure took his sweet time about it, though. Pansy had to relieve me, so I could go relieve my bladder a time or two. We never let it out of our sight though. We know what's what," she boasted.

"So what did Ace do with the Band-Aid?"

"He had someone pick it up with tweezers and put it in a Ziploc bag. That was according to procedure, wasn't it?"

"Sounds right to me."

"He said he might be back to ask more questions, so we shouldn't leave town." She laughed. "As if we're going anywhere."

Suddenly I remembered to ask, "Oh, Mamie, how did the appointment go with Arlo?"

"Oh, yeah, I wanted to fill you in on that. We pulled it off, and Freezia didn't suspect a thing. It was a blast. From what Arlo said when I talked to him later, he thinks it's just normal aging." After a long pause, she added, "I hate to think she'll get worse than she already is, but I guess we'll shoot that horse when we come to it."

I couldn't stifle a laugh. This was one cagey lady.

The rest of the day I spent switching back and forth from writing book two, to adding more things to the list of clues in Bonnie Hunt's death.

As I got ready for bed later, I wondered exactly what had killed her.

TWENTY

I woke in the middle of the night, remembering I hadn't told Drew about the second call from Andreason or whoever was impersonating him. I wondered if I he'd consider it important enough for me to interrupt his work. Shoot, I'd need to write myself notes, to keep up with him at this rate.

I fished a pen off the bedside table, and wrote a note on my hand, to tell Drew about both Bonnie and Andreason.

I was starved when I woke again at seven and let the dogs out. When they got tired of running, I poured food into their dishes and fixed myself a bowl of Cheerios.

I was completely enamored of my new walking cast —clearly a boon to mankind. I could only thank the Lord and rejoice over my newfound self-sufficiency.

The meager winter sun had receded behind a cloudbank when I took the dogs for a short walk at eight, soaking up sunshine while it lasted.

I finished my chores by 9:30 and sat down at the computer, to put on paper what little I knew about Bonnie's death. I listed anything even distantly related, including people who might have a grudge against her.

The longer I thought about it, the longer the list became. Not only were there several employees whom she had loudly fired, but there were others she regularly antagonized, and even a couple of residents whom she had alienated. I didn't know much about her personal life, but I wondered about her relationship with her son.

I phoned Gertie Albers at the police station and asked if she could look up Ellis Hunt on the police computers. We had a tacit agreement that sometimes the police department needed a little outside help when they weren't doing it right.

Gertie took my information and called back a short time later, saying all she could find was a name, address and place of employment. Apparently, he lived in a condo in a middle-income neighborhood in the city and worked as a UPS delivery person. I asked her to check the computers for information about Bonita Hunt. It took her an hour to call me back this time. Her voice quivered with excitement when she spoke.

"Makkie, you'll never guess what I learned. Bonnie's Dad was Daniel Hunt—died six months ago, leaving her heir to the Hunt toiletries fortune. She was his only child, and guess who he left out of his will?"

I bit my lip, thinking. "He left Ellis out of his will?"

"He sure did. Some kind of trouble between them is the scuttlebutt.

"Anyway, that's a mighty good reason to want your mother dead, wouldn't you say?"

"Well, thanks, Gertie. You'll pass this info on to the chief, right?"

"I sure will. Thanks for the help."

I turned back to my computer. So we had a motive for Ellis to kill his mother, but how had he done it? I puzzled over that for some time. Could he have used a poison of some kind? It was odd that she would've locked the door while in the office. Unless she was in a meeting, the door was always open, so she could keep herself abreast of what went on in the building, ie.—spy on the residents.

Adding to my list of clues, I wondered if Ellis usually gave her birthday gifts. I called Mamie again, and asked her to describe the necklace.

"Well, it was pretty nice, heavy looking, probably fourteen karat gold, from what I could tell, and it had a section that spelled out MOTHER with a baby bootie hanging from it. You've seen them, haven't you? They're everywhere. There are some cheap knockoffs, but this one was the real thing. The bootie on her necklace had a lavender stone in it. Which birthstone is lavender, do you know?"

I told her I'd have to get back to her on that. I thought it was February.

I tried to think what the Band-Aid could have to do with it. Then I remembered an old Matlock episode where a man had implanted a toxin into a Band-Aid. He had given his victim a necklace and purposely scratched her neck while putting on the necklace, then put the Band-aid over the scratch, giving the toxin an immediate route into her blood stream. She had died within an hour, if memory served.

The smoker's trans-dermal patches use the same method of delivery, through the skin. Was it possible that Ellis had seen the same Matlock episode?

I called Gertie again and asked her if they were going to do an autopsy, and she said she was sure they would, since it was a suspicious death. I related the Matlock episode and my theory about trans-dermal delivery of a toxic substance, and said for her to especially have them note her neck and do a tox screen. She grew more excited as we talked, until finally I said, "Hey, Gert, you might want to load up a trans-dermal patch with Valium, and apply it to your neck right about now." I heard her deep guffaw just before I hung up.

Mom called and asked if she and Snooky could join me for lunch. I browned ground beef and whipped up a pot of chili.

Over lunch, I filled them in on the latest, surprised that they hadn't heard about Bonnie's death. What was the matter with the grapevine? It always worked great when I'd rather it didn't.

I told Mom about the Matlock episode where the poisoning had taken place, and she nodded.

"Hey, I saw that one myself. Isn't that the one where he was hit by a car, and they used trans-dermal patches to relieve his headache?"

"I had forgotten some of that, but I think you're right on the button."

Mom picked at a loose thread on her trousers as she said thoughtfully, "So if Bonnie was an heiress to a fortune like that, why do you suppose she didn't quit her job?"

"Well, when you're single, sometimes your job is your whole identity. Or maybe she was just waiting until the will was probated before quitting her job."

Again she nodded, looking pensive. "That certainly is an angle to pursue. I think we can find out if the will is still in probate or not."

Snooky hadn't had much to say up to that point, but he put down his soup spoon and met my gaze.

"You know, if the fortune is large—I don't know the exact amount—it can take a long time to get through probate. It would also be good to see if this Hunt kid has made any recent major purchases, you know, bigger than normal for his income."

Mom beamed at him and said to me, "Isn't he amazing?"

Snooky smiled and blew a kiss at her across the table. I could see they were still crazy in love, and it made me laugh. "You two are adorable."

After pushing her plate aside, Mom said, "Okay, now tell me about Freezia's neuro exam. I've been on pins and needles to see if the whole ruse worked or if she figured it out. I know Freezia acts squirrelly sometimes, but she's not stupid."

"Well, Mamie said Freezia didn't seem to have a clue and was very cooperative when Arlo enlisted her help. He couldn't find a thing wrong, except normal aging. Mamie's comment was if it's normal aging, she hates to see what will happen next, but she'll kill that horse when she comes to it."

After lunch, Mom and Snooky offered to drive me over to Primrose to get a glimpse of Zoe's new house. She and Bryce were probably still in Switzerland on their honeymoon.

I couldn't resist. It was only about fifteen minutes from Azalea, but when I saw it, I exclaimed, "Mom, you didn't tell me it was a mansion." It was an ivy-covered brick three-story, a copy of a charming European design I'd seen in a magazine.

"Well, the inside isn't nearly as grand as the outside."

"But still," I said. "It has to be the most expensive property in the entire township."

She sighed. "I suppose, but I guess Snooky and I just aren't that impressed with wealth, are we, dear?"

"Not much," he agreed.

They dropped me off just in time to take a call from Drew, and I hurried to tell him about Andreason's call and Bonnie's death. He wasn't that interested in Bonnie, but he really zoned in when I mentioned that the dead man had called again.

In a concerned tone, Drew said for me to let the machine screen calls and not to get caught talking to him again. I didn't voice my fear that he already knew where we lived, since he'd been here at least once before.

Drew said he thought it would be several days before he'd be home, but he was on the cell phone if I needed him.

Drew's agency has bought their agents high tech, security encrypted cell phones, costing in the range of $1500 apiece, known to get a signal when the regular cells fail. I found that thought comforting.

I called Gertie again. "Hey, Gert, sorry to bother you, but I have something else that might be helpful." I related Snooky's idea, suggesting that they look at whether Ellis Hunt had made any unusually large purchases recently. I also asked her to find out whether

Daniel Hunt's will was still in probate. She seemed tickled pink to play go-between.

A short time later, I picked up the mail and found an envelope, addressed to me in big block letters, obviously not normal junk mail, and with no return address. I was hesitant to open it alone. I phoned Mom, who said she'd be right there.

Within ten minutes, Mom had Sheriff Duffy Murdock in tow, knocking on my door. Pouting, Duffy said, "You know, you guys are becoming the talk of the town. What is it this time?"

Mom looked daggers at him. "Keep a civil tongue in your head, Duffy. Remember, I'm the mayor, and if nothing else, my office deserves a little respect."

Duffy shuffled his feet like a humble school kid then held out his hand. "So let's see what you've got."

I handed him the letter, and he shrugged. "This looks harmless enough. What's the big deal?"

"You know, if you'd listen instead of talking, you might just learn something. Makkie had a phone call from the alleged dead man. You tell him, dear."

I related the incident, and his mouth was gaping when I finished. Mom said, "You can close your mouth now, Duffy."

He did. Then he said, "Why didn't you notify me at the time this happened?"

Mom frowned. "Knowing she'd get attitude from you? Why would she?"

He opened the envelope and used a pen to slide the letter out. He didn't touch the paper except with his fingernails.

He read it in silence, which was fine with me. Then he said, "It's supposedly from the dead guy. He wants the DVD back and says if he doesn't hear from you within forty-eight hours, he'll be paying you a visit."

"Good grief," I replied, feeling anxiety rise in my chest. "Why can't this dead guy stay underground with the rest of the dead guys?"

Mom looked at me and was ready to say it, but I beat her to the punch. "I know. I'm packing."

"You know, dear, it might save time in the long run if you just keep a packed bag stashed in the closet."

"Now there's a thought."

Duffy seemed to feel put upon, having to wait for us to get ready to go. Mom looked at him square in the eye and said sternly, "I've forgotten, just when does your term end?"

At Mom's, I called out, "Hey, Snooky, I'm home."

"Hi again, sugar," he said, laughing as he looked up from his newspaper.

Mom said, "She got a letter saying if the DVD isn't returned within forty-eight hours, he'd pay her a visit."

"Who? The dead guy again?"

I nodded. "One and the same."

He frowned, shaking his head. "He's pretty active for a dead guy, isn't he?"

It was so pathetic that we couldn't help but dissolve into laughter.

A short time later, we found an old re-run of "Matlock" on television and really got a kick out of it. We had a new reverence for the show, since it had shed new light on Bonnie's murder. Snooky made popcorn and we finished up the evening rooting on another would be millionaire and then joined Robert Stack, hoping to 'help solve a mystery'.

By now the dogs were pretty nonchalant about being shuttled back and forth between our place and Mom's. They curled up in bed with me, just as I remembered that I hadn't phoned Drew about my change of venue.

I woke to the fragrance of Mom's pancakes and sausage. I couldn't recall when I'd had such great pancakes, but I knew I'd better watch it, or that lost five pounds would no doubt find me again.

Gertie called to let me know that Ellis Hunt's financial transactions had been scrutinized. Within the past two days, the UPS deliveryman had apparently purchased a home in Aspen, and one in Palm Springs, as well as part interest in the Denver Broncos Pro football team. That just about clinched his conviction right there, I imagined.

It was Friday, and the citywide winter garage sales were on tap for today. They had been the brainchild of some bored-out-of-her skull housewife, who was sick of living in a small town with nothing to do during winter.

It was a good thing that nearly all the homes in Azalea have garages, because otherwise the idea would have died an early and chilly death. But most people have a walk-in door and choose to add space heaters to keep the clientele from freezing to death. Some offer free coffee or hot chocolate and occasionally even Christmas cookies.

Citywide garage sale day is a wonderful opportunity to visit with neighbors who have been staying in out of the cold. And there are some great buys, too. Mom and I left Snooky reading his Wall Street Journal and drove down the street, looking for signs.

The first sign was in front of Kylie Sheldon's house. Kylie is actually more Zoe's friend, but we get along great. Her husband Brad is an OB-GYN who consults at the Memorial, delivering the occasional baby and doing scheduled surgeries. So of course, she has the means to redecorate her home at regular intervals, giving us die-hard garage salers designer stuff for pennies on the dollar.

Mom and I decided we would be content even if Kylie's was the only sale in town.

Entering her toasty garage, I loosened my down jacket and looked around. Her garage is a two-car, so it offers plenty of space for the great stuff she's sick of.

Mom headed toward the decorator items on the left-hand table, while I went to the right. Old books, hundreds of them, were stacked on the table. With a puzzled gaze, I looked at Kylie, who explained, "I've decided to collect cookbooks instead."

I didn't actually ooh and ah out loud, but it was only because I was gritting my teeth, trying to keep still.

With my arms overflowing, I started a pile on the checkout table, including a Dick, Jane and Sally reader in perfect condition for only three dollars. I knew they went for seventy at rare book auctions. On top of that, I picked out a set of early McGuffy Readers, also perfect, tagged at ten dollars. After adding several colorful primary spellers and arithmetic books to my pile, I was a very happy camper.

I veered toward Mom, who had an armload of stuff already. Clearly giddy with delight, her face could barely contain her grin. Perusing that table, I saw a set of copper pans, all perfect, perched in a pile next to a pot rack in copper and brass—and all for ten dollars.

Shelly Keith, from Primrose, had been eying the same set from across the table, but she who hesitates is lost. I had them in my arms in a flash. It's a good thing it's a civilized society. Shelly shrugged and turned to look at something else.

Next I spied a section of beautiful clothing, in my size. Not that I have a lot of use for designer things, but I couldn't resist the one and two dollar price tags calling my name. Just when I thought I'd seen everything, Kylie brought out a natural color antique wicker, folding screen, priced at twenty dollars. I was in as close to glory as one can be on earth, as I added the screen to my pile, paid for it, and I toted my stash toward the car.

Mom giggled. "We can quit and head home if you're ready. I can die happy now."

At home, we sorted and thrilled over our finds. Mom had found a Louis Vuitton suit for three dollars in beige and black. She modeled it for us, and Snooky and I whistled at her, laughing as she blushed and giggled. She had found a beautiful new Christmas tablecloth, exquisite, with poinsettias sparkling all over it for two dollars, as well as a cedar-lined hope chest for ten dollars, which she decided was her buy of the day.

"Mom, are you sure your designer suit isn't the buy of the day? I mean, it looks beautiful on you."

She replied thoughtfully, "I suppose it might be if I were more thrilled with the idea of wearing suits."

We discussed whether we should stop now or keep shopping. Unable to resist a pull that rivaled an ocean tide, we were off again, coming home later with everything we could possibly need and a few things we didn't.

We'd picked up lunch from Peking's Express, and Snooky said he'd send us junking more often if it meant he would be rewarded with Chinese.

I called Drew after lunch, and his first words were, "Honey, are you okay? You never call unless something is really wrong."

"I'm okay."

I told him I was at Mom's, because of a letter from the dead guy, and he said, "Good. Stay put. I'll be home tomorrow, so feed me when I get there, will you?"

I couldn't help but laugh. Poor baby. Sometimes in the field, the guys have to live on rations they would never settle for at home, and sometimes they just take whatever they can scrounge. He had once mentioned that they ended up living for a week on nothing but cold cuts, chips and soda. No wonder he was so desperate to be fed.

TWENTY-ONE

I started the day with a sinus headache and immediately hot-packed my face. I had dealt with sinus infections before, even ended up hauling an IV pole to my wedding rehearsal, so I knew better than to take it lightly. I swallowed some herbs from Mom's stash. She isn't as sold on them as I am, but keeps the basics on hand just in case.

I called Suse Reilly, whose delivery date had come and gone, and asked the dreaded question. "Are you still home?"

She laughed. "Here I was spotting and on bed rest, and now I'm three days overdue. How's that for the ultimate irony?"

"Well," I asked, "how are you feeling?"

"You mean besides the fact that my feet are swollen, I can't breathe lying down, and my maternity clothes don't fit anymore? Great—just great. And how, may I ask, are you?"

"Compared to you, I'm bored. So how's the nervous father doing?"

She laughed. "Oh, he's a riot, watching me all the time, out of the corner of his eye, as if I might explode."

"Did you finish your Lamaze classes?"

She laughed. "We did, and it was a scream. The first couple of weeks we got the oddest looks, and one really young guy remarked, "I didn't know people your age even did it anymore."

I laughed. "Is there anything I can do for you?"

She said, "Just keep me laughin'. It's what you do best, right?"

After a beat, I asked, "Did you hear about the unexplained death at the nursing home?"

"No, but I'm listening."

I hit the highlights, and she said, "So what's the punch line?"

"What punch line?"

"I thought this was a joke."

"No. It's not a joke."

"Okay, start again and tell me what happened. This time I'll really listen."

I did, and she said, "You mean you think it was murder?"

"That's what it looks like to me."

"What on God's green earth happened to safe and rustic small town living?"

"I honestly don't know," I said, shaking my head. "And now that I think about it, every single murder in our town was due to greed. How's that for something to think about?"

Suse had to hang up to go empty her bladder, and I thought I was glad not to be in her shoes. Then again, maybe not.

Early that morning, Mom had put a big roast and all the fixings in the slow cooker, so when Drew came in at four, she handed me a container with hot food for my hungry man. In the car, he said, "I'm sure glad it's only a five-minute drive home, or I might have starved to death within a twelve inches of a feast."

He tossed his duffel on the bed. "I'll take the dogs out and give you time to get it on the table." It was the shortest doggie romp on record, after which, he ate like a starved man and held out his plate for seconds.

Feeling playful, I said, "Seen one too many cold cuts this trip?"

He sighed. "Enough to last me a lifetime. You'd think with a government budget like ours, we'd at least get breast of turkey or ham, but no, they give us generic baloney on bread—cheap white, dead bread. Now you understand why I'm starved."

"I'll have to speak to the FBI director about that."

He said doubtfully, "I'll bet you don't even know his name."

I shrugged. "You're right, I don't." Not that it mattered.

Drew started a fire and put on my Christmas music, before turning to me. "This time, I'm doing this for *my* mental health. Otherwise, *I* may shortly need tranquilizers."

Food wasn't the only thing Drew was starving for. He kept looking in my eyes, repeating the same refrain. "I'm so glad to be back. I'm beginning to hate this job." After a beat, he asked fretfully, "How could that be? I used to think it was the best job in the world, baloney notwithstanding. Now I dread leaving. Kiss me."

He started kissing me, and I returned the favor. It was sweet.

Later we lay there talking, holding each other, and I said, "Were there any women on this detail?"

"Yup, and as usual, they were demanding, disruptive, and completely obnoxious. Is that what you wanted to hear?" His eyes twinkled with mischief.

"Yup," I said, "you get an A plus. Now kiss the teacher."

He tipped up my chin and said seriously, "You still feeling a little insecure having me around other females?"

"I just need to hear that they hold no appeal for you, so keep on telling me, okay?"

"Not a problem," he said as he sighed contentedly, snuggling deeper into my arms.

I woke first, leaving Drew to sleep, let the dogs out and sat down to check my e-mails. *How did this guy get my e-mail address?*

I stuck a thermometer in my mouth as he slipped out of bed and headed toward me.

"Honey, what's going on?" Drew laid his palm on my forehead.

I took the thermometer out just long enough to say, "Sinus infection."

He blew out a puff of air and caressed my cheek. "You need to get in to see Arlo, sweetheart." Not if I could help it.

Gesturing, I said, "Honey, come and read these e-mails. There's one here you'll be interested in."

Drew stood behind me, yawning, as he read, "'This is not a joke. Your government is the one paying for the biological weapons being produced by Smith, Darden and March.' Signed, a *friend*."

Drew shifted immediately into agent mode. He made a copy of the e-mail and tried to send a return message. He wasn't sure it was received, but wanted to stay on top of it, just in case the *friend* wanted to keep talking.

He left for the office a little early, motivated by this new information. He asked me to call if any other e-mails were sent by the same *friend*.

Elvee Reilly called at 8:30, saying they finally had their beautiful baby girl. He assured me that everyone was fine, including the new Daddy, and I told him to give them a kiss for me. I planned to visit after lunch.

Marla Kelly called from Shady Oaks a short time later. "Makkie, I need transportation for a new resident, Pauley Jenks. He needs to see his orthopedist in Kansas City on the twelfth. Are you available?"

I said, "Marla, I really love the residents, but I don't think I'll be available to transport anymore."

After a long pause, she argued, "But I just gave you a huge raise."

"You sure did, but if you'll pardon me for saying so, there are some jobs that are not worth doing, no matter how much they pay."

"So you're asking me not to call anymore?"

"I am."

"I can't believe you. After all I've done for you. You know what a state we're in right now. We need all the help we can get."

This woman would make a great used car salesman.

"Well, Marla, I don't know what to tell you."

She huffed as she said, "Could you just do it one last time, at least?"

"I really can't, but I have an idea."

"Spit it out."

"Well, I need to consult with some other people before I do that, but I'll get back to you if it works out, okay?"

"Just make it snappy, will you?" she sniped.

I set the phone down quietly, then made a call to Freezia Harcourt, asking whether she and her 'all girl orchestra' would like to make some good money transporting people from Shady Acres to doctors' appointments in Kansas City and points in between.

"Well, only a few of us can still drive. Five of us, to be exact, but we're all excellent drivers. How many would you need?"

"As many as I can get, as a pool of drivers."

She sounded totally bewildered. "A what? A pool?"

"Freezia, a pool of people means there are several to choose from. If one can't do it, another can."

"Oh, I see. Well, when would you need us?"

"You'd be working for Shady Acres, and the first appointment is on the twelfth. I'm not sure of the time yet. What do you think? Think the girls will go for it?"

"I'm definitely in, if the roads aren't icy. And I know road conditions would be a consideration for all of us."

"You wouldn't be expected to drive on icy roads."

"Wow, this could be another great ministry, and we could make some money at the same time." She was trilling with excitement when she hung up.

I called Marla back a few minutes later. "I think I have a group of five ladies who would be willing to drive if the money's good enough."

"Yeah, well, who are these good people?"

"They're friends of mine, and you're lucky to get them. The only condition is they don't drive on icy roads."

"That means they might not drive for months around here," she snorted.

"Take it or leave it, and they get twenty bucks an hour."

She nearly choked on her words. "Why, that's highway robbery!"

"Listen, Marla, it doesn't matter to me one way or the other, but if I were in your shoes, I'd take me up on this deal. Just think of the Medicare paperwork it'll save you."

"I need to meet with these people first, before I say yes, you know."

"That's no problem. I'll give the group leader your number and the two of you can set up a meeting. How's that?"

"Do I have a choice?" she pouted out loud.

"You can hang up right now if you want."

"What I want is for you to drive for us."

"Sorry. That's not going to happen. Now," I said, quietly, "what do you want me to do?"

"Call them."

I hung up and was tickled when I dialed Freezia's number.

"Freezia, you need to call the Shady Acres social worker. I've already talked to her and she's willing to pay you each twenty dollars an hour."

She said in excitement, "I'm sure they'll need us to get physicals and stuff, but I know we'll pass with flying colors."

I wasn't so sure about that, but that was between them and Marla.

After lunch, I went to visit Suse and her beautiful dark-haired infant. "Oh, Suse, she's beautiful. She looks just like you."

She smiled, gazing in tenderness at the new baby daughter asleep in her arms. "So far you're the only one who thinks so."

"What? You mean to say somebody thinks she looks like Elvee?"

"Oh, you know how guys are. They just say what they think the other wants to hear."

"Listen, Suse, this is a no-brainer. Elvee has a thin face, with freckles and reddish hair—what there is left of it. She has your beautiful complexion and eyes. She's a carbon copy of her mother. Trust me on this."

Neely walked in a few minutes later and seconded the motion.

After admiring the baby, Neely said, "So what would you like us to get for Rachel?"

I said, "I don't think she's up for much more of Peter Rabbit."

"Neely said, "Well, there's always Winnie the Pooh."

Suse laughed. It was great to be together again.

Neely and I left together, and when we got to her car, we agreed that what the new parents needed most was a night out on the town, a gift certificate to their favorite restaurant, and the two of us to babysit. Neely volunteered to do the legwork to get the gift certificate.

By the time Drew got home at five, I had the table set with candles and my good china. His eyes narrowed in confusion. "Have I forgotten our anniversary or something?"

I laughed. "No, no occasion, except that you're home. These days that's worth celebrating."

I piled his plate with comfort food, lasagna, salad and garlic bread. As we cleaned up the dishes, he asked, "Any word from our *friend*?"

"Oh, honey, I was out all day and forgot to check when I got back."

"Well, I'd better go check now then, hadn't I?" He seemed a little miffed.

"Sorry, honey."

"Don't worry about it," he said gruffly.

Still feeling feverish, I took a sponge bath, aching for a shower. I was trying to decide how many limbs I would trade for one, but decided that would defeat the purpose.

A few minutes later, I looked at Drew, still staring at the screen, scrolling through our e-mail, when he said, "Nothing new, so not to worry."

"Well, that's good, because for a moment there, I thought you were angry with me."

He said nothing, but looked at me, chagrined. "I'm sorry, honey. Really. I guess I have trouble getting out of my agent mode, but I don't ever mean to hurt you." He stood and pulled me into his arms.

I hugged him, laying his head on my shoulder, and rubbed his back.

His last words before going to sleep that night were, "If I seem crabby, it's because I can't get a handle on this DVD deal."

I prayed silently, before we slept. *Please, Lord, settle this, will You, so we can put the issue to rest?*

TWENTY-TWO

The next morning dawned warm and sunny for December, and I felt like I could conquer the world. Looking at the calendar, I realized that Christmas was quickly approaching and figured I'd better get busy. I called Neely and she said she needed to go shopping and that Saturday would work for her.

Planning to go grocery shopping, I made a list of Christmas dishes I thought Drew would like, but realized I had never asked if his family had any favorite foods or holiday traditions he'd like to carry on.

At the Piggly Wiggly, I immediately noticed Noogy Gotsch's ancient, but distinctive red Schwinn bike. I watched from outside the window as she piled a huge stack of paper-wrapped magazines on the checkout counter. I stood close enough to identify them. *Redbook, Look, Time, Ladies' Home Journal,* and I thought I detected my favorite, *Country Living* on the bottom of the stack. She paid for them proudly, hustled them into a grocery basket, and pushed it toward the door. I panicked. She'd nail me in seconds if she saw me.

The only hiding place I could see was behind a blue U.S. Post Office drop box, and I made it just in the nick of time. I had seen the glint in her eye, as she thought *sales*. I've often wondered who ended up with all those magazines.

I felt stupid, sliding out from behind the mailbox a few seconds later, when I ran smack into the mailman, Cal Steadman, whose mother, Maybelle is one of my friends from Shady Acres. He has amazing laughing brown eyes, a thin, wiry frame, and a warm personality. He had evidently come to empty the box. He looked toward where Noogy had sped away, and winked at me with a knowing smile. "Don't worry, Makkie, if anyone asks, I'll just say you lost a contact lens, okay?"

Simultaneously, we burst out laughing, but it was the warmth crawling up my neck that made me bite my lip in embarrassment.

I finished my shopping in record time and didn't realize until later that they had been playing Christmas carols in the store. No wonder I had actually enjoyed marketing for the first time in history.

I had just finished unloading groceries when the phone rang and I answered to hear Zoe's voice.

"Hey, Makkie. We just got back from Switzerland, and guess what? I broke my leg skiing."

I hated myself for it, but the first thought that popped into my head was, *There is a God and He loves me.*

However, I said, "Oh, Zoe, I feel for you. My cast is supposed to come off next week if all goes well."

"Does yours itch?"

"It sure does, and there's not much you can do about it. Where exactly is your leg fractured?" I asked.

"I broke my left fibula just below the knee."

I thought, *she has a cast at least mid-thigh. That must have made for an interesting honeymoon.* But I said, "Does it hurt?"

"Not much anymore, but it sure was painful at first. They had to Life Flight me off the mountain."

After a little more small talk, I almost said, out of long years of guilt, that I was sorry I'd missed her wedding. But I caught myself just in time, and decided it would be a lie. A white lie, but a lie, nevertheless, and hypocritical besides.

When Zoe asked what we were doing for Christmas, I said that Mom and Snooky were coming to the cottage for Christmas dinner.

"Oh, well, never mind then," she said, and I knew she wouldn't stoop so low as to join us, and I was right. It was sad, but her social climbing gene was going to keep us apart for the holidays.

We got an e-mail from Drew's brother, Michael, who wanted to know if they could come for Christmas. Drew had been able to share Christ with Michael a few weeks earlier, leading him to the Lord, and I imagined they coveted time together, now brothers not only in the flesh, but in the spirit. I e-mailed back to come on ahead and planned to shop for more groceries.

Michael is five years older than Drew and had been the victim of their abusive father. They had been driven by the scars of their youth, but both seemed miraculously healed after their life changing Holy Spirit experience. Michael's life in Boston precluded frequent visits, so I wanted to do everything in my power to make this the best Christmas ever.

Mom was tickled pink to hear Michael and Cindy would be here for Christmas. She gave me her recipes for her cornbread stuffing and a delicious cream cheese/ cranberry salad. (A possible Recipe for Hot People?) I felt as giddy as a kid, anticipating their quickly approaching visit.

Neely and I set out, along with the rest of the world, to do Christmas shopping two Saturdays before the holiday. When the lines were miles long and the buyers worse than crabby, I shook my head, telling Neely, "Just shoot me if I ever even think about waiting so long to shop for Christmas."

With a look of chagrin and a nod of her head, she agreed. "That goes double for me."

In men's furnishings, I found Drew a pajama ensemble, in silver gray silk, with a matching robe. It was on sale, forty percent off, just about what it should have been marked in the first place. I also found him an onyx initial ring, which I had the jeweler inscribe with, *All my love forever, Makkie.*

Neely and I ate at Dayton's Treat, just north of the city, and it instantly became her new favorite, since she's a huge fan of the anything to do with the 1950's.

Monday I had an appointment to get my cast checked, but Arlo said the x-rays looked perfect, and picked up the cast saw, ready to remove it.

He laughed when he saw the relief on my face. "You're looking much more optimistic. Getting your Christmas wish early, Makkie—getting this cast off?"

"You can say that again."

He grinned. "And it's just my luck to get to play the part of Kris Kringle."

He was fishing for compliments, so I planted a kiss on his cheek, and said, "Satisfied, Santa?"

"It'll do in a pinch," he said with a chuckle.

I was giddy with relief when it clattered to the floor. My first thought was that I might not exit the shower until Christmas.

Drew came home that night and saw I was minus my cast, and he was as thrilled as I was. We made it a point to get in the shower together and wash each other's backs and hair. It felt so good to be under that warm water that I really hated to leave. But Drew promised to make it worth my while, with a massage and some cuddling.

I could tell he was excited about Michael's upcoming visit, and I had to ask, "Honey, I want this Christmas to be perfect. Do you have any family traditions or special foods you'd like me to include?"

He frowned and shook his head. "The only holiday tradition I recall is Dad getting drunk and making Mother cry." After giving it some thought, he added, "I guess we'll have to make our own traditions. Are we up for that?"

"Sounds good to me," I said, as cheerfully as I could. It would definitely take some Holy Spirit impact to erase the painful memories of Christmases past.

The next afternoon, Neely and I went to visit Suse and take their gift, a gift certificate to their favorite place—Salvatore's Italian Restaurant in Kansas City. The attached note said we were available to babysit. *This will be fun.*

Suse called after Elvee got home and asked if we could watch Rachel the next night, since they had a ton of Christmas shopping to do.

When we arrived at the appointed time, Suse was all dressed up, and I thought Elvee looked overjoyed at the prospect of an evening alone with his wife.

Neely and I were excited to have a newborn to care for, remembering babies as a cuddly, appealing and distant memory. The new mother, who was nursing, had pumped and refrigerated copious numbers of four ounce bottles.

We sat through the introductory babysitting course, with points of interest noted, including the location of diapers, wipes, burp pads and myriad emergency numbers.

We learned that you never microwave cold milk, but run it under hot tap water for about a minute. By the time orientation was over, the strain was showing. We had to scoot the happy couple out the door, with reassurances that I was an RN, and we were experienced babysitters, albeit from forty years before, but since that was neither here nor there, we skipped that part.

Peeking in on her, we couldn't contain our glee. Baby Rachel looked angelic, asleep in her crib. But looks, unfortunately, were wildly deceiving. She woke up shortly, screeching loudly, demanding to be fed, and threw us into an anxious frenzy.

Trying to take control of the situation, I said, "Listen, Neely, it can't be that hard. We were both old hands at this at age thirteen, so let's just take a deep breath and think positive." When Rachel only screamed louder, I sighed. "Forget thinking positive. Pray, will you?"

Neely warmed the bottle in the microwave, forgetting the lesson, but only for fifteen seconds. We shook it and tested it on our respective wrists, then hurriedly stuck it between Rachel's tiny, pursed lips. We were expecting her to sigh and coo with pleasure, at being rocked and fed, but clearly, she knew this rubber nipple was *not* her mother. She choked and cried constantly, when the bottle gave her more milk than she could handle. I walked up and down with her, trying to comfort her, only handing her off to Neely when I needed a break. She watched, looking dumbfounded, when nothing we did could calm the distressed infant.

In fact, Rachel cried, off and on, mostly on, all evening, and I nearly joined her after a while. I frowned, wondering if Suse had ever bottle-fed Rachel, or if we were all hapless and unwilling guinea pigs.

When the bottle was gone, Rachel cried some more. I tried to burp her, patting her back like I had learned in seventh grade Family Life classes, but no burp issued forth, only stomach rumblings, gas and spitting up. Neely and I looked at each other, and said simultaneously, "No wonder they were so anxious for a night out."

Suse called after two hours, crying, saying she missed the baby and had had a letdown of milk after hearing a baby cry in the restaurant, leaving her soaked down the entire front of her new dress. I understood and suggested they might all be happier, (I didn't say *and so would we*) if they backpacked her on their next Christmas shopping expedition.

Suse cheered up immediately at the suggestion, before promising to hurry home. Fortunately for us, they arrived soon afterwards, and I asked how they had enjoyed their dinner. Suse said it was fine, but I insisted on details, until she hesitantly admitted that she couldn't eat anything with tomato sauce, as it bothered the baby's digestion. So she had had plain spaghetti with clam sauce and salad. *Bummer.* Our Christmas gift had been a flop. Well, we had tried. Maybe next year, we could treat them to a weekend at the Crown Center or something, if they could leave Rachel by then. Preferably with someone else.

As I drove Neely home, I sighed. "I'm fried. How about you?"

She agreed she was definitely fried, but also starving.

I smiled. "Hey, just so the whole evening's not a total bust, how about getting some Chinese?"

Over won ton soup and egg rolls, we puzzled over the baffling incident, wondering how one small infant could stupefy two mature women. We'd had this down pat in 1962. We had a good laugh over it, but decided the whole humiliating experience would simply remain our little secret.

TWENTY-THREE

I started my Christmas baking early the next morning, beginning with sugar cookies in the shapes of stars, bells and, not surprisingly, Rudolph. I frosted some, decorated others with colored sugar and nonpareils and stuck them all in the freezer, and then started on the candies, which were harder to resist. The peanut clusters and chocolate-covered pretzels turned out great, but Mom's divinity recipe, predictably, refused to turn out as good for me as it does for her.

I had a fire going in the fireplace and my carols on, praising the Lord for His gift of Jesus, with the smell of baking in the air, when suddenly the phone rang. Oblivious to danger, I forgot Drew's directive to screen calls. After giving a cheerful greeting, I stiffened as I heard, "This is Manley Andreason. I tried to stop by and pick up my DVD last night, but you weren't home. I want that DVD."

"Listen, mister," I said, as I took a deep breath, "I don't know who you are, but I doubt very much that you're Manley Andreason. He had a head injury that would've left him severely brain damaged if he survived at all, so quit playing games with me."

I bit my lip, unable to believe I had said that. How dared I? I cringed, dreading what would come next.

"Okay, lady," the voice got tougher, "so you know he's dead. So what? One way or the other, we're gonna get that DVD back."

I breathed a quick prayer and said confidently, "We turned the DVD over to the FBI and the Centers for Disease Control in Atlanta. So go away and leave us alone."

"You think you're getting off that easy?"

I was shaking when I said, "You do what you have to, but you won't find the DVD in our possession. You can believe it or not, but you already searched here, remember?"

He said nothing for a moment, and my mind once again wondered why the scandal hadn't been picked up by any of the wire services.

"I'll have to get back to ya." As he hung up, I laughed. *He'd have to get back to me?*

I was so shaken by his call that I let a pan of brownies scorch and had to toss the whole thing down the disposal. The smell in the cottage reflected the change in the air—thick tension and burnt chocolate.

I called Drew, who said he'd call Washington and see what was up with the investigation.

"You know, maybe we should get some sharp reporter in on this."

"We may have to if nothing breaks soon."

I cleaned up the kitchen, opened the windows for a time to let the smell dissipate and threw in a load of laundry. I dusted and vacuumed, feeling greatly relieved to be out of my cast.

I let the dogs out about noon and decided that tomorrow I'd attend quilting and catch up on the latest.

I sat at the computer after lunch and worked on book two for a while. It was coming along nicely, and I felt satisfied with time well spent. A short time later, I put my mind and typing fingers to work on *Recipes*, adding Mom's cream cheese cranberry salad.

I made a pot of chili, which helped dispel the eau de burnt, and had it simmering in the slow cooker when Drew walked through the door. Seeing the look on his face, I knew something was wrong.

Abruptly he said, "Who do you know at the Kansas City Star newspaper?"

"Well, nobody personally, but I have great respect for one of their reporters. She seems to be a class act, yet gets to the bottom of an issue. You probably know who she is. Her name is Casey Steele."

"Call her."

I frowned in confusion. "You mean me? Call her? She doesn't know me from Adam."

"Do it anyway. Otherwise, we'll never blow the lid off this story."

"But Drew, what can we tell her? We gave up the DVD."

"We'll figure out something."

Casey Steele turned out to be a savvy woman, the kind who usually intimidates me, but when I made the call, I found her to be a gentle, compassionate woman. After only the first cursory facts, she said, "Tell me where you live. I'll be there as soon as I can."

With her shiny dark hair blowing in the wind, she was at the door in less than an hour with her tape recorder, notepad and camera crew, who waited in the van, just in case she needed them.

We related the pertinent facts and handed her copies of e-mails from our *friend*. She was pumped as she jotted notes, but I knew sooner or later she would ask for the DVD, and that would be a problem.

She looked at Drew. "So where is the DVD now?"

I started to say we had turned it over, but to my total astonishment, Drew produced it out of his jacket pocket and handed it to her.

"I made a copy just in case." Looking at me, he said, "I couldn't tell you, hon. You were already in enough danger."

I hugged him, knowing he had won the day. The overwhelming evidence on the DVD would clinch the story.

Casey said, "I don't think your names should be mentioned, for obvious reasons. You guys have done enough already. With what you've given us, we'll break this story wide open."

She grinned, shook hands and ran to the van.

Drew sat down, and I asked, "So are we out of it now?"

"I sure hope so," he said with an audible sigh.

The chili had been simmering long enough to fill the house with its fragrance, and sniffing, he said, "Mmm…what do I smell? Chili?" It was a Drew Livingston favorite.

I nodded, dishing up a big bowl, and handed the salad across the table.

Looking hungry, he said, "Do you know that chili is one of my favorite foods?" He had only told me a thousand times.

I nodded. "Well, that's a good thing, since I like to make it."

After our meal, we made a fire and I dug out some marshmallows that we toasted on long weenie forks, laughing as they caught fire, eating them while they were too hot, burning our tongues, and licking our sticky fingers afterward.

The next morning was gray, the skies filled with the promise of new snow. I was hoping for a white Christmas, but I thought an inch would be sufficient. I couldn't help putting my order in early.

I was reading the newspaper when an excited Gertie Albers called from the police department, saying they had the results from Bonnie Hunt's autopsy. Her death was attributed to anaphylactic shock, from prolonged exposure to Penicillin. The route of entry was transdermal, as we had thought, and the Band-Aid the source of the toxin.

Only a person who knew the victim's medical history could've known about a Penicillin allergy. It was so rarely used anymore that for anyone to get it accidentally was unthinkable.

Gertie added, "A Penicillin allergy was never noted on her employment records, possibly because it's almost never prescribed anymore, and that vastly decreases the chance of her killer being someone from the nursing home. Since she wasn't known for being open with anyone, it's also quite unlikely she would share something so personal.

"Which brings the spotlight to her son, Ellis. He was high on the suspect list from the beginning anyway, since he had method, motive and opportunity. So now they'll be bringing him in for questioning. Unless some major new evidence comes up to the contrary, it looks like they've got their man. Just thought you should know."

I was relieved to hear that justice would be served.

I had planned to attend the quilting session the next morning, but after one glance at my list of things to do, decided I couldn't spare the time.

I had to run to the city to finish Christmas shopping, since I hadn't yet come up with gifts for Michael or Cindy. Knowing it would be hard to shop for someone I didn't know well, I stopped by Drew's office to ask for suggestions. He dictated, as I listed on my hand, Michael's interest in football, golf and wine collecting. He said he wasn't too familiar with Cindy's preferences, but from the looks of their home, he thought she and I shared some of the same taste in decorating. *Ooh, this could be fun.* Before I left, he recalled seeing her collections of Santa Clauses and snowmen.

I spent several hours browsing through shops, looking for just the right gifts. I knew the moment I saw it that I would get a wonderful musical snow globe with movable children building a snowman, for Cindy. I asked for a bag with handles and continued adding to its contents as I shopped.

For Michael, I finally found a classy golf shirt in tan, burgundy and hunter green, with a matching cap, socks and hand towel. Unfamiliar as I am with golf, I had to ask the salesman what the towel was for. Amazingly, I learned that it was for sweaty hands. Would wonders never cease?

I'd been giving Mom the same thing for years, either a fluffy terry robe, or a set of bath towels. This year I wracked my brain, wanting to try something new. I found exactly what I was looking for as I walked past a window decorated as a home office. A gorgeous brass gooseneck lamp would be just the ticket for her office. And for Snooky, I chose a fancy sterling silver magnifying glass. Perfect.

I found a leather purse for Neely and a bottle of Pleasures perfume for Suse. For Mouse and Libby, I bought soft fluffy throws in pastel plaids. Taking advantage of sales, I got some great buys. Among throngs of other shoppers, I strode toward my car, with packages hanging from every digit, as well as a huge bag full of Christmas wrap, and ribbons.

The proof of my love for my family was that I, who despised crowds, braved the droves of shoppers and crawled home in bumper-to-bumper traffic, just as noisy sleet began to fall. I was more than grateful to finally pull into my own driveway at six P.M.

For some reason, I flipped on the television as I walked in the door and saw Casey Steele being interviewed by KC Channel 4 News reporter Glen Jones. The ticker tape monitor at the bottom of the screen flashed, *Late-breaking News,* which it repeated every couple of seconds. The interviewer asked Casey for the latest, and she said, "This is Casey Steele, reporter for the Kansas City Star.

"This reporter has come into possession of evidence that several top officials of United States government have been diverting millions of dollars in tax funds to pay Smith, Darden, and March Pharmaceuticals for the development of illegal biological weaponry.

"The United Nations enacted a world-wide ban on the development of such weapons in March of 1975. Investigators from the United Nations will begin to look into these allegations immediately. The world will be watching to see what action is taken to insure that this illegal and potentially deadly activity is stopped. We'll bring you more information as we get it. Back to you, Glen."

I was proud to see her stand up for what was right. Couldn't have hurt a bit to get a scoop like that either.

As Drew flew through the door, he hollered, "Did you hear the news broadcast on KC Channel 4?"

"I just heard. Can you believe it? Somebody actually did their job for a change."

"Restores my faith in human nature, what little there is left of it," he said with a pleased smile.

Mom and Snooky came over as soon as they heard, and for the first time in weeks, we could finally relax. At suppertime, I put the chili pot on the table, saying, "I hope everybody likes leftovers."

With a big grin, Snooky said, "Why honey, everybody knows chili tastes better the second day."

Mom said she had gotten a call from Gertie Albers at the police station, who wanted us to know that, according to company records, the security people, on orders from company officials, were responsible for chasing, beating, and ultimately causing the death of Manley Andreason. I was relieved when she said the company memo ordering Andreason's death was now in the hands of authorities. Those responsible were facing murder charges, and the company would also lose any future possibility of government contracts. It cheered my heart to hear that they were paying for their greed. We never did find out the identity of the friend who sent the e-mail.

It was four days before Christmas when we heard that Ellis Hunt would be spending his holidays as a guest of the Missouri State Board of Prisons.

As soon as the weather cleared a little, I took plates of goodies to my elderly friends who aren't able to bake anymore.

At Shady Acres, I encountered Dabney Franklin in the hall, smiling. "Oh, it's always so much fun when you stop by. Really livens things up around here. Mmm…what have we here? Christmas goodies?"

I nodded. "It's that time of year again, right, Dabney?"

His eyes twinkled as he asked, "Did you bring more of those chocolate covered pretzels I like so much?"

I smiled. "How did you guess? Listen, if I give you your treats now, promise you won't eat them all before lunch? Otherwise the director of nursing will have my head on a platter." After a beat, I added, deadpan, "She might even hit me."

He laughed. "You're a riot, girl." When I continued to look questioningly at him, he said, "Oh sure, I promise. Thanks." I left him with a Merry Christmas and a big hug, to go search for my next quarry.

Maybelle Steadman was just coming out of the public restroom, where I knew she wasn't supposed to be, and she dropped her chin, looking guilty as sin. "You won't squeal on me, will ya, honey?"

"Maybelle, you know me better than that, I hope. Heard anything about a new administrator yet?"

"Oh, haven't you heard? Peetry's daughter, Betsy McGill, is coming on board." Peetry is the mail carrier, who has delivered Mom's mail for thirty odd years, and is a friend of the family.

"Oh, I'm so glad to hear it. She's a very caring person."

"You don't have to tell us. We're thrilled."

She led me to her room, motioned toward the plate of goodies, and said in a hushed tone, "Do you know I have to hide this stuff? Otherwise I'm afraid my roommate could die of a diabetic coma. Trouble is, she can sniff out chocolate better than any bloodhound I know. I've thought about getting a small combination safe, that only I know the combination to. What do you think?"

"Sounds like a great idea."

I handed her the small Christmas plate, heaped with goodies, and she laughed, her eyes twinkling with delight. "I've got to go easy on this, hard as it is, or I'll lose my girlish figure." She sent me on my way with hugs and wishes for a happy holiday.

Mamie Harcourt had just come out of the beauty shop, all dolled up, and I wolf-whistled at her, "Whoa, Mamie, got a hot date?"

She laughed. "Don't I just wish…"

I followed her to her room, where she closed the door behind us. "That isn't what I think it is, is it?"

"It is, but let's just keep it between you and me. Lots of diabetics around would die for this stuff, and we don't want that to happen."

She sighed. "I can think of a few diabetics around here I wouldn't mind seeing bumped off."

I laughed. "What on God's green earth are you talking about?"

"That new guy, Mather Gillette, is scoutin' for a wife now that you're spoken for, so when I see him comin', I run the other way."

I grinned. "Well, maybe he thinks you're cute."

She frowned, scrunching up her nose. "Listen, I'd rather die, if you don't mind."

I handed her the plate of treats, and she gave a dreamy smile. "Oh, divinity. I haven't had divinity since 1945. My mama used to make it when I was a kid. She sold it at holiday time and used the money to buy gifts for us kids. It sure brings back sweet memories." She bit into a piece and smiled, closing her eyes. "It tastes just like my mama's."

"I assume that's a good thing?"

"It sure is. She was a great cook. Mmm…I'll have to make this last. Thanks, sweetie."

My last stop was Shuggie Heinz's room. Her son, Ian, was visiting. I stayed just long enough to wish them both a Merry Christmas and to give her a big hug.

As I was ready to leave, she said, "Say, Makkie, was it you who set us up with that group of little old ladies who drives us to doctor appointments?"

"It was, and I completely forgot to ask for a report. How are things going? Any scuttlebutt?"

"Well, those folks are almost as old as we are, and boy, do they fly low. You know that Freezia Harcourt? I know she's Mamie's girl, but Mamie says she doesn't want to hear what kind of trouble her kid gets into. But I told her anyway at lunch the other day. I said, 'Mamie, you know what that kid o' yours did, takin' me to the doctor to get my toenails clipped?'" Freezia is seventy-years old, and Mamie is over ninety.

"And she said, 'I'm closin' my ears to this, I tell ya.' So I just yelled a little louder, 'That kid o' yours got caught speedin' between here and Primrose, going over eighty miles an hour. Lead foot, that's what she's got.'"

I laughed and laughed, before I finally answered. "Maybe she'll learn to slow down, when her whole paycheck goes to pay the speeding ticket."

"Let's hope so," said Shuggie, with a forlorn shake of her head.

I made my way home in a think bank of fog. It made me wish I still had my '67 Chevy Impala with the fog lights mounted on the front. Maybe I could talk Drew into buying me some for Christmas. Grabbing a pen from my coat pocket, I jotted it down on the back of my hand.

I spent the next few hours wrapping packages and digging out my stash of Christmas decorations. The beautiful artificial tree that had been dwarfed by my tall apartment ceilings would be perfect for the lower ceilings of the cottage.

I spent the rest of the day putting it all together. I arranged limbs, untangled and replaced dead bulbs and finally strung them on the tree, along with my collection of wonderful old world ornaments. I added shiny white balls decorated with gold wire ribbon and then added tinsel. The outcome was one I had only dreamed of. The movie *The Enchanted Cottage* immediately sprang to mind. There was something about this cottage that made everything look exactly right—almost too good to be true.

I'd have to remember to mention that to Drew.

He came home early the day before Christmas, as I was leaving for the airport to pick up his brother. I said excitedly, "Oh, Drew, they let you off early. That's the best gift they could give me for Christmas."

I had spoken too soon. I could tell it wasn't good news by the look on his face. He frowned. "We've just been ordered to leave for Alabama, and I'm not sure how long I'll be gone. I am so bummed I can't see straight. The first time Michael and I have the chance to be together, to say nothing of my first Christmas with my bride, and I'm going to miss it."

"Well, Michael and Cindy will be here for several days, and we'll ask the Lord make a quick end to this assignment, so we can have you back ASAP. Okay?"

He looked at me wide-eyed. "You're being awfully sweet about this, love."

I was bitterly disappointed, but didn't want him to feel bad. "Well, it doesn't help to complain, because as they say, *stuff happens*."

He was throwing things into a bag, while I packed a thermos of steaming chili, crackers, carrots and apples, along with a Hershey's kiss or two. He kissed me long and hard and said, "I've got to be ready to take off in a half hour, and as usual, I'm running late."

"Be safe, sweetheart," I yelled as he roared out the drive. I had to get a move-on myself, or be left to park in the far parking lot at the airport.

The drive at dusk was not my favorite, since, in the thick fog, people left their high lights on, practically blinding me in the oncoming traffic.

I was at the airport a half-hour before their arrival time. However, when I entered the terminal, the monitor reported that their flight had been delayed due to fog. I approached the nearest ticket counter, as a line formed behind me, and I asked, "So when is the Boston flight supposed to arrive?"

After consulting his computer terminal, the distracted thirty something male said, "They haven't left yet as far as I know. They're fogged in just like we are."

I didn't know what to do next. Should I wait for Michael and Cindy or go home and try to call them?

After a few minutes' thought, I compromised and dialed the information operator, who gave me Michael's home number. When I called, Michael answered. "We're fogged in worse than any time in recorded history. No wind at all, which is odd, because Boston always has tons of wind this time of year."

When I asked him what he thought I should do, he said, "It doesn't look like we'll get out tonight, and maybe not even tomorrow. I'll tell you what, when it looks like we'll get to leave, I'll phone, but don't you worry about picking us up. We'll grab a rental. I can't have my new sister waiting indefinitely."

"Are you sure, Michael?"

"Absolutely. I'm sorry you wasted your trip. Give my little brother a hug, and tell him we'll be there soon."

He hung up before I could tell him Drew wasn't here either.

I drove home in the glare of what resembled thick pea soup. Not a single breeze was stirring, so who knew when the fog would lift.

In the rear view mirror, I saw bright headlights zooming toward me, and I frowned, unable to imagine who would speed in such awful road conditions. I couldn't say how it happened, but he was in my lane in a flash, and instantly I tried to maneuver out of his way.

Suddenly I found myself in a vehicle doing a three-sixty, and ended up on the very edge of the shoulder, with the other car no longer anywhere in sight. I was hyperventilating, big time, when a car stopped behind mine. A minute later, a state patrolman knocked on my window and motioned me to roll it down. With a look of concern, he asked, "Are you okay, ma'am? I saw that idiot coming up on you." He tapped the radio attached to his jacket. "Ironically, his recklessness caused an accident a half mile up the road only seconds ago. Lucky you were able to get out of his way."

As my heart raced, I sighed in relief. "I don't happen to believe in luck, officer, but I do believe God had His hand on me. I have no idea how I got out of the way in time. All I know is that my wheel was turning."

He looked at me oddly, his brow furrowing. "Ma'am, are you sure you're all right? You look kind of green."

I nearly hit him as I threw open the door and scurried a couple of feet away before vomiting. I pulled out my hanky, embarrassed. "I'm sorry, Officer, it just came on so suddenly."

"No harm done. Do you think you're all right to drive?"

"I'm fine. Thanks for stopping."

After sticking a piece of chewing gum in my mouth, I was back on the road as soon as I could squeeze into the stream of slow-moving traffic. Treacherous black ice made it necessary to creep home at twenty-five miles an hour.

It was more than an hour later when I finally pulled into our driveway, stiff from tension in my shoulders, grateful to finally relax. The December evening was frigid but with no wind and no moon.

The dogs were ecstatic at seeing me, and I let them out, turning on the lights in the cottage. The exquisite

Christmas tree lit up as well, since I had plugged it into a switch.

It was like a glimpse of heaven, ethereal, in the dim light of the room and even more so after I took my glasses off to rub the sore bridge of my nose. I built a fire, turned on my carols and got into my pajamas on this, my first married Christmas Eve in thirty years, and sat alone, but not really. The nativity of the Christ Child was resting beneath the tree, with the star of Bethlehem shining down—The Reason for the Season. I noticed Drew had left my snow globe on the coffee table. I picked it up and turned the key, shook it, and listened as the music tinkled, *While Shepherds Watched their Flocks by Night,* entranced as the tiny sheep and shepherds moved round and round.

I sang along as tears of gratitude filled my eyes. I paused when the music stopped, thinking about the past year. So many things had happened in twelve months, including some that were hard, and yet I had many reasons to be thanking the Lord.

I picked up my Bible and read Luke 2: *And there were in the same country, shepherds abiding in the fields, watching over their flocks by night.*

And lo, the angel of the Lord came upon them, and the glory of the Lord shown round about them and they were sore afraid.

And the angel of the Lord appeared unto them, saying, Fear not, for behold I bring you good tidings of great joy which shall be to all people. For unto you is born this day in the city of David, a Savior which is Christ, the Lord. And this shall be a sign unto you, that you shall find the babe, wrapped in swaddling clothes lying in a manger. And there was with the angel a multitude of the heavenly hosts praising God and saying Glory to God in the highest, peace on earth and good will toward men. And it came to pass as the angels were gone away from them into heaven, that the shepherds said one to another, Let us now go even unto Bethlehem and see this thing which has come to pass, which the Lord has made known unto us. And they came with haste, and found Mary and Joseph, and the babe lying in a manger.

The miracle of God's love coming in the form of a baby has never ceased to amaze me. I sat with tears trickling down my cheeks, unable to understand what it means to love that much.

I went to bed, snuggling with my pets, thinking about the animals that surrounded the manger on that night so long ago.

TWENTY-FOUR

When I woke alone Christmas morning, the house was cold. Had the furnace broken down or a fuse blown? I pulled my terry robe around me, turning on the lamp, sent the dogs outside, and went to find the fuse box. It was in the wall of the laundry room, and sure enough, a breaker was tripped. I reset it, and set about building a fire in the hearth. It couldn't have been more than fifty-five degrees in the house. In fact, I thought I saw my breath.

I wondered if the Christmas lights could've overloaded a breaker. I'd have to get Drew to check it out when he came home.

The cottage warmed quickly once the furnace kicked on, and I was even more grateful for heat, when the dogs came in, bringing a blast of cold air not to be believed.

I made some hot chocolate and turned on the tree lights, leaving the curtains drawn against the cold. The windows in the cottage are charming, but not triple layer insulated, and today, they were definitely feeling their age. Not unlike myself.

Drew called to wish me Merry Christmas and to ask if Michael and Cindy had arrived. I explained that the fog had cancelled their flight, and I hadn't heard from them yet. He said he was in Tennessee, on a layover, and should be home mid-afternoon.

I stuck the turkey and fixings in the oven all throughout the day, and in no time, the fragrance wafted through the house. My only regret was that Ernie wouldn't be with us this Christmas. But I knew that in reality, it was I who should be envying him, spending his Christmas in heaven.

I made Mom's recipe for eggnog and set in the fridge, called my friends and wished them Merry Christmas and set the table as festively as I could manage. Mom and Snooky had sent over a huge poinsettia, and I set that on a decorative runner in the middle of the table, and finally went to shower and change.

I had called Mom earlier, and we had decided to schedule the meal for six. She said they'd be over in plenty of time to help.

A car drove up, and I expected it to be Drew, but when I answered the door, I found Michael and Cindy, their arms heavily laden with gifts. We hugged and cried, and I said, "I thought you were going to call when your flight was ready to leave."

"I was, but they called our flight suddenly, with just a short window of opportunity, between fog banks, so we just left. Sorry."

They oohed and aahed over the cottage and had just settled down with eggnog when Mom and Snooky blew in. The frigid gusts wafted through the door, sending everything blowing that wasn't nailed down.

I had just finished the introductions when Drew arrived, with his arms full of gifts, and his duffel, precariously perched under his arm. Frantic, he said, "Oh, I'm dropping this big one! Oh-oh. Catch the green one, it's fragile."

Michael rushed to his rescue, and soon they were hugging and blinking away tears, trying to make up for lost years, it seemed to me.

Over dinner, we visited, and I was tickled by the warm banter of conversation among us as we got acquainted.

Since everyone was too full for dessert, we moved the celebration to the living room, where Snooky read the Christmas story from the book of Luke, his eyes moist with tears. We harmonized on some carols, and I found myself growing very fond of Michael and Cindy, who both sang with enthusiasm to the Lord.

After the fire had died down a little, we began to open gifts and exclaim over each surprise. I was totally overwhelmed by the lovely things that ended up on my lap.

The first one was from Cindy, with a note enclosed that read, "*Makkie, I have a deep fondness for you, for this special reason. I have known the Lord since my sixteenth birthday and married Michael in rebellion from God. I came back to the Lord when I was thirty, and have been praying for his salvation ever since. When you sent Drew to Michael the night you were hospitalized, I knew it had to be a gift, a sacrifice to the Lord, and I knew you were praying from your hospital bed. I had been praying for years that the two of them could get together, sort out the past, and let the Lord heal them. Because of your gift that night, my prayer was answered, and the two of us are finally one. Thank you, sister of my heart. Love, Cindy.*

I was weeping openly as I rose from my chair and hugged her.

She smiled. "Now open your gift." I pulled from the package a long, camel cashmere sweater that had to have cost a fortune. I started to shake my head, but she gently pushed it back at me. "It's not a fraction of what I feel. Now go put it on."

I did, and it was the softest thing I had ever touched. I blinked at my reflection in the mirror, unable to believe that anyone would give me such an expensive gift. There were still tears in my eyes when I modeled it from the doorway.

Drew smiled. "You look beautiful, sweetheart."

A short time later, Drew came and sat beside me and handed me a tiny box, wrapped in gold foil, with a shimmering, white ribbon. I looked at him, and he said, "Open it." When I opened the box, I found a gold eternity band, encircled with diamonds. The inscription said it all, and I cried as I read, "To the woman of my dreams, with all my love, Drew."

Everyone smiled as I dried my eyes.

Shortly, Drew handed me a heavy package, which turned out to be a set of fog lights for my Taurus wagon. No one believed me when I said I was thrilled to have them. I couldn't even remember mentioning it, but then I couldn't remember a lot of things these days.

Drew said, "I saw a notation on your hand several days ago."

There was a small, but heavy package next, also from Drew, that revealed a set of one, two and five-pound weights. "To build up your upper body for shooting," said the card. Everyone thought that was just too romantic. From Mom and Snooky, I received a shimmering, crocheted ecru shawl.

Mom was tickled with her new brass lamp, and said, "Oh, Makkie, this is the perfect gift for my home office."

Snooky hugged me, holding his magnifying glass up for all to see. "You know I've had my eye on one of these at the local antique emporium in Primrose. Now I won't have to buy one. Thank you, Makkie."

By ten, we were all exhausted, and everyone pitched in to help tidy up the mess. Mom helped me make up the sofa bed, with a down featherbed and comforter for Michael and Cindy, and I laid out extra blankets and fresh towels for our guests.

I kissed Mom and Snooky good night and sent them on their way. The only one missing was Zoe.

I just couldn't harbor any anger for her tonight. I was wishing I could phone her, but thought the hour too late. The phone rang right next to my ear about five minutes after I had crawled into bed, and I knew it would be Zoe, before I even picked it up. As much as we disagree, we had never been apart a single Christmas. And anyway, Christmas is the time for forgiving.

Zoe spoke hesitantly. "Makkie, I'm not waking you, am I?"

I was surprised to hear her voice concern. It was something new.

"No, Zoe, I wasn't asleep."

Drew sat up on one elbow to listen.

Zoe said quietly, “Makkie, I miss you, and I want to wish you a Merry Christmas.”

“Merry Christmas, Zoe. You know, I was just thinking that it’s lonely when you’re not here for the holidays.”

“Really?”

“Zoe,” I said, quietly, “I love you. I’ve always loved you and I always will.”

I could hear her sobbing quietly, and then she sniffed and sighed. “Even when I’m such a pill?”

I smiled, hearing her admit it. “Even then.”

Timidly, she asked, “Are you guys doing anything tomorrow?”

“Drew’s brother and sister-in-law are here from Boston, for the holidays. Why do you ask?”

I couldn’t believe what I was hearing.

“Well, don’t tell Bryce I said this, because I don’t want to seem ungrateful, but rich people have no idea how to celebrate Christmas. I don’t know exactly how to explain it, but it’s like they are all dead and just haven’t been buried yet.”

All I could say was “What?”

Zoe laughed a little nervously, before she admitted, “You know, I have always been so jealous of you, because you love life and God and Mom so much. It just sort of oozes out of every pore, and I couldn’t compete with that, so I despised you, I guess. But since I’ve been away, I haven’t seen that *aliveness* anywhere else, and I guess I just don’t want to feel dead like them anymore.” After a beat, she asked, “Is this making any sense at all?”

I hesitated. "I think so."

She continued, now weeping softly, "I'm tired of trying to be perfect and failing. I'm tired of being demanding and thoughtless. I know I am, so you don't need to say anything. I just don't know how to be any other way. Know what I mean?"

"Zoe, is Bryce there with you?"

"He went to the University, to catch up on some work."

"On Christmas Day?"

"Don't worry, it's what he does. But I guess I'd like to sit down and talk, just the two of us, maybe at Mom's in the morning. Could we do that?"

"Of course, and I'll even eat bacon and eggs if you want to fix it."

"Are you kidding? That stuff'll kill you."

I couldn't help but laugh.

She said, "Meet you there at eight, okay?"

"I'll be there."

Hanging up, I was so excited that I couldn't wait to tell Drew, and I could hear Michael and Cindy still talking quietly, so I told them about Zoe's request. They said they would pray for a miracle, and I sighed.

"Okay, but just so you know—It needs to be on approximately the same scale as the virgin birth."

TWENTY-FIVE

At seven AM, I phoned Mom and told her of my appointment with Zoe.

"I knew it! I just knew it! I asked the Lord to do something miraculous in her heart this Christmas, and…" She paused. "Oh, bless the Lord and all that is within me, bless His holy name!"

When I arrived at eight, Zoe was waiting for me in her car in the bright zero degree morning.

I frowned. "Zoe, why didn't you go in? You could've frozen to death out here."

"I can't believe Mom would even want to see me again, after the way I treated her at the wedding."

I gently laid my hand on her shoulder. "Zoe, Mom is crazy about you. Don't you know that?"

"Really?" she asked, her eyes wide with wonder.

When we walked through the door, Mom and Snooky were nowhere to be seen. I had a sneaking suspicion they were on their knees in the bedroom, so I led Zoe into the guestroom where I had spent so much time last summer. She sat on a pillow on the floor and I sat beside her, praying silently, waiting for her to find her way.

Finally she said, "Makkie, I've been so lonely and miserable that I even considered suicide."

"Oh, Zoe," I whispered, taking her hand in mine.

"You can't imagine how horrible it is to be depressed. It's the worst thing I can recall, even worse than losing Cappy."

"I think I understand."

She shook her head. "You can't understand unless you've been there."

I was silent, listening as she went on, "I thought if I married into money and prestige, it would fill my emptiness. I thought if I drowned out my own misery with shopping and traveling, spending time with people who looked so together, maybe I'd feel as good as they look. Only, you know what?" She paused and then said, "I saw some of them when they don't have their happy faces on, and underneath, they're just as miserable as I am." After a long beat, she added, "I was so disappointed. I was almost in despair, wondering how anyone can keep going with no hope, and I just had to talk to you."

She continued, "I know what I am. I'm a miserable human being—and I can't help but hate myself. So how is it you can love me?"

My own tears started to fall. I held her as tears streamed down her face. There were no words for a moment like this.

After a time, I whispered, "Zoe, is it all right if I pray for you?"

"Okay," she said weakly.

"Lord, right now it's hard to know exactly how to pray, but You say You intercede for us when we don't know how to pray. Have Your way, Lord. We know You are able to set the captives free from depression and to be the lifter of our heads, so we come asking, and will wait for Your answer, in Jesus' name."

We sat there in comfortable silence, until she whispered, "That's another thing I've been jealous of. You talk to God as if He were your next-door neighbor, like you're talking over the backyard fence. How is that possible? I don't get it."

"What is it you don't understand?"

She sighed. "Oh, I know all the stuff they shoved down our throats as kids, but it always seemed so insincere and pushy, I just decided I wouldn't give it any thought. Threw the baby out with the bath water, I suppose." After a beat, she said, "Tell me, specifically, how this relationship thing works, in a way that I can understand."

I silently prayed, *put a coal to my lips and words in my mouth.*

After a short pause, I said, "Well, the truth is still the truth, no matter how it's told, right?"

"Of course. It's a no-brainer."

"Well, that's just the point. The truth that you heard in Sunday school was right, whether they said it appropriately or not. Is that a fair statement?"

"So you mean I have to re-evaluate what I heard?"

"Yes, only this time, if you do it with an open, willing heart, God will actually show Himself to you."

After a beat, she gave a sad smile. "You know, nobody's ever told me this before."

"I know," I said, looping one of her curls around her ear.

Looking horrified, she asked, suddenly, "You don't think it's too late, do you? You know, that I'm too far gone?"

"Absolutely not."

There was a pause while she was thinking, before she said, "You know, I think knowing God because I choose to, of my own free will, might be something to see, don't you?"

"I do. I really do."

"Well, what are we waiting for? Tell me what to do."

"Well, Zoe, you just talk to God, ask Him to forgive you, and tell Him you want to be His child, with a brand new heart. Just say it in your own words."

She began haltingly, with tears streaming down her cheeks. "God, I knew about You when I was a kid, but I never really made Your acquaintance. I didn't understand what I was going to be missing all my life, but I can't live without You anymore. Are you listening, God?" She continued, "I have so little time to change, and I can't do it alone. I need You to do it for me, because I hate who I am without You. Yours sincerely, Zoe Webster."

I smiled. It was said with such a tender child's heart that I just knew that God wouldn't be able to resist. Besides, He had drawn her, hadn't He?

I looked at Zoe, whose tears had begun to dry, and saw something new in her eyes. She hugged me and said excitedly, "I know something has changed. I don't know exactly what, but something." Then she laughed, "What do you know about that?"

She stretched and smiled. "Let's go find Mom and Snooky. I need a hug."

They were waiting, wide-eyed in the living room, and Zoe couldn't make it to Mom fast enough. She threw her arms around her waist, and laid her head in her lap and wept. "I love you, Mom, I really do."

My precious, white-haired mother had tears running down her cheeks, as she said, "You don't know how long I've waited for this moment. I've been dreaming of it for fifty-four years."

Zoe looked puzzled. "Really?"

"Since the day you were born and I dedicated you to the Lord, I've prayed for you to understand how precious you are to God and to us. And today He answered my prayer."

Zoe started crying again, now sobbing loudly. "Mom, I'm sorry I treated you so shabbily at the wedding."

Caressing Zoe's cheek, she said, "Never mind, darling. Everything is forgiven, forgotten, as far as the east is from the west."

Zoe smiled. "I remember hearing that. I remember that phrase. As far as the east is from the west, so far hath He removed our transgressions from us. Is that right?" She smiled, a contented child's smile that I had never seen before.

Mom smiled. "That's exactly right. Mrs. Craig had you memorize that in the first grade. Do you recall?"

"Not exactly, but I do remember the verse."

Snooky, who had always been a little afraid of Zoe's moods, was suddenly on his feet, gently pulling her into a warm embrace.

"Hi, Dad," said Zoe.

"Hi sweetheart," said Snooky, and we all dissolved into laughter. It was music to our ears.

Zoe left a little later, but not before she said, "We all have lots of years to catch up on, so don't anybody go anywhere." I couldn't help wondering what Bryce would think of the new woman who wore his ring.

I was anxious to get home. Drew threw open the door, taking my coat, and they all looked at me expectantly. "Give," he said.

"This was definitely a God thing, a move of the Holy Spirit. You were praying, weren't you?"

They nodded. Smiling, Drew said, "It seemed like a tiny window of opportunity. Besides "Unsolved Mysteries" was showing re-runs."

They sat enrapt as I related the miraculous events of the morning, and we all basked in the power of God's Spirit. There was nothing, absolutely nothing as great as living in the center of God's will. Anything else surely had to be an anticlimax.

Zoe brought Bryce over after lunch and winked at me, to let me know she wanted him inside God's family as well. I gave her the thumbs up sign, silently reassuring her I was on the job, praying.

We had a lovely visit, though I thought Bryce was a little confused by the change in his wife. I even wondered, *who are you and what have you done with my sister?* Facetiously, of course.

I had a tiny inkling of the kind of friendship awaiting us, and I couldn't wait to help it along.

Michael and Cindy flew back to Boston early the next morning, and within two days, Drew got a call to report that they were job hunting in the Kansas City area, because, all of a sudden, Boston seemed overcrowded with strangers, and as Michael said, "Home is where *you* guys are."

The new year came entirely too fast, and soon the holiday decorations were tucked back into their boxes for another year.

Zoe and I spent a lot of time talking during those first weeks of the new year. She picked my brain on every conceivable subject, like a baby bird, starving, and rearing to fly, her spiritual walk deepening daily.

One morning, while we were talking, she said, "Makkie, Mom mentioned that you went through a deep depression and have been on an antidepressant. Why didn't you tell me?"

"I knew it would all work out."

"Well, I love you all the more because you've already been where I am now."

The highlight of January, as dubious as it may sound, was the Azalea First Memorial Fellowship of God's first annual Winter Beat the Blahs Sale, followed by the ham and bean dinner. In our advertising, we had put in fine bold print that besides ham and beans, we would serve lasagna, salad, and garlic bread, as well as a myriad of homemade pies, donated by the excellent Fellowship of God cooks.

By mid-January, people around here are so bored that even non-attenders eagerly clean out attics and basements in search of junk to donate to the sale. The signs were up, the ads in the paper, and, according to the weatherman, the Lord was promising to hold off a major storm system until the following day.

The church annex was appropriated for the dinner, since the merchandise was displayed on tables wall to wall everywhere else. The fragrances of the food emanating from the kitchen drew people in from the outdoors. Probably the result of the kitchen exhaust fan, which ran constantly to vent the heat that kept us Hot People drenched in sweat.

There were tables of wonderful kids clothes, which numerous moms sifted through, and emerged beaming —with a sack full for a dollar. Other tables held summer treasures, including old buckets, rakes, trowels, worn gardening gloves and seed packets leftover from whenever, which were snatched up quickly, by those who could only dream of spring.

One table held some rare items indeed. A pole lamp, in perfect condition, from about 1975, lay horizontal beside its three avocado green fiberglass light covers. Not at the top of my want list, I left it for an elderly woman who simply glowed at its discovery. I watched as she hauled it off as if it were the Olympic torch.

There was a wide variety of nice costume jewelry, some furniture, fishing tackle, a lawn mower and tables of odds and ends.

There were hosts of Tuppermaid canister sets, in the ever-popular harvest gold and avocado green. I got rid of those colors in 1974, but figured they must be favored by someone, since nary a one remained when I took my second look around an hour later. Unfortunately, the Popsicle molds weren't going anywhere.

The sale was a sell-out, an out an out miracle in itself, since most of the junque was simply junk. The ham and beans didn't taste half so bad accompanied by lasagna smothered in tangy spaghetti sauce, with garlic bread and salad. The pies were gone by half past one, and the committee members once again shook their heads, marveling at the grace and blessing of God, who does all things well.

There was, fortunately, a youthful clean-up committee, because the rest of us were pooped. The whole day netted a whopping $972.14. And praise God, the amount we had allocated to haul off the remnants wasn't needed, because there was nothing left but a few garbage bags full, which were tossed directly into the dumpster.

The money was raised to benefit the Azalea First Memorial Fellowship of God's Women's Aid Society and Orphan's fund, whose recipients would, I was certain, feel overwhelmed and blessed.

The only suggestion Freezia had at the end of the day—was that at next year's mid-winter shindig, we should auction another quilt, which sounded totally exhausting to those of us who overheard.

Drew thought the idea of turning the ham and bean dinner into a lasagna meal had been a winner. He himself had consumed several overflowing plates full. From the glove box, I noticed him ferreting out a bottle of Tums as we drove home, and knew he was regretting his lack of self-control.

Michael had called the previous evening, saying he had snagged a job with a brokerage firm in Kansas City, and that they would be flying in to look for housing. We were excited, looking forward to growing close and growing old with family.

As we drove home after the fundraiser, it seemed to me the night stars were twinkling extra brightly, and I felt extra blessed. I thought back to my life a year ago, and marveled at the way God works when we give our whole selves to Him.

That night, cuddled up in front of the fire with our furry menagerie, while the Christmas lights twinkled brightly, I mentioned to Drew that if felt like we were living in *The Enchanted Cottage*.

He kissed me and smiled. "I'm not sure how scriptural that is, but you know, I can't imagine being any happier than I am right now. I feel like I'm in a dream, loving you the way I do, and I hope I never wake up."

I smiled and nodded my sleepy head. How could life ever get any better than this?